SUBMERGED SECRETS

What was the cause of the handsome and noble Lord Ramblay's callous cruelty toward all those around him, including Maggie Trevor?

What was the real identity of the ravishing Blanche Haversham, the toast of Regency society and the woman who claimed to be Maggie's best friend?

What was the true goal of dashing Captain Morrison, who gallantly guided Maggie through the hothouse jungle of the fashionable elite and was so close to winning her love?

Maggie was in over her pretty head in a whirlpool of mystery and deceit—and now only her heart could save her. . . .

THE ADMIRAL'S DAUGHTER

More Regency Romance from SIGNET

The Admiral's Daughter

by Judith Harkness

A SIGNET BOOK

NEW AMERICAN LIBRARY

TIMES MIRROR

For Donald,
with love and laughter

NAL BOOKS ARE AVAILABLE AT QUANTITY DISCOUNTS
WHEN USED TO PROMOTE PRODUCTS OR SERVICES.
FOR INFORMATION PLEASE WRITE TO PREMIUM
MARKETING DIVISION, THE NEW AMERICAN LIBRARY, INC.,
1633 BROADWAY, NEW YORK, NEW YORK 10019.

SIGNET TRADEMARK REG. U.S. PAT. OFF. AND FOREIGN COUNTRIES
REGISTERED TRADEMARK—MARCA REGISTRADA
HECHO EN CHICAGO, U.S.A.

SIGNET, SIGNET CLASSICS, MENTOR, PLUME, MERIDIAN
AND NAL BOOKS
are published by The New American Library, Inc.,
1633 Broadway, New York, New York 10019

First Printing, April, 1980

1 2 3 4 5 6 7 8 9

PRINTED IN THE UNITED STATES OF AMERICA

One

THE HOUSE TAKEN by Admiral Trevor and his daughter upon the famous old officer's retirement from active service had much to recommend it. Situated well up on a stretch of rising ground, it afforded an excellent prospect of the surrounding hills and of the gentle River Orre as it wound its placid way among the pleasant farmlands of Sussex. On the north a wall of ancient cypress protected it from winter wind and summer heat alike, and in the evening was full of the trilling of nightingales. The house had thirty rooms, and was just that combination of grandeur and comfort which an elderly man, having spent his life in the service of his country and his King, might have welcomed for the passage of his old age. The Admiral's study, a well-appointed apartment on the second floor, possessed a charming view of the grounds, and beyond, of the rolling hills and river. Here a man more fitted to such an occupation might have stood for hour upon end gazing out over his property and congratulating himself upon his good fortune in discovering so delightful a situation for his retirement.

But Admiral Trevor was no great lover of views, nor of any of the other amusements favored by country gentlemen. His days were passed in recording the details of his many victories over Napoleon's fleet, and in the year since he had removed from Portsmouth, scarcely a glance had been accorded either the view from his window or the shrubberies directly beneath it. It was astonishing, therefore, that on this fine, bright October morning, he should have been stationed before that very window for nearly half an hour, staring down into the labyrinth of hedges below. On his handsome, fierce old countenance was a glower not unlike the one once said to have frightened a whole school of pirate ships off his bow without any aid of cannon. The little mutterings and sounds which now and then issued from his throat were further proof that the sight of the earth, just beginning to be touched with gold and crimson, afforded him no joy at all.

The Admiral was not a man to hide his presence. By dint of courage and strategic brilliance he had risen from a penniless ensign to the highest rank in His Majesty's Navy without benefit of either friends or family; after a lifetime of command, he was hardly one to be found cringing before his own window in his own house. And yet the Admiral's huge frame did seem to be enfolded in the window draperies, and looked for all the world as if he was desirous of concealment. A guilty look now and then passed over his face, making a very comical effect in combination with the great shaggy gray eyebrows, the ruddy weathered jowls, and hawklike proboscis. For some time now his face had been working with emotion— whether from anger or distress it was difficult to discern— and when his great hammy fist was raised as if to smash through the leaded windowpane, the extent of his feeling was evident.

"Idiot!" he fairly choked. "Dyspeptic young coxcomb! Reminds me of a colicky sheep." "By God!" he muttered suddenly, an idea causing him to leave the protection of the draperies and press his nose almost against the chilly glass. "By God, I hope she ain't encouraging him!"

A mirthless laugh hinted at the absurdity of this notion, but the terrified look did not leave his eyes at once.

To the disinterested observer, it might indeed have seemed that the Admiral's worst fears were justified. Directly beneath the spot where he had positioned himself for better observation, a scene was being enacted which might have softened a less cynical heart. There, walking among the neatly pruned hedges was what any casual observer might understandably have taken to be a pair of lovers. The young gentleman of the pair was waving his arms about in a most eloquent fashion. He was an ungainly looking fellow, whose extreme height and thinness forced him to bend nearly double to address his companion. His face was long and thin and pale, his eyes too small, and his mouth too large. His appearance was not much improved by an ill-fitting jacket and pair of trousers which, though evidently new, displayed more attention on the tailor's part to speed than elegance. His companion, whose expression was hidden from view by a very comely bonnet of forest green (a cloak of the same shade being flung about her shapely shoulders), appeared to be immersed in an examination of her slippers. Just at this moment, however, she lifted her gaze to the young man's face and a look of intense pain was visible in her expressive hazel eyes. The corners of her mouth were twitching slightly.

The Admiral, however, was prevented by distance from seeing this minor point of his daughter's attitude, and when he saw her mouth open slightly, as if to say something, and the young man, ignoring her, break forth into an even more violent seizure of waving arms and eloquent glances at the sky, he could contain himself no longer.

"Good God, Maggie!" he burst out, heedless of the fact that he was now standing in clear view of the pair below, "make him stop! If you encourage him at all, he shall never have done! What! Ain't it enough that we must all be subjected to his pedantic sermons every Sabbath, without his haunting the very house and grounds? By Jove, is this what I brought you to the country for? So that you might be plagued by the attentions of a knavish curate?"

A sound—half growl, half groan—followed this speech, and the Admiral, seeing that his breath had fogged up the windowpane, made an ineffectual swipe at the glass with his handkerchief. The effort seemed too much for him, however, and turning away with every appearance of a man defeated, he went to his desk. The memory of the curate's unctuous expression, however, lingered for some while longer in his mind.

"There's nothing for it, my dear," he muttered to himself, after a moment. "I'd as soon see you dragged and quartered as subjected to that imbecile's company another day."

So saying, the Admiral lowered himself into an armchair, and taking pen and paper from amid the heap of notes and documents upon his desk, commenced to write a letter.

It is unfortunate the Admiral had chosen just this moment to turn away, for had he remained a little longer, he would have been privy to a drastic change in the scene below. Mr. Wayland—for such was the curate's name—

had been holding forth for the better part of half an hour
without pause. His speech, rehearsed that very morning
before his glass, had included all those graceful metaphors
and references which the young man had culled from his
readings upon the subject of love. The clergyman had a
very high opinion of his own eloquence, however, and had
taken certain liberties with some passages. One, in particular, which had struck him upon reading it as very pretty,
having to do with a young lady's likeness to a summer's
day, had had to be altered to allow for the actual time of
year and to make space for one of Wayland's favorite
themes, a variation of one used often in his sermons.

"Beautious creature!" he had cried out, as soon as he
had been received and a walk among the shrubberies suggested. "Delightful, charming vision! So like in every aspect
the dawn of a fair autumn morning! Walking across the
meadow from the vicarage, I imagined you, tending your
lovely rose garden, so like an angel! The clarity and sweetness of your expression is exactly what I imagine the Virgin
Mary must have worn when she was approached by the
Angel Gabriel! So like a saint in the way you devote
yourself to your father's comfort. Ah, what a blessing it
would be to have so solicitous a hand upon my own brow!"

"But I assure you, Mr. Wayland," Miss Trevor had interjected here, in an astonished voice, "that my father has
very seldom the benefit of my hand upon his brow! And
while you are very kind, I doubt I bear any resemblance
whatsoever to either the Angel Gabriel or any other saint.
I am afraid I am not the least bit saintlike—as indeed you
ought yourself to know. Save for wishing most earnestly
that I could be better, I am afraid few girls are less saintly
than myself." As if in an afterthought, she added, "And
roses are not in season any more, you know."

Mr. Wayland suppressed his annoyance at this interruption, which seemed to him to have little to do with
the point of his speech. With a coy expression, he begged
to contradict her.

"You do yourself a great injustice, my dear Miss Trevor.
Allow me, a man of God, to say that I have seldom known
a more virtuous young lady in all my life. Why, did not
you nurse poor farmer Drummond's lady back to health
with your own sweet hand? I think you are really too
modest!"

"I did send her a leg of mutton now and then while she was ill, and visited her as often as I could. But as to bringing her back to health—why, I think the surgeon must be thanked for that!"

Once more the curate was forced to suppress his real feelings and said with a great effort at patience, "Ah! This is just the kind of modesty I like! Most young ladies would have taken credit for everything themselves. But you—*you*, Miss Trevor, have such a keen devotion to the truth, and are so exceedingly modest, that you will not be thought better of than you deserve. Even, I should say, than you *think* you deserve, though others may disagree!"

Mr. Wayland, however, was not one of these. He had very little belief in Maggie Trevor's saintliness, and no desire to continue an argument with her upon the subject. As to her maidenly modesty and devotion to the truth, he heartily wished she had less of it, for it was continually causing him irritation. Try as he might to flatter her, she would not listen, but only stared at him with those clear eyes in a way that suggested she either did not understand, or did not wish to. If he paid her a compliment, she would instantly turn it around, which made him appear foolish, and to appear foolish was the curate's greatest dread. Had it not been for his acute desire to advance himself, Mr. Wayland would certainly never have subjected himself to the humiliation which his courtship had entailed.

The curate was not a man of huge perception, but in the matter of his own career, he was cleverness itself. Early in his life he had determined to be a member of the clergy, for it seemed to him that calling could best satisfy his constant urge to hear his own voice, and (presuming everyone else on earth loved the sound as dearly as he) he was desirous of increasing his audience. He wished, besides, to succeed someday to a bishopric, and with the same vanity which made him believe he was superior to other mortals, he had little doubt of one day securing one. Yet he was now two and thirty, and still held a living in a minor parish of Sussex. He was without family or influential friends, and possessed only those personal attributes herein described. Even Mr. Wayland understood that if he was to advance himself, he must have some aid from others.

For some time he had pondered what to do, but without

finding any satisfactory solution to his dilemma. And then one day, as if in answer to his prayers, he had learned of Admiral Trevor's coming into the neighborhood. The Admiral was renowned throughout England for his victories against the French usurper; he had been decorated by the King himself, and acquired during his career a handsome fortune. Though without any of the consequence of birth, he had carved out a position for himself second only to a peerage—a connection with such a man could only help the curate. And when Wayland heard that the Admiral also possessed a daughter—a young lady said to be handsome, clever, and rich—his way seemed clear. Even before he had laid eyes upon Miss Trevor, the curate had determined to marry her, and had he discovered that she was in fact a wretched hag, his determination should not have been decreased.

Such was the clergyman's complacency that he did not for a moment doubt of his success. With the stubbornness (some might say blindness) of his nature, he had set out to woo her, but even Mr. Wayland understood that some formalities must be observed in this courtship. Having never been moved by any passion stronger than the one reserved for his own dear self, he was forced to resort to novels for advice on how to court a lady. From these he gleaned that the proper way of going was to slowly woo her by means of many pretty speeches, made over a protracted period of time. At the end, on the day selected for the final conflagration, he found that he must fall down upon the ground—either full-length, as the ancients were fond of doing, or on the knees, in the manner preferred by more civilized beings.

The first part of the task was completed. For six months Wayland had trudged across the meadow to the Admiral's house on every day the weather did not make him fearful of muddying his boots. His speeches had, at first, been written down and then rehearsed before his glass, much in the way he practiced the delivery of his sermons. But at last Mr. Wayland discovered he could as easily extemporize upon the spot, and with a great deal more freedom. This last was especially necessary if he was to deal with Miss Trevor's annoying habit of contradicting him at every turn. But the curate would not be put off, and if he ever suspected that his attentions were unwelcome, he gave no hint of it.

Today in particular he was determined not to be distracted from his purpose, for this was the day for which he had worked so long. If Maggie Trevor wished to turn aside his compliments, then he would turn them back. Suppressing his mounting irritation, therefore, he said:

"Besides, you know, I did not mean actual saintliness. It is only a figure of speech. And yet I do really like your modesty; it is a most becoming attribute in a young lady. Pray, don't blush! Nothing is so fitting in tender womanhood as a disinclination to be overpraised. And yet I would equally say it is a lover's prerogative to contradict the lady he admires. Pray, what is a gentleman's function, if not to serve as a mirror for his beloved, so that she may see all the flowering beauty he invests her with reflected in his eyes?"

Mr. Wayland was very well pleased with this simile, and paused for a moment to let it hang in the air. He did not expect a response—indeed, he was prepared to answer it at some length himself—and was therefore displeased at hearing his companion interrupt yet again:

"You are much too kind, Mr. Wayland! And I cannot listen any longer to so much flattery. In truth, I find it most painful."

"Ah! And you *ought* to be pained, too, dear lady, at seeing a man's heart lying open before you, waiting only to be thrust aside by one little gesture of your hand, or made whole and happy with a word! You see before you, Miss Trevor, a man whose destiny hangs in the balance!"

The time had certainly come, thought the curate, to fling himself to the ground. He had really hoped this interview might have been held indoors, for he had bought a new pair of breeches for the occasion, and had no wish to muddy them. A recent rain had left the ground damp, and here and there were still some puddles in the grass. Mr. Wayland accorded the ground a doubtful glance, but seeing that they had by now reached the bottom of the garden walk, and that Miss Trevor was on the point of turning back, he took one quick breath and fell to his knees, making simultaneously a lunge for the young lady's hand.

Almost instantly Wayland regretted his action. A stab-

bing pain shot through one knee, and he realized—too
late—that he had knelt upon a jagged pebble. With an
heroic effort, however, he disguised his agony and proceeded at as rapid a rate as possible:

"My dear Miss Trevor! Surely you cannot mistake my
meaning! So much delicacy of feeling must long ago have
recognized my admiration for you! One glance must have
told you, even on the first day of our acquaintance, what
I felt on looking into your eyes! For months I have strug-
gled against my own emotion, weighing the duty of my
office against my weakness as a mere *man,* and at last
I could not pretend any longer to be master of myself.
A clergyman's chief joy ought to be in a single-minded
pursuit of holiness; but a man—oh, a man, Miss Trevor!
A man is not whole until he knows the comfort and joys
attendant upon the company of the woman he loves! Ah!
What a relief it is, at last to say what is in my heart!
Say you will be my wife!"

Mr. Wayland had a look of sublime ecstasy upon his
face as he gazed into the startled countenance of his
companion. Unable to grasp her hand on his first attempt,
he now made another essay, but Maggie managed just in
time to move her arms behind her back.

"Mr. Wayland!" she cried out, "what on earth are you
doing? Do, do please get up upon your feet! This is a
most extraordinary performance! Indeed, sir, you had better get off the ground at once."

The curate would no doubt have been glad to oblige
her. The ground was certainly very wet, and very cold
as well, and the agony of his knee was increasing every
moment. But having come this far, he was not about to
relent. With a stubborn look, he said,

"I will stay where I am, ma'am, at least until you have
heard me out. A man in love has as great a right to
kneel upon the ground as any other. Only say you will
do me the joy to be my wife, and I will get up as quickly
as you like!"

"Then I fear you will be on your knees a great while,"
replied Miss Trevor, "for I cannot marry you, though your
asking does me great honor."

Mr. Wayland was astonished. He thought for a moment
as clearly as he could, under the circumstances, and at
length stammered, with an incredulous look:

"Can it be you do not *wish* to marry me? Perhaps you consider the living I hold too paltry for you! It is true I have not a great deal of worldly fortune to offer, but then, I have all the fortune of Heaven! Do not you consider Heaven a greater temptation than this dull earth?"

Maggie smiled enigmatically. "Is it a place in Heaven you are offering me then, sir? I had thought it was a place at your side." Her expression might have troubled Mr. Wayland, had he happened to notice it.

"Both, both, my dearest love!" he now positively wailed, for he thought he could not bear the pain in his knee another moment. "Both by my side on earth, and in Heaven afterward! Oh, do, do, *do* please say you will be my wife!"

The misery in Mr. Wayland's voice was so intense that Maggie, gazing down upon him in astonishment, could not help but be softened. She had never supposed Mr. Wayland had any feeling in his heart greater than a love of his own voice, but now she wondered if she had been mistaken, and regretted having teased him for so many months. His face was twisted up in agony, his eyes were red, as if from crying, and his fingers clenched and unclenched in the air. In a kind voice, she said:

"Dear Mr. Wayland, you must not take it so much to heart. I cannot marry you, nor anyone else. I am honored that you would think of me, but my duty is to my father, for I am certain he needs me a great deal more than you. Even had I the desire to marry, I could not. What else could a young lady want, beside the company of her dearest friend, a house of her own, and the freedom to do as she likes? No, no, I cannot marry you, but I thank you for the honor you do me."

After some moments of utter disbelief, a cunning light came into the clergyman's eye. "Oh, I see what you are doing! I have heard that young ladies count it as a point of pride never to accept the first offer. They like to bide their time, and after they have had their fun, they give in, as they always intended doing."

Maggie was at her wits' end. "But I assure you I have no such intention, Mr. Wayland! I am the most plain-spoken creature you will ever meet, and detest all manner of deviousness. If I wished to marry you, you should know it without any doubt. My refusal is likewise definite; I shall never consent to be your wife. Now you had better get up off the ground."

But Mr. Wayland would not budge. His knee was numb, and his mind determined.

"If you dislike the vicarage here, Miss Trevor, I should mention—though it is not yet a certainty—that I have hopes of a better living. It is such an excellent situation in every wise, affording not only an increase in stature, but proximity to one of the best families in England, that even you, Miss Trevor, cannot scoff at it. No, no! Pray let me finish! The park is very grand, and the lady of the family has hinted that, should I take the living, I and my family would be welcome to use it. Besides, we should have the advantage of a close association with the family, who are a very tonnish kind of people, fond of music, with a great deal of society always about them. You should be privy to the wittiest conversations, the most stylish arguments—so much amusement, in fact, I am certain even you cannot dislike. Perhaps you might even be on intimate terms with the daughter, who I am told, is a most elegant young lady."

"So much inducement," replied Maggie in a dry tone, "could hardly persuade me to love anyone. Had I the advantage of a husband whose tastes I shared, I should want no further company. And without the first requisite, every other recommendation is superfluous. My decision, Mr. Wayland, will not be changed. And now, I must beg you to get up, for I have a great deal to do indoors, and must give up your company."

Mr. Wayland had no choice, at this, but to rise to his feet and accompany Miss Trevor back to the entrance of the house. This he did with so sullen an expression, and so strong a feeling of resentment in his heart, that the pain in his knee was as nothing in comparison. Sly creature! She would lead him on in this fashion, and then reject him! So like a woman! He made no attempt to speak, and for once, Maggie had the whole length of the walk to make conversation. Her bright, impersonal chatter, however, was kept up without any of the joy it might have afforded her—only for knowing she had managed to get a word in edge-wise while in the curate's company—at another time. When they had reached the terrace which surrounded the south entrance, Mr. Wayland stopped.

"My company," he said with a great bitterness, "cannot

please you very well, Miss Trevor. I shall not burden you with it any more."

And with a stiff bow and a last accusing look, the curate turned upon his heel and hobbled off across the meadow.

Two

IT HAS BEEN said that the history of mankind is divided equally between the sublime and the ridiculous. Surely as many great wars, resulting in untold horrors and death, had their beginnings in a comedy of errors as those begun by the thoughtful decisions of wise men. Individual lives are often conducted in the same fashion.

The unfortunate Mr. Wayland, limping back to his vicarage across the meadow, could hardly have guessed what a dire effect the sight of him had had upon Admiral Trevor. Most certainly he could not have imagined that one look at the Vicar, with his hair plastered down upon his prematurely balding pate and his arms sawing the air in eloquent gesticulation, had caused the stern old officer to revise his opinion of an ancient quarrel.

Many years before, when the Admiral had been a penniless ensign, he had fallen in love with a young lady from one of England's noblest houses. Though herself without fortune, Miss Ramblay had been the favorite of her uncle, the family's head and a Viscount besides. Lord Ramblay had opposed the match from the start, and when it looked as if his niece would not give up her attachment, he had written her out of his will and out of his heart. He had intended leaving her a handsome legacy, but his pride was such that he could not bear any hint of disobedience, and when the young people married despite him, he would not hear her name mentioned in his presence. Young Trevor soon began to make his mark in the Navy, and his fortunes grew in proportion to his rank, but still a bitter resentment persisted between the two families. Even after Mrs. Trevor died, shortly following the birth of a daughter, her husband carried on the feud, refusing to recognize his wife's relations and growing angry at the mere mention of the Viscount's name.

Maggie Trevor grew up without any knowledge of her cousins save that they were very rich, and very proud, and cared nothing about her. She had heard how cruel they had been to her mother, and harbored a natural bitterness against them, encouraged by her father.

Some time ago the old Viscount had died, and an only son had come into the title. Admiral Trevor heard the news and paid it no attention, for his feelings were firmly fixed. A letter arriving soon afterward from the new Lord Ramblay, in which was expressed a keen regret for his father's conduct and a warm desire to see the quarrel ended and harmony restored between the families, had been torn up and was never answered. And yet the matter had been in Admiral Trevor's mind increasingly of late, and he had begun to regret having missed the chance to renew his relations with his wife's family.

Admiral Trevor was very proud, and very stubborn, too. On his own account he could never have been induced to change his opinion of the Ramblays, but for his daughter, who was the joy of his existence and the pride of his old age, he would have done almost anything. For two and twenty years Maggie had been his sole companion, advisor, and confidante. She had nursed him in times of sickness, and provided a home where he was proud to entertain his friends and fellow officers. She managed his house and filled his idle hours with laughter. She was generally considered to be clever and beautiful, but to her father she was the very perfection of womanhood. If anyone had dared hint to him that she had her share of flaws, like other mortals, he would have bellowed out in rage. He loved in her that same fiery independent nature which he himself possessed, but the refinement and sensibility, which she had inherited from her mother, he held in awe.

For his daughter's sake he had bought a house in Sussex, although the country bored him to distraction, so that she might be the daughter of a landed gentleman. He had hoped, in removing her from the society of officers at Portsmouth, that she might marry a more eligible man. But the neighborhood in which they now lived offered no improvement: quite the opposite, for where at Portsmouth there had been a constant round of dinners and dances, outdoor fetes, and a continual stream of callers, here there was hardly any amusement at all. He dearly wanted her to marry well, even if it meant parting with her company himself—even if it required forgetting his old quarrel with Lord Ramblay. The Ramblays he knew to be among the first families of the *ton*. Elegant, fashionable, and worldly, they could offer Maggie entrance into great society, where the Admiral believed she naturally belonged.

Having that very morning witnesssed his beloved daughter in the company of possibly the hugest idiot in England had done much to sober him. He had been forced to wonder what would happen to her if she remained here with him in Sussex. Hideous though the possibility seemed, was not it altogether likely she would one day be, if not an old maid whose chief diversion lay in visiting about the neighborhood, the wife of just such a pedantic coxcomb as the Vicar?

"By Jupiter, I have been a selfish wretch!" he thought to himself. "Placing my own pride above Maggie's future, and in securing to myself her company, perhaps sacrificing her happiness!"

The thought eased the way to writing the letter, which otherwise would have demanded more masking of his real feelings than the Admiral was capable of. The letter was posted that very afternoon, and within a fortnight he had his reply. Lord Ramblay's letter was written out upon a sheet of heavy parchment that bore the family crest. The hand was at once bold and fine, but the tone so distant, even in its civility, that the Admiral was a little chagrined. While there was nothing absolutely cold about it, yet it had not that warmth which the former letter had possessed in abundance. The Admiral, however, set more store by action than innuendo, and when he saw that the Viscount had appended an invitation to his daughter, he could not criticize anything in the rest of the communication. The invitation was all Admiral Trevor had looked for—had even hinted at—and when he had done reading, he went at once to find his daughter.

Maggie, driven indoors by a heavy shower which now beat rhythmically at the windows, was discovered in the music room laboring over her pianoforte.

"What a pretty air that is!" declared the Admiral as he walked in, for he was a great admirer of Maggie's talents.

Maggie replied with a rueful smile, "How lucky it is you are my father and have not an ear for music," she laughed.

"For if you had, you would know how badly I play, and if you were not my father, you would not hesitate to tell me so!"

"Nonsense, nonsense, my dear!" replied the Admiral in a jovial tone. "No one plays so well as you! Everyone was always saying so at Portsmouth!"

"At Portsmouth no one had ever heard anything better. But I am afraid if they had, they should have seen me for what I was—a great enjoyer of music, without any real proficiency of my own. I do really wish I could play better, for it would be a great pastime now we are in the country."

"You are very fond of music, my dear, ain't you?" inquired the Admiral, finding a chair for himself near the instrument.

"Oh, no one could be fonder of music than I am," replied Maggie. "That is—fond of the performances of others, when they are worth liking. It is a great pity I cannot play better, for I have taste enough to perceive what is excellent, but not skill enough to imitate it."

The Admiral would not hear of this, but he inquired if his daughter would not be delighted by the opportunity of a great deal of good music and to enjoy, besides, a great deal of good conversation.

"I do not know of anyone who could resist such a combination of delights!" responded Maggie playfully. "But, have you come in only to tease me, Papa? I hope you have not, for there is no one who talks well in the neighborhood—unless you count Mr. Wayland, who makes up in quantity what he misses in quality—and only the Miss Durbens play to any degree."

"Ah, Mr. Wayland," moaned the Admiral, his face growing red. "I wish you would not mention him, my dear! But, I did not come in to tease you, nor to discuss that pompous fool. I came to tell you of an invitation you have received."

"An invitation, Father?"

"To Essex."

"To Essex!"

"And then to London, for the winter season."

Maggie was too astonished to say anything for a moment.

"But I know no one who lives in Essex, sir!"

"But you ought to do. Indeed, had it not been for my stupidity, you should have had friends there these many years. But I shan't leave you in suspense, my dear. The

invitation is from your cousin, the Viscount Ramblay, who
very kindly requests your company for the whole winter."

"Not the Lord Ramblay you detest, Papa?" cried Maggie
in amazement. "I thought you would never speak to him
again!"

"And so I should not have, only this is not the old cur-
mudgeon, but his son."

And then the Admiral recounted the whole story of the
correspondence, only changing, for Maggie's benefit, the
date of the first letter, which, out of desire to conceal his
own vanity, he reported as having come a few weeks before
and inspiring his own reply. Maggie was all astonishment
at the news of the reconciliation, and happy admiration of
the son who would bridge the gap initiated by his father.
She would not rest until she had seen what sort of letter
he had written, and the Admiral, having only the second
to give her, and that one so cold, endeavored to put her off.
But Maggie would have her way, and in the end the
Admiral was forced to hand his correspondence over.

The letter was read at one glance, and then read over
with greater care. On finishing it, Maggie said nothing, but
her father exclaimed:

"Is not it an admirable piece of work? I never knew such
a fine letter!"

"To be sure the hand is very good," replied Maggie with
some restraint, "and the paper is the best parchment."

"But the invitation!" cried her father impatiently, "is not
it generous?"

Maggie did not respond to the question, but asked one
of her own: "I suppose you wrote him a long letter, and
were very open?"

Astonished, the Admiral replied his letter had been as
long as it ought, and that he had been as open as possible,
considering the circumstances.

"Just so," thought Maggie. "Papa has written one of his
long letters, begging my cousin to introduce me to Society.
And in response, he has got this: a short, cold, civil piece
of writing, sent more from duty than desire. Lord Ramblay
does not want me for the winter, he only wants to assuage
his guilt. He would be delighted if the invitation were refused, which he cannot hope it will be."

But to her father, she said: "Do not you think the tone
a little cold, Papa? If I was my cousin and wished to heal

such a breach as existed between you and his father, I should be a little more warm in my solicitations."

"Oh!" cried the Admiral, "It is only his way. His first letter was in the same style, though much longer. He is one of your noble young what-d'you-callums—I suppose he would behave the same, no matter what. But the invitation, my dear! What do you say? Is not it a grand one?"

Maggie knew her father very well, and from long observation of him, she could detect what was in his mind no matter how he endeavored to conceal it. She saw now that it was his dearest wish that she should go to Essex, and then to London, but a vague unease prevented her desiring the visit herself. To go to London for the winter was indeed a happy thought! To spend the time in the company of friends, who loved her company and longed to see her, would have been her greatest delight. Who could think otherwise? So much entertainment, so many new faces, such an altogether delightful prospect! But to go, only to be a burden to people who did not want her and had only asked her out of a sense of what they *ought* to do, rather than what they *wished*—what a different kind of prospect!

"I had rather not go, Papa," she murmured.

"What! Not go to Town with Lord Ramblay? But of course you must go! I will not hear of your not going! What! Refuse such an invitation!"

Maggie saw that she was beaten, even before she had begun to struggle. Torn equally between a desire to please her father and a deeper loyalty to him and his long-standing prejudices, she could only say she would make the journey, and wonder inwardly what kind of a torture it would be.

But the Admiral was beaming, for he could not have suspected her doubts. "Go! Of course you shall go, and gallivant about the place to your heart's content! Why, I wish I could be there to see their faces when they glimpse you! I suppose they expect some country cousin or other! Imagine what their surprise will be, when they see you are the finest young lady in the place!"

Maggie smiled at her father's complacency and said nothing. He rattled on, talking of plans for the journey, and at last went off to write his letter to Lord Ramblay to say when she would arrive.

"For it does no good to dawdle about, child! One had better strike while the iron is hot, as your Mama used to say! I shall tell him you will be there within the fortnight, so you shall have a week or two at Essex before going on to Town."

With these words the Admiral strode out of the room, conscious that he had done all he could to secure his daughter's happiness, and certain of her ability to impress all her cousins with her elegance and beauty.

But Maggie, passing the afternoon in what ought to have been the delightful business of looking over her wardrobe for the journey, felt none of her father's delight. With the help of her maid she had laid out all her clothes upon her bed, and now, standing looking down at them with the desultory drumming of the rain in her ears and a great many thoughts waging war in her head, she felt suddenly exceedingly low.

"A fine country cousin I shall make, indeed!" she said to herself, holding up before her in front of the glass a jonquil silk dress she had thought very elegant when she had had it made up in Portsmouth. Now it seemed to her plain and drab, and the place where it had been altered a month before was painfully visible. She made a mock curtsey, and grimaced.

"I hope you are satisfied, Cousin," she said. "Now you see what a fine piece of work you have made! You did not want me to come and now you are sorry for inviting me! Five decent gowns to my name, and the best of those not fit to be seen at Almack's!"

This was a very different Maggie Trevor from the one who, for so many years, had scoffed at spending above fifty pounds a year to dress herself. She had never cared much what she wore so long as she was neat and comfortable, and, because she possessed a beautiful carriage and was tall and graceful, with a proud way of holding her head, the Admiral had often marveled at how well she looked. She hated frills and furbelows, for they made movement difficult, and Maggie was in constant motion, even when she was still. Her few jewels—a cameo or two, a slender necklace of diamonds and pearls, and an amethyst pendant that had belonged to her mother—were hardly ever worn, save for the most formal occasions. Now she keenly regretted having held so low opinion of those females who spent half their lives wondering what they should wear in the other half. Oh! Not for herself, to be sure—what cared she if

Lord Ramblay disapproved of her? But the idea that her father might be included in her own embarrassment was too painful a thought to bear. No, for *him,* she now slumped down upon her bed, the jonquil silk still clutched in her hands, a mortified expression in her face at the thought of how she would compare to those elegant women to whose company her cousin was no doubt used.

It was not alone on account of her clothes that Maggie felt so low. Her knowledge and attainments, though great enough at Portsmouth, where she had been accounted among the most accomplished young ladies in the town, were not, she knew, sufficient for the likes of her cousins and their friends. She had a great love of reading, and had devoured a great many books in her life, but without any kind of formal guidance or discipline. Her taste in drawing and music sprang more from her innate understanding of what a thing ought to be than from training, and while she delighted in everything beautiful she saw or heard about her, she could not have told anyone why. No one knew better than she that her manner of playing the pianoforte was more like doing battle with the music than performing, and, conscious of the fact, she was loath to display her skill before others, try as her father would to coax her into it. Her patience was so limited, and her enthusiasm so great, that she could not be persuaded to practice above half an hour together before the beauty of the day or some other occupation called her away. When she had failed to master a whole concerto in that time, or even the first movement, she would say, with a rueful smile: "Clearly I have no talent in this direction. Let others, who have real skill, perform—I shall enjoy the lesser talent of appreciating their accomplishments!"

Such had been her attitude throughout her life, and, while she had lived twenty-two years very happily with the philosophy, she had now to regret it.

"What an awkward wretch they shall think me!" she lamented. And with such kinds of self-criticisms and worries she passed an hour in futile misery. But Maggie was a girl so little given to regretting what she could not change, and her disposition was so inclined to happiness, that more than an hour she could not give to such remonstrations. At the end of that time she stood up with a determined light in her hazel eyes and a mischievous smile on her lips.

Glancing into the mirror, she held up the unfortunate jonquil silk once more, and proceeded to do a fast jig about
her bedroom. At the end of this exercise she was laughing
inwardly, and her face was animated with amusement.
Stopping now before her glass, she made a grimace at her
own reflection, which returned to her the sight of a young
lady radiant with good health and a joy in living, her thick
auburn hair coming down a little from its pins, her hazel
eyes dancing, and her generous mouth curved up at the
corners.

She would not make herself miserable on *their* account
any longer! What, was she to feel ashamed, only because
she had never cared enough about what she wore to have
a closet full of gowns in the latest style? Was she to lament
the fact that she was not an expert, either at the pianoforte
or the drawing table? No! What were such accomplishments in comparison with a warm heart and a desire to be
liked? "Let them take me as they find me!" she declared
out loud. "I shan't do anything to make them think better
of me in that vein. If they count fashion and music above
common courtesy to their relations, I shall not mind being
despised by them!"

So saying, she set about her packing with a renewed
vigor and good humor. Having once decided to do nothing
extraordinary in the way of improvements to her wardrobe,
Maggie almost went so far as to turn away one gown for
the fault of its possessing too many silk ribbons, which
very nearly made it verge upon the stylish. If, in the natural
defiance of her temperament and her loyalty to the Admiral, she was a little more determined to dislike her cousin
than she might have been, one very great advantage of the
journey did occur to her. Mr. Wayland, for all his avowals
that he should not plague her any more, had been nearly
as omnipresent as he had been before his proposal. To be
sure, he had not called at the manor house, but Maggie
had not been able to walk into the village without seeing
his resentful countenance. On the previous Sunday he had
walked right past her in church without so much as a
glance, but his face was so full of his feelings that Maggie
would really have preferred one of his lectures. To be
removed from *that* would be a comfort indeed, and she
hoped that by the time she returned from her visit he might
have forgotten his bitterness and forgiven her.

There was much to do in preparation for the journey, for Maggie had the whole house to see to, and the servants must be given instructions for the period of her absence. Nearly a fortnight was required for this, and one day— nearly the last one before she was to quit Sussex—a servant came to her as she was in the storeroom with the housekeeper.

"Mr. Wayland is here from the village to see you, miss," said the maid. Startled, Maggie demanded if this was really the case. She could not conceive of his pride allowing him to visit her so soon after he had been rejected. Only the most urgent business could have brought him, she was sure. Thinking there must have been some death, or that an illness had broken out among the local residents, she went upstairs without pausing to tidy her hair or change her frock.

Mr. Wayland was waiting in the morning room. His manner, as he bowed, was stiff and formal, and the elaborations of his greeting so pointed that they seemed to be meant as a punishment. Hemming and hawing for a shorter time than usual, however, the Vicar commenced:

"I should not have intruded upon you, Miss Trevor," said he, in the self-important tone which was his wont, "if I had not had a great piece of news to impart. I would not for all the world have disturbed you in any other case."

Maggie murmured that she would never consider the Vicar an intruder.

"How kind you are!" declared the clergyman, but with a look that contradicted his utterance. "You were not once so kind," his eyes seemed to say, but, much to Maggie's relief, his lips were soon occupied in saying something else.

"I came, in short, merely to tell you, for I thought you might still have some interest in the case, that I have received the living I mentioned to you."

"How very fortunate for you!" cried Maggie. "But I do not recall any such living. Perhaps you did not mention it to me?"

Mr. Wayland was very sure he had mentioned it, mentioned it, in fact, at some length and in detail. But he only smiled icily, and said, "Oh! I thought you knew all about it. It is the very living I had hoped for, and now, through a lucky stroke, I have got it just at the time I wished most to be removed from the neighborhood."

This last was muttered with an accusing look, and Maggie saw at once that the chief purpose of the interview was intended to be a punishment of herself.

"How delightful! I hope it is a good situation?"

"As excellent a one as I could wish," pronounced the Vicar primly. "Indeed, even had I not the *desire* to live elsewhere, I should have been happy to take it, for the post itself is among the most important in the vicinity of London, and the family one of the finest in the whole kingdom. The park and grounds are, as I believe I mentioned, most beautiful. The castle is ancient, but has many modern conveniences, and the whole situation is so advantageous for a man of my tastes that I am quite overjoyed. The lady of the family is, besides, so exceedingly condescending, such an elegant personage in every wise, that she has offered me the use of the park at any time, and hinted that I shall be almost a member of the family."

"How very fortunate for you!" cried Maggie, as warmly as she could. "It will be a great thing to have such friends in a new home. And where is the living to be held?"

"In the county of Essex!"

"In Essex!" Maggie had just been considering the irony of fate, which was to remove Mr. Wayland from the vicinity just when she had no need of his removal. "What a coincidence, for I go to Essex myself the day after tomorrow, on a visit to my cousins."

The coincidence struck Mr. Wayland as ironic, too. However, since he was now in a position to patronize his old inamorata, he determined to be generous.

"How astonishing! It is likely your cousins will not be within easy reach of my new living, or I should certainly invite you to drive in our park. I think you would be most pleased with it, for the land has been laid out very cleverly."

Maggie expressed her regret that, since she would certainly be occupied a great deal with her relatives, she could not take advantage of such a generous invitation. Mr. Wayland passed a quarter of an hour enumerating all the many points on which he might be congratulated for obtaining so choice a living, and when he felt he had punished Miss Trevor enough, he rose to go. His manner seemed to relent a little at the door, however, for as he had his hand upon the knob, he turned around and inquired in what part of Essex Miss Trevor would be.

"I go to Ramblay Castle, near Debbens," replied Maggie, not at all displeased, after all Mr. Wayland's boasting, to be able to claim her relatives as inhabiting a castle themselves.

But Mr. Wayland appeared to have been taken suddenly ill. His small eyes grew round in disbelief, what little color there had been in his cheeks drained away, and clutching at his heart, he spluttered—"Ramblay! Good God! It is the very location of my living!"

Three

THE FIRST PART of Maggie's journey to Essex was accomplished without incident. Riding in the comfort of her father's chaise, with her own coachman at the reins and her maid beside her, there was little to occupy her mind save the passing scenery and a general apprehension at the prospect of meeting her cousins. It had been arranged that Lord Ramblay's carriage should meet her halfway, at the posting house at Dartmoor, and as the chaise clattered its way over the potholes of the Great North Road, raising behind it a huge cloud of dust, her uneasiness increased. Now at last she would see for herself what kind of man the Viscount was—whether his letter had been, as her father claimed, tempered by a natural restraint of manner or whether, as she really hoped was not the case, he was really just the kind of cold, indifferent man as his style of writing made him seem.

Gradually the verdant undulations of the Sussex countryside, with its clay hills and misty pastures, began to give way to a different kind of view. The farther north they progressed, the more regulated the landscape became. Flatter and more cultivated than that of Sussex, it seemed to have fallen a great deal under the ordering influence of man. Where the south had been soft and wild, here the neat fields and meadows were layed out in regular patches of color, with only the intermittent interruption of a narrow stream or woodsy copse. The day had dawned very clear and fine, with one or two wispy clouds in the azure expanse of sky. Maggie, who had traveled little over this part of the country, watched the changing scene with fascination.

The posting house at Dartmoor was among the busiest in all of England. Situated just at the junction of the Great North Road and the Bath Highway, it attracted

every kind of conveyance going either north or west, to
London or the Midlands. As the Admiral's chaise drew
toward it, a great hum of activity became visible. Post boys,
vaulting off their lathered mounts, paused barely long
enough to catch a breath before leaping onto fresh horses
and tearing off again. Chaises for hire, elegant private
equipages, and two stage coaches crowded the yard, while
the various coachmen, some in livery, some in the crudest
leather jerkins, shouted orders with equal bravado to an
ostler leaning up against a post. The ostler was evidently
more fascinated by the droning of some flies than all their
impatience. Almost at once Maggie's ears were assaulted
with a din of voices and her nostrils with an equally riotous
concoction of odors. As they turned into the yard, a servant
in yellow livery stepped before the horses, nearly causing
them to bolt and bringing forth an incoherent volley of
abuse from the coachman. But in short order they had
driven into the yard and taken their place in the line of
carriages waiting for fresh teams.

The yard was so full, and the likelihood of finding Lord
Ramblay's chaise amid the fray so slim—if indeed it had
arrived at all—that Maggie determined upon taking some
refreshment in the coffee room while they waited. A sign
above the door advertising the finest of beverages and
viands to be found anywhere in the kingdom had evidently
done its work; the entranceway was crammed to overflowing with bodies of every description waiting for a place at
one of the overloaded tables. There seemed little hope that
Maggie and her maid would secure seats, but in a moment
the landlord of the inn, recognizing a lady traveling with
her servant, had procured them a place near the window,
through which they could observe the hubbub without.

Cider and some slices of mutton were brought forth and
quickly devoured, for they had begun their journey at day-
break and it was now past three o'clock. Much improved
by this nourishment, Maggie leaned back to watch the hum
of activity about her. It had been a full year since she had
seen so much humanity all in one place and the sight was
immensely diverting. She was a great lover of every form
of life; no pastime pleased her half so well as observing
the lowest and loftiest kinds of human beings all going
about their business, with all the peculiarities and eccen-
tricities of their natures. It seemed to her that elevation of

station had no effect upon man's foibles, and for this fact
she was very grateful, being fonder of laughter than almost
any other activity she could think of.

Thus occupied, she had whiled away a quarter of an
hour in a most delightful fashion when her eye, chancing
to stray in the direction of the door, lit upon the figure of
a man who was leaning in the entranceway. The gentleman
—for his dress, though dusty from traveling, proclaimed
him to be one—had evidently been staring at her intently.
Maggie flushed a little at the smiling admiration in his eyes,
and turned away. But the gentleman apparently felt no
such embarrassment. He continued to watch her with half
a smile, and when she glanced back again in several moments, held her gaze with his own. Maggie was not so
displeased as she might have been: the gentleman was in
no wise impudent, but so merry-looking, so fair and tall
and brown, that it was clear he felt only an open admiration for her. Maggie smiled at him, and he smiled back.
His regular features were lit up in a delightful look of
pleasure. But now Maggie saw him signal to the innkeeper,
who came over at once, and the two were bent together
in conversation. Maggie's gaze returned to the scene in
the yard.

But in a moment the gentleman and the landlord were
standing at her side, and with a very civil bow and a dis-
arming apology, the gentleman wished to know if he might
be allowed to share her table. There were no other vacant
chairs in all the house, and the gentleman, who had ridden
that morning all the way from Portsmouth, had still three
hours left in his journey. With another bow, and a boyish
grin, he admitted to being "exceeding starved" and claimed
no other state but the direst danger of starvation could have
persuaded him to intrude upon her so unceremoniously.

Maggie had been feeding hungry sailors all her life. She
could not now deny a man at once so pleasant and so civil.
The news that he had come from her old home made her
doubly generous, and in a moment the gentleman was
ensconced beside her. He astonished her at once by introducing himself as Captain Morrison.

"Oh!" cried Maggie upon hearing this, "you are exactly
what I would have wished for! A naval officer with a
knowledge of Portsmouth. It is my old home, and I have
a great yen to hear all about it."

The Captain was all eagerness to oblige her, but begged pardon for his ignorance of the city. His usual port of call was Liverpool, and only a battered hull had made him put in at Portsmouth for repairs. There he had been not above six weeks, and having overseen the chief part of the damage mended, was en route to London to take his leave. Six weeks, however, appeared to have been sufficient time for Captain Morrison to make the acquaintance of every one of Maggie's old friends. His amiable manner must have recommended him at once, thought she, upon hearing his amusing accounts of the seaport's inhabitants, told all in the most open and humorous style. Captain Morrison appeared to be one of those rare souls who is capable of putting everyone at their ease. His own manner was so lacking in self-consciousness that it was impossible to feel awkward in his presence. He listened with a keen interest to everything he heard, and replied with great sincerity, but without any of that lugubrious gravity that dampens a conversation. His features radiated with good-humor and candor, his smile was quick and his laugh quicker, his mind agile, and his sensibilities just. Maggie liked him at once, and still more so when, upon hearing her own name mentioned, he exclaimed—

"Miss Trevor! You must be Admiral Trevor's daughter! I should have known at once by your knowledge of our profession that you were not a mere civilian! What a happy chance this is, indeed, for I have long admired your father, and had two or three years ago the good fortune to meet him. In my belief, he was the chief cause of our victory over the French—in truth, a more able strategist we have not had since the time of Drake's victory over the Armada."

Maggie could hardly hear this without feeling twice inclined toward liking the young officer. Any praise of her father was balm to her ears, and when she saw his admiration of herself increase with the knowledge of her parentage, her feelings were firmly fixed.

Very happily they passed another half an hour in further conversation, while Captain Morrison made short work of a leg of mutton and two mugs of ale, laughing at his own appetite. It was discovered they had all of the same tastes and interests, and, upon hearing that his new acquaintance was shortly to be in the capital, it was agreed they should meet again. So happily occupied, and diverted from her own worries by the merry conversation of the naval captain, Maggie had almost forgotten about her cousins. But now, seeing Captain Morrison glance sharply out the window giving onto the yard, she was reminded of it.

"Why!" she said in some surprise upon seeing his face grow pale and a hard look come into his eyes, "is anything wrong?"

Her own glance followed his, and took in only the usual commotion of the yard, which was now focused upon a sleek phaeton and a team of lathered horses.

The Captain shook his head and smiled at her. "No, no— I only thought I saw a man I know. It reminded me of a most unpleasant affair, but one which I had rather forget."

Maggie looked at him curiously, but the Captain had turned away from the window and was making a pointed endeavor to take up their conversation where it had been interrupted. She saw by his look that he did not wish to explain himself, and though she saw his eyes dart now and then to the window, she suppressed her own curiosity.

After a little while she herself looked out the window, hoping to see some signs of her cousin's carriage.

"I cannot imagine why there is so much delay," she said. "I was to be met by my cousin's chaise two hours ago— and still there is no sign of it."

Captain Morrison very civilly offered to go out into the yard and make some inquiry, and was just getting to his feet when a commotion at the entrance to the coffee room drew both their attentions. In amazement, Maggie saw that the trouble was caused by her own coachman, who, gesticulating violently in her own direction, was being barred from passing by the innkeeper. Exclaiming at this, she began to gather her reticule and gloves to see what the matter was, when at that moment the coachman broke out of his captor's grip and rushed toward her.

"Miss Trevor!" he cried almost incoherently. "There's a varmint outside claims your horses belong to 'im! He's gone and snatched 'em, good and proper, while I was fetching a brush from the stables! I'd almost done hitching them up to your new chaise, when they was sudden gone and disappeared!"

The coachman paused for a moment to catch his breath, his eyes nearly popping out of his head at this outrageous information. Maggie, however, who had caught only half of his words, and these so mysterious that she had not the least idea what he was talking about, only stared back at him, urging him to calm himself and explain what had happened once more.

"There, there, my good man," cut in Captain Morrison, patting the fellow on the arm. "You had better tell us again what occurred. You say Miss Trevor's horses have been stolen?"

"Plain in me own sight, your lordship!" exploded the coachman with fresh energy. "Plain in me own sight and under me own nose, this 'ere bloke come up and snatches 'em off the 'itch! Dashed impudence, *I* call it, after we'd waited half the day for 'em as it is!"

Captain Morrison glanced inquiringly at the young lady, who explained, "I was to be met halfway by my cousin's chaise, sir. No doubt the man has been mistaken—perhaps he adopted some other man's team thinking they were my cousins."

"Mistake!" blurted out the coachman, with a reproachful look at his mistress. "Mistake, miss! I hope I've got more sense than that! I've only driven for yer father these last three and twenty years! Mistake, miss! What do you take me for, that I have not sense enoug' to find your cousin's team in a stodgy posting inn?"

Again Captain Morrison urged the man to calm himself, offering to go out into the yard to help him recover the team, if indeed they belonged to his mistress's cousin. The coachman seemed satisfied by this suggestion, and began pushing his way back to the door with Captain Morrison close upon his heels. Maggie, pausing only to collect her belongings and wait for her maid, followed just behind.

But the ladies, detained by an excited crowd in the hallway of the inn, were delayed for several minutes and emerged at last into the sunlit yard in time to witness a most amazing scene. There in the middle of the yard was standing the distraught coachman, making furious gestures at another carriage servant, who, with a stubborn expression and no sign of paying attention to the former, was continuing to hitch a team of handsome dapple-grays to the very phaeton Maggie had seen earlier from within the coffee room. Captain Morrison had a restraining arm upon the man's arm, but just as the ladies caught sight of them, the coachman broke out of the officer's grip and made straight for the other servant. With a cry he leaped upon the other man, and there followed a battle of fisticuffs, with limbs all tangled up in each other, and teeth digging into flesh, until the two fell into the dust in a mass of squirming feet and limbs. Just at that moment a cry came from within the doorway of the inn.

"What the devil's going forward here?" came a deep voice, whose owner was for the moment invisible. But even this rather mild expostulation appeared to have an effect on the coachman's opponent, for he instantly ceased wriggling in the dirt, and, though he did not get to his feet, made no further resistance to Admiral Trevor's coachman. The latter, taking full advantage of his enemy's paralysis, instantly swept down upon him with a fresh volley of punches and kicks.

"What the devil are you doing, man?" came the voice again, this time directly behind where Maggie and her maid stood. Maggie turned around in time to see the speaker step out from the crowd that had gathered around the entranceway. The gentleman was above the average in height, and a beautiful cape of deep brown Scottish worsted was thrown about his broad shoulders. Everything about his dress, from the fine, crushed leather of his Hessian boots to the snowy white linen cravat knotted simply at his throat, bespoke the gentleman's pedigree. His was not the attire of a dandy, nor even of a Corinthian, yet there was that in his carriage and in the quality of cloth and lines of his garments that could not be mistaken. What struck Maggie, in the time she had to study his appearance, however, was not the gentleman's attire, but his face. It was surely the handsomest face she had ever seen, and would have been absolutely beautiful had not the features possessed so marked a quality of masculinity. The brow was high and finely made, the aristocratic nose perfectly chiseled, with nostrils now stretched out by indignation. The cheeks were high and well defined, the jawline strong, and clefted deeply in the chin. But the whole, regular formation of features, framed in a thatch of messy dark waves, was ruled over by the eyes. Those eyes were so dark that they looked absolutely black, and were now shining with annoyance. Deep-set and widely spaced, they stared out upon the scene from under the thick dark brows with so much frowning authority that Maggie instinctively took a step back. She was wise to do so, for the gentleman, having paused only for a second in the doorway, now strode past her without so much as a glance in her direction. She would not in the least have been amazed had he trod over her in his determination to get into the yard—so strong was his aura of arrogance. That arrogance was the one displeasing quality in the whole face, but it was so marked that Maggie instantly disliked him. She was not insensible of masculine beauty, and would otherwise have been struck by his handsomeness, but this air of having the whole world at his command made everything else about him distasteful. So absorbed was Maggie in contemplating this, that she barely noticed the scurrying figure that hurried in his wake—a small, thin, bent man with a wizened face. He was dressed all in black, and carried in his hand a small black bag.

The first gentleman was now standing over the squirming coachmen.

"Here, Jason, what are you about? What do you mean by this? Get up at once—I have no time for your tomfoolery."

The gentleman spoke no louder than he might have in a drawing room, but his accents were so laden with irony that the servant instantly took fright.

Admiral Trevor's coachman, however, evidently felt no such cowardice. Leaping to his feet, he began to pound upon the gentleman's chest with his fists, all the while yelping abuse.

" 'Ere! Tike this, your worship! I 'ave no doubt but it was *you* approved this piece of villainy! What are you about, man? Ordering your man to steal me own mistress's horses?"

The gentleman stared down at the battling coachman in amazement, and with one calm movement of his arm, thrust him aside.

"What on earth are you doing, my good man? Here, leave off your fisticuffs, if you will be so kind. As to your mistress's horses, I assure you I would not touch them. This team is my own." Turning to his own servant, who had by now scrambled to his feet, he continued: "If you are quite through, Jason, I would be obliged if you would climb up. As I informed you, we have no time to waste with any further of your foolishness."

And with these words, which were spoken to the dire amazement of the Admiral's coachman, the gentleman handed his companion up before him into the box, leaped up himself, and in the wink of an eye was driving out of the yard.

"What!" muttered Maggie to herself, when she was calm enough to speak. "I can hardly credit what I have just seen!"

And stepping out into the yard, she noticed for the first time that Captain Morrison was nowhere in sight. In a moment he was by her side, however, exclaiming angrily at the piece of arrogance he had just witnessed.

"Never in my life have I seen anything like it! And yet, knowing the gentleman, I can believe it a little."

Maggie instantly demanded who the man had been who was capable of such incivility.

"Why, it is the Viscount Ramblay, a most arrogant and unamiable man," replied he.

"Lord Ramblay!" Maggie was too amazed to say any more for a moment. "Lord Ramblay—are you absolutely certain, sir?"

The officer regarded her inquiringly.

"As certain of that as I am of my own name, Miss Trevor—why does it amaze you so?"

And now Maggie, with immense mortification, was forced to explain that Lord Ramblay was her cousin, the very man whose chaise she had been waiting for!

"Good God!" exclaimed Morrison, understanding causing him to blanche in outrage and amazement. "Your cousin is Lord Ramblay? The very devil! Why, had I known that——"

"But what could you have done?" demanded Maggie bitterly. "He cared nothing for anyone save himself! Kind as you are to think of it, it is plain to me that any interference would have been ignored. I can hardly believe it still!"

But Captain Morrison was lost in his own thoughts, which, from the dark expression in his eyes, were not very happy ones. At last he said, "But how is it you did not recognize him yourself, Miss Trevor?"

And then Maggie narrated to him the history of her father's quarrel with the late Viscount, and how it had been resolved so recently, adding, with an ironic smile—

"I had no reason to think well of my cousin, Captain, even before this moment. His invitation was so perfunctory, and wreaked so thoroughly of duty rather than desire, that I cannot imagine he remembered he had sent his team for *me*. Indeed, I have no doubt but that he has forgotten I am to visit him!"

Captain Morrison stared at her incredulously.

"Forgotten! But, indeed, perhaps you are right. From what I know of him, he is so altogether selfish and hard a man that it would not amaze me much."

Such an account of the man Maggie had been dreading to meet all day could hardly have been calculated to make her complacent. And yet she would not absolutely discredit her cousin until she had inquired further of the stable keepers. Captain Morrison, when she proposed the scheme, seemed of her mind as well, for though Ramblay was an arrogant and cold-hearted fellow, there was no one ruled by duty so much as he. No, no—though he might treat *others* badly, it was doubtful he would be really uncivil to a cousin.

The officer's inquiries were rewarded, for in short order he returned with the coachman—who had recovered his composure a little—to say that he had found the Viscount's chaise, which had been towed away to the back of the stables, and that a team of Lord Ramblay's horses were waiting within. They were not, it is true, so fine a group of beasts as the ones their owner had just dashed off with, and yet they were fresh, and well equipped to make the journey. At the officer's orders, they were now in the process of being hitched up, and Lord Ramblay's coachman and postillions—whose whereabouts during the period of the quarrel was something of a mystery—were readying themselves for the journey. They had seemed none of them surprised to hear of their master's recent presence at the inn, though they would offer no explanation for it, and were unperturbed at hearing what had gone on between Miss Trevor's coachman and the Viscount. Captain Morrison explained this amazing show of indifference by saying—

"I suppose they are more accustomed to your cousin's manner than we are, Miss Trevor. In any case, you are assured of being on your way within the half hour."

Settled at last in the elegant comforts of her cousin's

vehicle, Maggie had ample time to contemplate her cousin's astonishing behavior. But not even the luxuriousness of the chaise and the attentiveness of Lord Ramblay's servants could assuage the resentment she bore that gentleman nor erase from her mind the tale Captain Morrison had told her as they waited for the carriage to be readied.

Four

CAPTAIN MORRISON had unfolded his tale—or rather, those bits and pieces of it which Maggie was forced to take in lieu of a more complete narration—only after some little prodding from the young lady. He seemed at first reluctant to cast any aspersions upon her relative, showing thereby a delicacy of feeling which directly increased her esteem of *him*, even as it diminished her regard for Lord Ramblay. But at last, when she had told him the extent of her own knowledge of her cousin and the history of her family's quarrel with his father, he consented to tell her a little. From the expression in his eyes and the restraint of his manner, Maggie was sure he did not tell her *all*—and yet it was enough to strengthen her own misgivings about the Viscount.

The Viscount had been known for some time to the naval officer, without, as the Captain said, any of that intimacy which might have attended their relations had they been born into the same rank. Lord Ramblay was not one of your democratic aristocrats, it seemed; he could not feel easy with the acquaintance of one from a humbler background, and though they had frequented the same balls and clubs in the years before Morrison's induction, they had not shared more than a passing acquaintance. Yet it had been enough to show the younger man a little of the other's style.

"Yes, yes," Captain Morrison had muttered, when he heard Maggie's description of the letter which had been written to her father, "I can well credit it. Ramblay never cared for any comfort but his own, and if, in doing his duty, he makes himself easier, his duty he'll do. But I don't think it springs from any *love* of duty. Do not misapprehend me: there never was a more dutiful man on earth—but neither, I think, one with a colder sense of how

35

to perform it. I only tell you this because you are to depend
so much upon his company, and though I have but known
you this last hour, I cannot help believing you are as
ill-disposed to coolness as I am."

Maggie nodded eagerly at this, not without a certain
satisfaction at hearing the Captain join their two natures
under one description.

"Ah! I think there is nothing more distasteful, unless
it is a really cruel heart; and I cannot help but suspect
that where there is a nature given to iciness, it has not
far to go to outright malice."

Captain Morrison gave her a deep look on hearing these
words.

"Just so," he murmured, so softly that Maggie barely
heard him. He stared out for a moment at the scene before them, the muddy, trammeled grass of the yard, the
stamping of a post horse not ten yards from where they
stood, and the aquamarine sky floating over the distant
meadows beyond. He wore a moody look, and his clear
eyes were clouded. Gazing at him, Maggie was struck
afresh by the amiability of his countenance, even at this
moment when he seemed lost in thought. His was a fair-
ness born less out of golden curls and pink flesh (for his
hair was a pleasant disarrangement of curly chestnut
waves, and his complexion tanned from months at sea)
than from a particular disposition of features. His brow
was high and broad and clear, his mouth nearly as full as
a woman's, and a deep cleft in his chin prevented the long
lashes of his eyes and the dimple on one cheek from making him seem feminine. There was strength in his look,
but it was a strength of harmony and good humor, rather
than fierceness. His face was made for laughter, just as
his shapely legs in their well-worn Hessians, and the neat
waist and shoulders in the heather-brown tweed riding
coat, seemed formed for dancing.

"I suppose," he said, after a moment, "you are acquainted with the story of your cousin's marriage?"

Maggie replied that, so far from knowing the story, she
had not even known Lord Ramblay was married.

"Ah!" The Captain gave her another look, and looked
away. "He ain't married any more. He was, however, for
nearly two years—if you call it a marriage where the
partners are bound only by vows, and where all the inti-

macy of thought and feeling which, to my mind, is the very heart and soul of the state, is lacking."

"I am exactly of your mind!" she exclaimed warmly, pleased beyond everything at this declaration of Morrison's, which exactly matched her own view. "A husband and wife ought to be as a two-headed beast, each with his own mind and thoughts, which enrich the other's, but sharing one heart, and one attitude toward the great issues of life. Without such a kind of unity, there is nothing to keep them together but a promise."

"And a promise without any deeper intent is worse than none at all."

Again he paused, and again Maggie attempted to draw him out.

"But were they then so ill-suited to each other? Why marry at all, if there was no love between them?"

"Oh, there was love—love enough, at least, on the lady's part," replied Captain Morrison cryptically. "*She* was born to love. A sweeter, more devoted nature I have never known, nor one with a greater capacity for feeling, though her physical strength was as tiny as a kitten's."

Maggie would liked to have inquired into all the particulars, to have asked the officer what his knowledge was of the match, and what had ensued, for by his look he knew a great deal. But she contented herself by saying, "I suppose it was a marriage of convenience. From what I know of my cousin's father, he cared nothing for anyone's feelings, and a more heartless custom than the arrangement of marriages I cannot conceive."

Morrison surprised her by saying in reply, "But it was not arranged by the old Viscount. As to convenience, I suppose it *was* convenient for Ramblay. I cannot conceive why else he might have taken a wife he neither loved nor liked. He treated her as one might treat a rare china vase which one has paid a great deal for, and thereby knows the value of, but which one does not like half so well as the guinea jug by the wash basin. It is kept locked up in a cupboard, along with the family heirlooms, and brought out upon occasion to be showed about to one's friends. Suddenly, on hearing it admired and coveted, it becomes prettier in the eyes of its owner; but the instant it has ceased to be admired, when the friends go away and no further compliments are heard upon its beauty, it ceases to be liked again. And so it is stowed away till such a time as its owner may again take satisfaction in knowing he owns it. Such was the kind of convenience Ramblay took from his marriage. But she—ah! *She* worshiped him, and I cannot believe it was more the coldness she received from *him*, than a lung fever, which carried her away so soon."

They had been standing in the shadow of the tethering wall while they talked, and now the arrival of a team of horses made them move out into the sunlight. It was warm for the time of year, but even as they had been talking the sun had crept lower in the west, and the shadows in the yard had begun to lengthen. Now a chilly breeze sprung up, fluttering the molten cape about Maggie's shoulders and sweeping her skirt against her legs. She would like to have gone inside, but feared interrupting this narration. Already her interest was so keen in the tale that she could have ignored the cold without any discomfort. She was shocked by this picture of her cousin, for though she might formerly have suspected him of egotism, of a pride born out of wealth and rank and a love of his own importance, she had not thought of crediting him with so much hardness of heart as this story showed him to possess. The tale brought up in her mind a most pathetic picture, and being of a warm nature herself, she could not help but cry out inwardly against the injustice it displayed.

"Why did he marry her, then?" she cried eagerly, when they had found a place in a sheltered corner of the yard, away from stamping horses and yelling black-stockings.

Captain Morrison shrugged. "Who knows what moves men to do half of what they do? We are a strange lot. I suppose in part he was stunned by her beauty—as nearly everyone was—and then, too, perhaps there was really some part of the collector's spirit in him. Anna—the lady's name—was coveted by every man with half a heart in London. She came to England, you know, from the West Indies, where her father owned half the fertile lands in the territory. She had an immense fortune, and was as sweet and unassuming as you please."

Maggie could not resist inquiring, with a smile, if Captain Morrison had not been in love with her himself, but the question, which had been meant in a lighthearted kind of way, was met with a sudden frown.

"I loved her, it is true," he replied instantly, "but not in that fashion. I met her when she dearly needed friends, and I was to her a kind of brother. At least——" and here the Captain paused——"so long as I was able to see her. Your cousin could not bear her having any friends beside himself, and though he so rarely availed himself. of her company, he detested the notion that anyone else should enjoy it!"

Morrison had spoken with an intensity altogether unlike his former manner. He seemed to have forgotten himself, and for a moment, Maggie saw a dark look come into his eyes. But as quickly as the mood came, it passed, and the officer, seeming to remember himself, smiled quickly, and turned the conversation to other matters. He appeared reluctant to continue in the vein, and Maggie would not force him to, although her curiosity was now at such a peak that it took all her self-control to keep from questioning him further. For a few moments they talked of London, and Maggie was soon caught up in her companion's descriptions of life in Town. His interests were so entirely her own, their tastes and affinities so similar, that she was more and more hopeful of a continuance of their friendship. Suddenly the prospect of a visit to the capital became attractive. If she was destined to be confined chiefly to the society of her haughty cousins, the promise of one friend who shared her own attitudes made the picture a little brighter. Her pleasure was very great, therefore, when, upon being informed that her carriage was ready, and when she had been handed into the luxurious equipage with her maid and the satin pillows disposed behind her shoulders by an attentive male servant, the Captain leaned in at the window and said, "I hope I may count upon seeing you in London?"

Nothing could have suited her better, and Maggie replied she would be glad of receiving him at any time. But at these words Captain Morrison looked doubtful.

"I think I shall not wait upon you, Miss Trevor, if you are to be with your cousin. He dislikes me so much for having been a favorite of his wife's that he would be enraged to hear I was acquainted with his cousin. However, if you are to be at Almack's, I shall certainly see you, and if you allow it, I shall claim the pleasure of your very first set of country dances."

So it was agreed, with a deep, interested look on the face of one, and a pleasurable flush on the cheeks of the other, that they should continue their acquaintance as soon as possible. The outriders and postillions were now arranged about the chaise, the coachman in his perch, and with a crack of the whip the carriage started off. Maggie had now as much time as she liked to contemplate her new acquaintance, and to recollect the story he had told her of her cousin's marriage. The former she liked better the more she thought of him, and the latter, contemplated with some animation of feeling, served to prepare her for the meeting she had dreaded all day. If this new aspect of her cousin did little to make her comfortable, at least it lighted the way for her, and what had begun as uncertainty as to his character, was pretty well formed into a determination to dislike him by the time the chaise turned in to a long elm-lined drive bounded on one side by a vast deer park and on the other by a stretch of ornamental waterways and wooded land. If her vanity had been soothed a little by the luxury of the carriage and the great attentiveness of her cousin's servants, her heart was more than ever set against the nobleman whose ancestors had devised this elegant pleasure ground.

Five

DUSK WAS ALREADY well advanced by the time the Viscount's chaise came into view of Ramblay Castle. Maggie's first glimpse of the mansion, lit up by what seemed a thousand candles in as many windows, nearly took her breath away. The castle was a vast building, with two great wings stretching out from a central construction, which, from its darker color and crumbling walls, appeared to have been the original edifice, constructed in the time of King John. It lay at the end of a stately avenue, lined on both sides by ancient elms, their crimson leafy glory just touching over the center of the road. A huge portico at the front of the castle, with room for three carriages at once, was sustained by twelve immense columns, and the main entrance was guarded by a pair of marble lions. Through the gathering dusk, Maggie could descry great terraces and balustrades giving off the modern wings, and a variety of flower gardens and walkways leading into a deer park.

She was amazed at first to see such a profusion of light, when she supposed only the immediate family was at home. Even in her first delight at seeing so much beauty, elegance, and symmetry of design, she could not help but be taken aback by such a display of wealth. It struck her as just the kind of display an arrogant peer might like, which might, in fact, serve to assuage his own pride more than any more practical need. She herself had never allowed a taper to burn where no one was using it—to see such a profligate waste of candlewax as this only served to remind her of her prejudice against the Viscount. She was not allowed much time to contemplate this idea, however, for the chaise had very soon drawn up before the mansion, and in the ensuing commotion of postillions dismounting, footmen running out to unload her baggage and carry it indoors, and the carriage doors being thrown open, every other concern but the immediate business of getting down and seeing that nothing was forgotten left her. She was not allowed to do much, for the servants were so numerous and so efficient that within the wink of an eye the carriage was empty and being driven toward the stables. Another moment saw the great front door swing open and the dignified figure of the butler appear. Her maid, who had been standing stock-still during all the foregoing business, evidently too amazed to budge, now grasped her arm in fright and whispered a question.

"Never mind, Marie," Maggie murmured back, with a reassuring pat, "you shall come with me, whatever they say."

And together the two women mounted the great marble stairway and passed the butler into the hall. Here was an even more extravagant array of luxury than the exterior of the building had promised. Gilt and crystal, silk and exotic marbles made up the whole; Maggie felt a fleeting sympathy, on finding herself in the vast and echoing hallway, for her trembling maid. Marie was still clutching her arm, a single bandbox clenched in her free hand and her eyes wide with awe. For a moment Maggie felt exactly like a pauper who has just had her first glimpse of Windsor Castle. The whole place was built on such a grand scale, and with such a regard for beauty at whatever price, that she might have been standing in the foyer of a cathedral rather than a private house. Here indeed was food for every twinge of esthetic hunger—one glance about the walls told her that every art of construction and design of painting, silversmithy, and sculpture had gone into the building of this castle.

The butler was now standing behind them, coughing. With a sudden start, Maggie realized he meant to take her cloak, and slipped it off.

"The other guests are all upstairs," he murmured, bowing, and, Maggie thought, glancing wonderingly at her dusty traveling costume. "Shall I announce you?"

And now for the first time, Maggie was aware of the distant sounds of laughter and voices. Whatever else she had envisioned of her arrival at Ramblay, she had never supposed she might come in in the midst of a dinner or a ball!

"Oh, no!" she exclaimed in reply. "I shall wait here for my cousin."

The butler bowed again, smirked a little, and retreated to his post beside the door. Maggie waited patiently for five minutes, until gradually the idea dawned on her that Lord Ramblay was not aware of her arrival. She was on the point of saying something of the kind to the butler when a doorway opened beside her and through it issued a plump and smiling woman in black.

The housekeeper—for her dress, and the ring of keys jangling from her waist, declared her to be such—had commenced speaking even before she was through the door.

"Oh, to be sure, to be sure!" she cried, with her tiny hands gesticulating in the air, "I had no idea you were here, miss! Pray forgive me! Indeed, here you are at last. I know you are Miss Trevor, my master's cousin, and this girl must be your maid."

The woman beamed back and forth between them, instantly comforting both. Maggie had begun to feel more awkward than she had ever felt before in her life until this plump and motherly presence had appeared. But now she began to regain her composure, and smiled back at the woman.

"Indeed I am, and I would be very grateful if someone told my cousin I am here."

"Tut!" cried the little woman, glaring at the butler, "has not he been told? Oh, la, miss—you must forgive us. Lord Ramblay has got a hunting party down from London for the week, and we are all in a tizzy below stairs. So many complaining ladies, you know—well, we shall soon remedy *that*, I assure you! Here, my girl," she said to the maid, "you must come along with me, and we shall lay out your mistress's evening gown, and I shall have Lord Ramblay down in a flash!"

Bustling off, but not before she had informed Maggie that she was Mrs. Black and at her service should she require anything, she disappeared through the same door through which she had come, Marie in tow.

Now Maggie was left completely alone, standing in the middle of that vast expanse of marble. Moment followed moment and, save for the ticking of a clock at the foot of the central stairway, not a sound was heard. Seeing a row of pictures hanging on a wall behind the sweep of stairs, she moved toward them with the idea of occupying her idle moments while she waited. The first in the series of huge portraits framed in gilt depicted a fat youth with round cheeks and wearing a ruffled collar. Beneath the portrait was the legend: "First Viscount Ramblay, 1563." The second Viscount was less spoiled-looking than the first, but not a great deal thinner. Maggie wandered down the room, alternately amazed and amused by the diversity of expression, face, and form in her ancestry. The last portrait was a rendering of the present Lord Ramblay's father, her mother's uncle, and this she gazed at with considerably more interest than she had accorded the others.

Lord Ramblay had been an exceedingly good-looking man, but so stern in his expression, and with such a haughty lift of his eyebrow, that the beauty of his face was almost defeated. The brow was high and broad, the eyes deep-set and sharp, the nose almost hawklike. There was something in the face that reminded Maggie of some likenesses she had seen of the early Roman emperors. The lips, for all their magnificent shape, had a cruel twist, and the set of the strong chin hinted at the stubbornness that had caused the rift with her own mother.

It was just as she was gazing up at this portrait, lost in contemplation, that she heard a step upon the stair, and whirling about, saw her cousin descending toward her.

Lord Ramblay had changed from his traveling costume into an evening suit of deep green satin, with a pearl gray waistcoat. He wore breeches, as in the old-fashioned custom, and pearl gray stockings set off his shapely calves. Everything in his manner, as he came down the steps, smiling at her, was dignified and elegant. But what struck Maggie most, after she had caught her breath on seeing again how extraordinarily handsome he was, was the perfectly amiable smile upon his face. The scornful frown he had worn that afternoon had vanished, changing the whole look of his features, and making them infinitely more pleasing.

"Why, Cousin!" he exclaimed, reaching the last step. "I am afraid you have been kept waiting through some oversight. I hope you have not been impatient—I see at least you are well occupied."

"Yes, thank you," replied Maggie, adjusting herself to

be wary of this new manner, which was certainly a false amiability. "I have been studying these portraits."

"A motley collection we have for our ancestry, eh?" smiled the Viscount, coming up beside her and regarding the painting of his father. But the picture held his attention only for an instant before he turned to regard her. This process was so prolonged, and so intense, that Maggie really thought she would begin to tremble under his eyes. She kept her own focused upon the picture of her cousin's father, but could not shake off the sensation of being looked through. At last she said, turning to him abruptly and staring him straight in the eye, "Why, what are you staring at, Lord Ramblay?"

The Viscount was instantly abashed, and lowered his eyes.

"I beg your pardon, Cousin," murmured he. "It is only that I did not expect—that is——"

"Perhaps you did not expect to see me again so soon?" inquired she pointedly, smiling at his amazement.

"I beg your pardon—so soon?"

"So soon after our encounter at the posting inn at Dartmoor," responded Maggie calmly, determined not to be made uncomfortable by those dark eyes, which seemed to look quite through her. "I suppose you did not see me, however—I was only one of a crowd, while *you* were the center of attention!"

Now Lord Ramblay had the grace to flush and glance at her uncertainly. But his composure was instantly restored.

"Why, I did not know we were there at the same time! What a pity—for I should have availed myself of the chance to know you sooner!"

"You seemed to be in quite a rush," remarked Maggie drily, turning back to the portrait. "I do not think you would have had time to know me very well."

"Oh, you are quite right," responded the Viscount, as if he had momentarily forgotten what business he had been on, but, having remembered it, was determined still to be chivalrous. "I was in a great hurry, on a matter of business. Well!" cried he now, as if to change the subject, "you are arrived at last! I hope you are not too weary from your journey to join us for tea. I have one or two friends staying here for a week's hunting, which is nearly over, thank God! But——" now Lord Ramblay looked at her uncertainly, for Maggie was smiling to herself—"if you are too tired—or had rather not—"

"Oh! But I should not miss it for anything!" cried the young lady, and then, turning to her cousin with an impudent look, demanded to know if by "one or two friends" he did not mean a hundred or more souls.

"Nothing like it," she was quickly assured, but with a little puzzled glance. "I am not one of your entertaining hosts, I assure you—rather the contrary. My idea of a large party is twenty at the most, and *those* I had rather do without."

This kind of talk might have gone on all night, if it was allowed, and to be sure Maggie would not have been less taunting. She had ample reason to dislike her cousin, and now with every word he uttered her determination to find fault with him increased. He seemed to her utterly without candor, for every word, every look, seemed weighed to please some ideal of civility. Lord Ramblay *was* perfectly civil—this she could not deny—and yet his manner was so stiff that it struck her as unnatural. The more they conversed, the more she detected that same devotion to duty above every other concern which had struck her about his letter, and which Captain Morrison's tale had only illustrated further. She felt, furthermore, a distinct uneasiness when he looked at her, as if he was endeavoring to read her thoughts. No matter that she was also trying to read *his*—in him, it seemed like arrogance. He struck her, altogether, as an arrogant, cold, and probably unfeeling man, whose charm was all reserved for the drawing room, or wherever else it might be admired by consequential friends. To be sure, *she* was not consequential, but then Lord Ramblay must have had some other reason for wishing to impress her. Had not she already witnessed the manner in which he conducted himself when he thought he was unobserved by friends?

Maggie had not been in the hall ten minutes with her cousin, but already her feelings were firmly fixed. Lord Ramblay fit exactly into the mold she had prepared for him—handsome, arrogant, rich, and cold. That he was also charming did not trouble her much. How easy was it to be charming, only in such a kind of intercourse! How much harder to prove oneself worthy over the long run—loyal, kind, generous, and selfless in times of trouble. With her

mind she decided to allow him still the chance to prove
he was other than what she suspected, but in her heart
she was determined to make the proving difficult. She
decided now to give him another opportunity to redeem
himself on the point of their mutual ancestor, and turning
to the portrait of his father, remarked upon his handsomeness.

"Oh, indeed—he was always considered a very fine-looking man," replied the Viscount, following her gaze.

"And yet there is such a coldness in the mouth—and a
stubbornness in the chin. *I* cannot value mere beauty
when it is marred by an evil temper."

"If you count a strong will and a ready temper as absolutely *evil*, Cousin, then I disagree. To me, a man ought to
have strength of character. A face that is flabby and soft
lacks manliness, however amiable it may appear. I would
rather a hundred times a face were ugly but with traces
of strength and resolution, than beautiful but without any
character in it."

"And yet," said Maggie, unable to disagree upon this
point, and irritated that her cousin had managed to turn
the conversation away from the face they were both
looking at, "if that resolution is so absolute that it results
in the breaking up of family loyalty and love, I should
prefer a face without any resolution, than one so for-
bidding."

Lord Ramblay now turned to her with a little smile in
his eyes, and replied: "Resolution, my dear Miss Trevor,
is only the means by which the human will is carried out.
Whether that will be thought beneficial or hateful depends
upon the persons affected by it. A man can only do what
he thinks right in his own conscience. If he does really
abide by that one code, then *I* shall never think ill of him."

"Even if his conscience makes him cruel!" thought Maggie. She saw now what her cousin's position was. He would
always defend his father in the end, no matter what he
might say otherwise to be civil. To her and her father, he
might admit the late Viscount's mistake—but in his own
heart, he agreed with him. This idea persisted in Maggie's
thoughts while she went upstairs to change her dress, and
only enforced her opinion of Lord Ramblay. If he would be
civil, then so would she—but more allegiance than that
she would not give him. And at whatever cost, she was

more than ever determined to discover the true story of
his marriage to Captain Morrison's friend. Hitherto she
had only thought her cousin cold and indifferent, but if
she found out he had been really cruel to his wife, she
would have every reason to hate him.

It was a little with the look of a battling goddess that
Maggie descended the stairs some while later. Her dark
hair was knotted up upon her head and fell down in little
tendrils on her neck. Her shoulders and bosom were bare
above a mauve silk bodice, and all she lacked to look
the part of a vengeful deity was a raised bow and arrow.
But Maggie, try as she would, could never look absolutely
threatening. There was that in her eyes, and about the
quizzical lines of her mouth, that more nearly approached
impudence than acrimony.

Six

MAGGIE SAW AT ONCE that the group was smaller than she had expected. Instead of the twenty or thirty souls she presumed a Viscount would assemble for a week's hunting, there were barely a dozen mortals ranged about the conservatory. The apartment itself was smaller and more cheerful than any other room she had so far seen in the castle, with high windows and a multitude of flowering trees growing in pots, giving the effect of a summer garden. A group of instruments stood in one corner, and the row of chairs about them gave evidence that the room was sometimes used for music. None of these was in use at the moment, though a very pretty young woman was sitting before the pianoforte and pretending to play, while three gentlemen stood about the instrument admiring her. The young lady threw back her head and laughed as Maggie came in the door, and she saw that one of the three gentlemen who instantly joined in was Lord Ramblay. He stood with one arm resting upon the instrument and the other hand upon his hip. He did not laugh so heartily as the others, but there was a smile upon his lips that suggested a great delight at the playfulness of the young lady. So enthralled was he, indeed, that he did not notice his cousin had walked in, and Maggie stood for some moments alone, in the middle of the room, before anyone seemed to see that she was there. Such an entrance was calculated to dash her spirits a little, and indeed to make her feel almost awkward. She could not very well shout across the room nor stamp her foot to draw attention to her presence. And so she stood, the crimson mounting in her cheeks, until the young lady's mimicry of the song was done and a little round of applause had died away. Then she started across the room to where Lord Ramblay stood, but was saved at the last moment from the humiliation of announcing her own presence by his turning about at that instant and exclaiming:

"Why, it is Miss Trevor! I had not expected you to join us so soon. Are not you weary from your journey?"

"Very weary," smiled Maggie, "of sitting in a carriage for ten hours. But certainly my condition is nothing that cannot be readily relieved by a little refreshment and a great deal of conversation."

One of the other men standing at the pianoforte, a gangly-looking fellow with immense whiskers and an apricot cravat, remarked jovially, "The tea you shall no doubt have, and the best in England—mark you, Ramblay has a special mix from Hunt's. But as to the conversation——"

The sentence was not finished, but it inspired a round of laughter from the other guests, who had left off their conversations, and were now all staring at the intruder. Feeling as if she had missed the point of a private joke, Maggie smiled good-humoredly.

"I hope you are not serious, sir, for I have traveled very far precisely *for* the conversation. My cousin is everywhere accounted so clever a man, and so witty, that it was my dearest wish to hear him speak."

"Well, no doubt you shall have plenty of *that*," said the unknown gentleman, grinning widely at his host. "For though Percy won't utter two words to *me*, he always has a clever *mot* for the ladies."

Lord Ramblay seemed to find nothing humorous in his friend's words. Frowning slightly, and still more so when a titter was heard about the room, he moved toward his cousin.

"Miss Trevor may not be quite done in, Whiting, but surely she is too weary to be amused by this sort of nonsense before she has been in the house an hour. Allow me," he said now, in a quieter voice, and taking Maggie's arm, "to introduce you to my mother. Then you may listen to Whiting's tomfoolery all you like, or any other of them. I must warn you that hunting is a most exhausting business; after a day in the field it often seems to me a man's good sense has been slaughtered as cleanly as the fox."

Maggie glanced at her cousin in surprise as she was led across the room. He might have spoken those words in a jesting tone, with the good humor of a host reprimanding an overly lighthearted guest, which the man in apricot did really seem to be, but there was a real coolness in his tone, something almost of irony. Lord Ramblay lacked that easiness of disposition, she thought, that marks the best hosts. Thinking this, she wondered why he bothered to hold house parties at all. Such kinds of affairs were generally thought equally amusing by host and guests alike. If there was so little enjoyment of them, they lost all their purpose.

The guests were arranged about the room in little groups; Maggie did not at first see the dowager Viscountess. But as Lord Ramblay led her across the floor, she began to feel a strange sensation, as if she was being watched. In a moment she saw why. Seated on a sofa at the end of the room was a woman older than any others in the company. Lady Ramblay was constructed upon so magnificent a scale, her countenance was so threatening, her bosom so high and heaving, her attire so rich, and the crown of hair piled atop her head and held in place by several dozen diamond combs, so high, that she gave at first more the impression of a royal barge than of a mere woman of between fifty and sixty years of age. At the moment Maggie glimpsed her, she was sitting upon her sofa as if it was a throne, and the several younger persons about her, courtiers. Maggie was in truth a little taken aback by the sight of her hostess, but Lady Ramblay apparently felt no consternation on seeing *her*. The Viscountess's lorgnette was held up to her eye, and she perused the young lady as she advanced on her cousin's arm as if she was examining a fish that was to be served her for dinner. Maggie might have been more embarrassed than she was, had she not been so tempted to laugh. As it was, her first sensation of awkwardness at being thus perused, without one flinch or one smile, was almost instantly erased by the anger that welled up in her bosom. That anger only increased in the moments that followed.

Having once surveyed her cousin, and showing no sign whether she was pleased or the reverse with what she saw, Lady Ramblay put down her quizzing glass, and, just at the moment when Maggie stood not three feet away from her, turned pointedly away.

"Indeed," she remarked, as if taking up a train of thought where it had been left off, "I cannot tell you what became of the Duke, although I have heard some people say he was killed at Waterloo. But *I* cannot credit it. He was ever a perfectly sensible man, where it was a matter of his own safety."

A little titter followed this remark, but Maggie could not tell whether it was the joke that was laughed at, or herself. Her own color was very high at being thus slighted, and with so little ceremony, but a glance at her cousin told her nothing at all. His expression was perfectly unreadable, and at once Maggie's anger was directed at him as well as the mother. They had now stood before the Viscountess a full minute, and Lady Ramblay was embarking upon a new story. Why would not her son interrupt? Surely he might relieve her embarrassment a little, even if he was the coldest man on earth. She felt utterly humiliated, and had not anger risen in her bosom as speedily as unhappiness, she might really have burst into tears.

The rules of conduct in this castle certainly differed from those she had been brought up to think of as the proper way of going. The meanest sailor at Portsmouth would not have dreamed of behaving thus to anyone. Yet here was a woman, accounted by everyone as elegant and admirable, who openly slighted an unknown cousin in her own house and before others. Had not Maggie scorned such conduct, she might have suffered more from it. As it was, she could not help but feel humiliated and her humiliation made her as angry at herself as at the Viscountess.

A moment of awkwardness in such a kind of situation will often extend itself in the mind of the one offended into an age, and after Maggie had stood for what seemed to her like a hundred years while her hostess ignored her presence, some comfort did come. There was a young girl seated next to Lady Ramblay on the sofa whom Maggie had not noticed at once. So small was she, so self-effacing in her manner, that she did not draw any attention to herself. She was pretty, the way a miniature porcelain figure is pretty—so tiny and frail that she seemed more like a doll than a girl. A look of horror had come over her face as soon as she saw what the Viscountess was doing, but she was evidently too timid to speak out. The color mounted in her cheeks as the large woman beside her talked along, glancing in evident pain between Lord Ramblay and his mama. At last she seemed unable to bear it any longer, and much to Maggie's astonishment, gave a tug to Lady Ramblay's sleeve.

The Viscountess glanced down in great annoyance. "What is it, Fanny?" she demanded impatiently.

"Here is my cousin, I think, Mama," murmured the young girl in confusion, her ivory cheeks growing red.

Lady Ramblay now had the audacity to glance up at Maggie and her son as if she had not seen them before. "Ah!" issued from her lips, and she was silent. But the lorgnette was again set in place, and her stare took in the young lady from head to toe. At last she seemed satisfied.

"So you are Captain Trevor's daughter!" she exclaimed at last. "You do not in the least resemble my husband's niece. She was not so tall, and had much lighter coloring."

Only a fierce reminder to herself that, if she was not a *titled* lady, she was a lady nonetheless, prevented Maggie from saying anything what she felt. She was rescued, indeed, from saying anything for a moment, for Miss Ramblay, coloring fiercely, burst out:

"Oh! But I do not agree, Mama. From the pictures I have seen of our cousin, I think they are perfectly alike!"

Lady Ramblay's cheeks took on an angry flush at this direct contradiction of her words, and from so evidently unexpected a source, but Lord Ramblay, who seemed to have found his voice at last, cut off what looked like his mother's rebuke, by saying calmly:

"You are both of you justified in your estimations, I think. Miss Trevor is certainly like her mother, though she is something taller, which must be owed to a resemblance to *Admiral* Trevor. Though I have never met him, I think so valiant an officer must be above the average stature of men, and it is fitting that his daughter ought to stand above most women, likewise."

Maggie had no wish to be the cause of a quarrel between mother and children, and, if she was instantly grateful to her cousin for oiling down the waters, and defending her as well, she was more chagrined than ever to think that she had come unwittingly to this castle to be made a mockery of by one relation and cause uneasiness among a family. It was plain that Lady Ramblay was determined to hate her—from what motive she could not guess—and that her son, in doing his duty, had not reckoned upon where his allegiance, dutiful or not, must lie.

One thing was certain, however: the little doll-like creature, Fanny, was the sweetest child she had ever looked upon. Her cheeks had not ceased to burn since the disagreement had commenced. Mortification shone in her eyes like tears, and those eyes, so huge and innocent and violet, now gazed with rapt admiration at her brother. Clearly Miss Ramblay considered his defense to have been as purely motivated as her own. Maggie, even while she doubted this, determined to love her little cousin. But the moment demanded her to swallow her own pride, if there was to be any hope of peace during her visit, and with the natural good-humor that had for a while deserted her, she said as lightly as she could:

"Oh! It is true, I am a great deal bigger than my mother was! Indeed, I believe I am inferior to her in every point, save perhaps one of strength. Strength is not often accounted a great virtue in a woman, but I have often had reason to be grateful for mine."

Lord Ramblay cast his cousin a curious glance, almost smiled, and said nothing. Miss Ramblay, too, seemed to have exhausted all her powers of conversation. She sat with her eyes cast down upon her hands, fiddling at a ribbon in her frock, her cheeks pale. Lady Ramblay was plainly bridling, but she seemed at last to lose interest in the subject.

"Whatever your strength," said Lord Ramblay now, "you must be pretty well exhausted after so long a journey. If you will excuse us, ma'am—" with a bow to his mother— "I shall take Miss Trevor away to have some refreshment."

Lady Ramblay nodded her consent, dismissing Maggie with a nod, and in a moment was lecturing the young people around her once more.

There was silence between Maggie and her cousin as they walked back across the room, on the part of one from such a mixture of emotion that she knew not what she *could* say without openly insulting her hostess to the lady's son, and on the other side, from some unreadable determination to be silent. Lord Ramblay did steal more than one glance at his relative as he led her back to the pianoforte, but his dark eyes were veiled, and if there was a hint of pain in them, it was no more than a hint. He might, at this

moment, have redeemed all the ill that had been thought
of him—unbeknownst, it is true, to himself—by making
some apology for his mother's incivility. Maggie almost
longed to hear him make such an excuse, for she had unaccountably softened toward him. His words, spoken on
her behalf a moment before, though not an absolute contradiction of Lady Ramblay's insult, and though lacking
something of that passionate cry for justice which had
made Maggie instantly love his sister, had seemed to spring
from a real desire to blunt the point of his mother's
tongue. If only now he would speak out, would make some
sign that he knew her feelings and was sorry for them!
If so, Maggie's natural generosity of spirit might have
erased her former ill opinion of him. Such an apology
might even have inclined her to discredit Captain Morrison's story, or at least to think of it with an open mind.

But no apology came, and though Lord Ramblay did
once open his mouth as if to speak, he shut it again at
once with an almost imperceptible shake of his head. His
silence, when he might so easily, so naturally have spoken,
only hardened Maggie's determination to dislike him, and
if that dislike now owed as much to her pride's having
been twice wounded at his hands, it was perhaps even
stronger than an unprejudiced opinion might have been.

"By Jupiter!" cried Mr. Whiting, as they came up beside
him, "are you escaped so soon, then? I should have thought
there would be a great to-do of kissing and long-lost
female cousin chatter between you!"

Maggie was prevented from replying by Lord Ramblay's
quick interjection, in a biting tone, of, "My mother and
Miss Trevor had never met before, Whiting."

Whiting looked taken aback and said no more. The
young lady at the pianoforte was in the midst of a song—
a real one this time—and Maggie noticed with amusement
that both her animation and her voice improved the instant
Lord Ramblay had come into view again. The song was
finished with a little trill, and the young lady accepted her
applause with smiles and laughter. Whiting and his friend
declared her the best thing since Mrs. Siddons, to which
she responded in a teasing voice—

"Silly things! You know I have not more than a little
creaking voice, and that my fingers are made of wood,

though I do hope I have not so frightful a countenance as she!"

The gentlemen all roared with laughter at this sally, and protested hotly the first point, while heartily agreeing to the latter. But the young lady was soon tired of the other gentlemen's admiration, and turning to Lord Ramblay, cried:

"Percy, you are quite uncivil! I have not been introduced to your cousin yet!"

The oversight was instantly amended. Maggie learned that the Honorable Miss Montcrieff—or Diana, as she begged to be known—was at Ramblay Castle with her brother, who was "not in evidence at the moment. You know he is swooning over that perfectly divine Miss Haversham."

It appeared Maggie ought to have known this Miss Haversham, but when it came out she did not, Miss Montcrieff turned with wide eyes to Lord Ramblay.

"Why, Percival! Where on earth do you keep your poor cousin? 'Pon my word, it is amazing to meet someone who has never even *heard* of Blanche Haversham!"

Maggie explained with a smile that she probably did not know anyone she ought to know, as she had been all her life at Portsmouth with her father. Her further admission that she had never been to London save once, when she had been a little girl and too young to remember anything, brought a smile to Miss Montcrieff's lips. It was not altogether a kind smile. Indeed, it had more than a little sneer in it, and when the young lady exclaimed at Lord Ramblay's having any cousin who did not frequent London regularly, and commenced teasing him upon the subject to secure his attention to herself, Maggie determined that her first efforts at amiability had been hypocritical. It was all "Why! And have you many other pretty cousins, Percy, whom you are keeping hidden in the wilds? Lud! How is a girl to trust you, when you are always keeping some secret to yourself, and such comely ones, on top of everything!"

Miss Montcrieff was the sort of young lady who, when she will, can be as charming as a June day. Her eyelashes, which were long and black, fluttered up and down over her teasing eyes; her lips, curled into the prettiest smile in the world, and her long neck, which was as white and slender as a swan's, bent attentively toward whomever she addressed. Miss Montcrieff in this state was as sweet as honey, but the instant she was displeased, or if for a moment she lost the attention of every man about her, her eyes grew dark and moody, her mouth formed into a pout, and her sweetness turned to petulance. She was one of those ladies who has been formed from birth to please men. She knew from instinct, as well as education, how to make them think they were the center of the earth, and any man who has ever known such a woman will attest to the irresistibility of such a creature, be she ever so homely.

All this was evident to Maggie after seeing Miss Montcrieff for barely half an hour. Miss Montcrieff was a disappointment, and her two swains, Whiting and his friend, were very little better. The hope that the rest of the company might reveal some greater minds and hearts was quickly dashed, for the serving of late tea, shortly thereafter, opened the way for her to converse with everyone in the party. Miss Montcrieff's brother was a very well-looking man, with fine features and a handsome figure, but these were all marred by the same petulance about the mouth and eyes, and the same whining voice, that characterized the sister. He had little to say to Maggie, for his attention was all directed at Miss Haversham, a tall, haughty-looking beauty with a cold smile, who only opened her lips twice all the evening, and attended to her suitor's continuous string of jokes and anecdotes with a distant, disinterested look. These two seemed perfectly content in each other's company, however, and if the sight of them made Maggie smile, the boredom of the one and the foolishness of the other apparently satisfied their different ideas of conversation.

The rest of the company was composed of married people, but the wives had as little to say to their husbands as the husbands to the wives. After they had, from courtesy, mingled about the tea table for a quarter of an hour, devoting the chief part of their interest to the lobster and cakes, they disposed themselves again much as they had been before, with the men all around the mantle boasting to each other about their day in the field, and the ladies gossiping in another part of the room. This monotony seemed to please everyone, for the distraction of a newcomer was barely noticed. Upon hearing that Miss Trevor did not hunt, the gentlemen were all silent, apparently at a loss for what to say to her, and the ladies, when they discovered she knew none of their friends and had no great expertise in the field of fashion, turned away with smiles.

For a while Maggie contrived to join in their conversations, but soon discovering that she had as little to say to them as they did to her, she contented herself with wandering about the room admiring the wealth of handsome artifacts disposed on every table and in a variety of cabinets.

The party had removed, after tea, to a drawing room of ample size, but not, as Maggie noticed from peering through a doorway, the chief one of the castle. It was long and narrow, with groups of chairs and sofas arranged to allow for several conversations going forward at once. On the walls were tapestries, one of which depicted a medieval hunting scene with a band of riders circling about a doe. An arrow had evidently just struck the beautiful creature, for she had fallen down upon her forelegs, and her delicate head on its noble neck was turned in bewilderment toward her murderer. Her great eyes were wide with pain and amazement, as if she could not believe she had really been struck, making an awful contrast to the expressions of pleasure on the faces of her pursuers. One of the hunters had his head back in laughter. Some others were conversing together, probably boasting of their conquest; but the one who rode in front, and who had actually killed the doe (for his arrow was still poised against his bow), had no expression upon his face at all. His eyes were dark and impenetrable, and only a tiny thread of light, which seemed to connect his own gaze with the poor creature's, gave a clue to his feelings. It was a depiction, as clearly as could be conceived, of man's arrogance, and Maggie, staring at the murderer, could not help but remember Captain Morrison's tale of her cousin's marriage.

"Do you admire it?" sounded behind her suddenly. Lord Ramblay's voice was unmistakable, and coming, as it did, in the midst of the thought she had been forming, it made her start violently. But the Viscount's face, when she turned around, was lightened by a smile. This expression changed his countenance remarkably, making him seem ten years younger than he had looked before and actually changing the color of his eyes. Maggie noticed with astonishment that these eyes were not black, as she had thought at first, but rather hazel, like her own, and with an even greater range of coloration. When they had stood in the hall together, his eyes had been dark and ominous, but now they were a mottled shade of green and ocher. She thought fleetingly that they looked like eyes that had seen a great deal, but whether of their own pain, or the pain of others, she would not hazard a guess.

"It is a remarkable piece of work," she replied.

"Oh! The needlework is exceptional, to be sure. I believe it was worked in Flanders some two hundred years ago. One is always amazed at the steadfast patience of those women, who could labor over such a thing tirelessly, for year upon year. But it is not the needlework that astounds *me*, so much as the sensibility of the artist. Is not it a moving study of a hunt?"

"As to that, Cousin, I could not say, or rather, my opinion would be of no value, for I have never hunted. But it is most certainly a moving study of *life*—and of death."

"And what can you know of death, Miss Trevor?" inquired Lord Ramblay, with a smile. "You, who seem so full of the very soul of animated life."

Maggie was a little discomfitted by these words, accompanied by a searching look. Was he mocking her? His eyes held her own steadily, but he seemed to be looking through her, almost as he had done on their first meeting. No doubt he had a very low opinion of women, and of women's capacity for serious thought, if he admired Diana Montcrieff as much as he seemed to do. The thought made her, unaccountably, wish to persuade him that she was not merely a scatterbrained female.

"I have known something of death, my lord," she replied with a challenging look. "I should have thought *you* would not forget that. I lost a mother once, as you lost a cousin."

Now Lord Ramblay pleased her by looking a little shamefaced. But his dignity was recovered at once, and he said:

"And I wish I had known what a loss I suffered by that death. Your mother was much loved in this house, and I believe, everywhere she went."

Maggie said nothing in reply, fearing that, if once the subject were opened, it could not help but lead to an argument. Lord Ramblay, it seemed, had the same idea, for he said, after a moment:

"They are setting up tables in the card room, if you will make a hand at whist. But perhaps you are too tired to play. Don't hesitate, if that is the case, to retire when you like. We observe hardly any formality at these parties. Indeed," he added softly, "I have very little say in what is or is *not* observed."

Maggie glanced at his face in surprise, wondering who had the authority to command here, if the master of the house did not, but she saw his look change instantly, and that rigid formality which had hitherto characterized his manner, return. With a little bow, and replying to her plea for an early retirement with a nod, he wished her good night and walked away.

Almost instantly she regretted that she had not taken advantage of his unguarded mood to inquire what he had been doing at the posting house in Dartmoor that very afternoon. She watched him cross the floor to Miss Montcrieff, who greeted him with a high, tinkling laugh, and a teasing look, but glancing in some annoyance at herself for having robbed her of her lover's company so long. Maggie smiled to herself. Miss Montcrieff had nothing to fear from *her*. Even had she not been his cousin, she could never have felt any love for Lord Ramblay. So much formality, such a guarded manner, was exactly opposed to her idea of amiability in a man. It is true that in that second when he had seemed to relax his guard, she had very nearly liked him. But the return of his former manner reminded her of what she knew of him, and even more, of what Captain Morrison had hinted.

Lady Ramblay was not in the room, and neither was Miss Ramblay. Forsaking the idea of bidding her relatives good night, therefore, Maggie retreated upstairs, glad of the immediate prospect of sleep, and glad too, to be allowed some time to her own thoughts.

Seven

LORD RAMBLAY'S GUESTS had been at the castle nearly a week when Maggie arrived. The following day being Saturday, and most of the party set to depart on the Monday, a greater hunting expedition than usual was arranged. The ladies, save for Miss Haversham, did not hunt, but some were persuaded to ride out for the start in any case, the day having dawned remarkably fine and clear. Miss Montcrieff consented at once, though she detested horses and considered fresh air an unfortunate necessity of life. But when Lord Ramblay inquired whether or not she desired a mount, she responded with a radiant smile that she would not be left behind for all the world, if "her dear Percy was not to desert them as he had done the day before."

Maggie, coming into the breakfast room in time to hear this little exchange, could not help but smile and demand to know if her cousin was in the habit of leaving his guests all alone very often?

"Oh, la!" exclaimed Miss Montcrieff with a pout, "he is an abominable host! Fancy asking us all to stay, when he has no intention of entertaining us above five of our seven days!"

This proclamation evidently did not please Lord Ramblay overmuch, for he frowned in annoyance at the young lady. Miss Montcrieff only laughed at him.

"If you loved us better, Percy, I am sure you would attend to your business at another time!"

"Believe me, my dear Diana," Lord Ramblay replied mildly, "nothing but the most urgent affairs could keep me away from my friends. Unfortunately, however, my steward regards his claims upon me as superior even to a day's hunting."

Maggie, helping herself from an elaborate array of dishes on the sideboard, could not resist interjecting lightly:

"I suppose your business was very pressing *yesterday*, Cousin!"

"Why, no more than usual, Miss Trevor. Why do you say so?"

"Because I should have thought it made you absent-minded." At her cousin's bewildered look, she continued, "No doubt you forgot, when you changed your horses at Dartmoor, that you had sent a team for me as well."

"Dartmoor!" cried Mr. Whiting, whose attention was equally divided between his calves' liver and the conversation going forward around him. "By Jupiter, Ramblay, you are a sly one, ain't you?"

"What do you mean, Whiting?" inquired his host with a smile. "Is not Dartmoor an admirable posting house?"

"Aye, if your way lies to the southwest. But I had thought you was going to Town. But p'raps I shouldn't say so, old boy," Whiting finished, with a significant smile.

Miss Montcrieff's interest, usually aroused only by those remarks addressed directly to herself, or made about her, was suddenly piqued.

"Whatever is he talking of, Percy?" she demanded, with a petulant look. "Were not you in London yesterday, as you told us? Why should you stop at Dartmoor, if it lies out of your way? And what," now her eyes were leveled accusingly at Maggie, "what in the world does Miss Trevor mean?"

Maggie watched her cousin keenly as he recovered the composure which had momentarily deserted him, and rising from his chair, replied evenly, "I suppose my cousin can best explain her own meaning herself. As to what I was doing in Dartmoor, it is perfectly simple. Mr. Belding, my steward, has been after me for six months to view a property in Highgate. As we were already on our way from London, and within easy reach of the property, he proposed we drive over to have a look at it together. Highgate, as you may recall, Whiting, is a dozen miles southwest of Dartmoor. The property, unfortunately, proved to be worthless—full of dead timber and prevented by a rocky soil from being easily adaptable to cultivation. Now I had better inform the stables what sort of mounts we will require."

With these words, which had been spoken, Maggie could not help but notice, with rather too artificial a levity, Lord

Ramblay quit the room. But Mr. Whiting had not done with the subject.

"I don't believe a word of it, Diana!" he cried teasingly. "If you ask me, your dear Percy is covering his own footfalls. Mark my words, he has got a pretty piece of muslin hid out in Highgate, and don't wish to offend your vanity! Fellow's been dashed mysterious lately, lurking about in posting houses and pretending to have affairs in Town, when everyone knows there is not a self-respecting lawyer left in London at the hunting season!"

Miss Montcrieff looked sternly at the young man. "How dare you say so, Freddy? I am sure Percy is the most honorable gentleman in England. *You* may have your fun if you like, but pray don't expect me to discredit *him*."

Young Montcrieff, who had hitherto found it impossible to tear his eyes away from the beautiful Miss Haversham, now felt it incumbent upon himself to defend his sister.

"Silly goose—he's only teasing you. Do shut up, Whiting, or I shall be forced to knock your block off. You know quite well old Ramblay's too much of a stuffed shirt to cut such a caper, even if he were *not* so much in awe of his mama. In any case, if you put such ideas in Di's head, she shan't stop whimpering about it for a fortnight."

Miss Montcrieff did not know whether to be angered or flattered by this defense, but having twice opened her mouth to protest, she settled into a petulant silence.

"*I* do not believe Lord Ramblay gives a fig for his mama's opinion," pronounced Miss Haversham suddenly. The lovely young woman's regal silence was maintained so perpetually, and with such an air of not caring what was going on about her, that every head in the room turned at the sound of her voice.

"Oh, come along, Blanche!" exclaimed Mr. Montcrieff, but with none of the certainty with which he had addressed his sister. "You cannot really mean that! I never in all my life witnessed such a mama's boy. 'Percy do this, Percy do that!'—" giving a comical rendition of Lady Ramblay's dictatorial manner—"and the fellow leaps as if he had got a hot iron under him!"

Miss Haversham, staring imperturbably at her left hand, continued as if her lover had not spoken. "No, he don't care for her opinion, I am positive. He strikes me as a

man with a great secret. He knows his own mind, at any
rate—better than you two."

Evidently unaware of the astonishment she had caused
her audience, Miss Haversham now rose briskly from her
chair and, throwing down her napkin upon the table, turned
to Maggie.

"Are you to ride out with us, Miss Trevor? If you like,
I shall have my filly saddled for you. She's a lovely mount,
if you have got a tender hand."

Maggie protested that though she loved a ride she had
never been on a hunt, and did not wish to hold up the
party with her ineptitude.

"Never mind. If you have got a drop of courage—and
I dare say you do from the look of you—there's nothing
simpler. If you can be ready in half an hour, I shall meet
you by the stables."

Without waiting for a reply, Miss Haversham turned
and quit the room, leaving in her wake a gaping Mr.
Montcrieff and a Maggie flushed with pleasure. Miss Haversham's surprising show of kindness was the first really
friendly gesture she had had from these people since her
arrival. Coming, as it did, from so unexpected a quarter
(for of all the ladies in the party, Maggie had first judged
the silent, proud-looking beauty to be the least approach-
able), it was doubly pleasant. But the prospect of acquiring
a friend among this party, and of a ride upon an excellent
mount, was not the least of the attractions promised. Miss
Haversham's remark about her cousin had aroused Maggie's curiosity. What could she have meant by saying Lord
Ramblay struck her as a man with a great secret? Surely
that secret could not really be what Mr. Whiting had
jokingly called "a piece of muslin." And yet she had
seen her cousin color deeply when the fact of his stopping
in Dartmoor had been mentioned, and for all his quickly
regained composure, Maggie could not help wondering if
indeed he had not something to conceal.

Breakfasting as quickly as she could, Maggie ran up to
her apartment and changed her muslin frock for the riding
habit which had done her service for five years. A glance
in the mirror made her grimace; in the elegant surroundings of this room, the skirt looked suddenly worn, while
a fringe about the bodice, which had once seemed like
ample decoration, struck her now as impossibly plain.

There was nothing to be done about it, however, and fastening her hat under her chin, she took a last critical look at herself in the glass before turning away. She was relieved, on her way through the house, to see still no sign of the Viscountess. Upon her inquiry, the butler told her that his mistress stayed in her apartments until noon, while Miss Ramblay, whom she had really hoped to have seen at breakfast, was at her lessons.

Maggie found the stables without trouble. They lay on the western side of the castle, hidden from view by a grove of elm and willow so ancient that the limbs of the trees had grown down to the earth and sprung up again in smaller growths. Their trunks were as massive as houses themselves, and the sunlight filtering down through their branches touched the ground in a fairy-tale effect.

Walking along the gravel path between the copse and a great marble balustrade running along the side of the castle, Maggie was struck by the peace and beauty of the grounds, where a dozen gardeners were to be seen scattered about the innumerable flower gardens and lawns. In the light of day the castle itself looked even more vast than it had the night before. The modern structures on either side the central building, which, from its deeper coloration and crumbling stone facade, was obviously the original construction, stretched out in the sunlight like the arms of a noble old beast. Here indeed was serenity and grandeur, elegance and taste of design. That so much beauty and quiet should harbor within it a party of such vain, foolish, and snobbish creatures was indeed a pity. And yet the idea made Maggie smile: Had not she often observed that a penniless boatswain, without any advantage of education or family, had sometimes more real delicacy of feeling than his betters? Human nature was full of oddities, a fact that pleased her as often as it amazed her. And if truth be told, she had been not a little cheered to discover that her noble relations were not much different from the rest of humankind. She had been afraid of finding them all cold and haughty, so elegant as to have hardly any trace of humanity at all. Instead, she had found Lady Ramblay as ill-mannered as a fish-wife, and very little handsomer. Miss Ramblay was a little mouse, too afraid of everyone to look you in the eye without a blush, although her passionate little nature had instantly won Maggie's heart. As for Lord Ramblay's guests, they were equally divided between foppery and vanity. Only Miss Haversham was a mystery. Her silences, which seemed at first to have sprung from haughtiness, now inclined Maggie to think she was deeper than her friends. But why such a beauty should submit to the attentions of the young dandy Mont-crieff, was beyond Maggie's comprehension. Lord Ramblay, too, was impenetrable, and it was Maggie's hope that a friendship with the former might elucidate a little her understanding of the latter.

Miss Haversham, in a wonderful scarlet coat and pearl-gray skirt, with a French plumed riding hat atop her black waves, was pacing back and forth before the stable door.

"Oh!" she cried, but without smiling, when she caught a glimpse of Maggie, "I had almost determined you would not come after all."

"But of course I have come! Did not I say I would?"

Miss Haversham stared, and at last seemed satisfied.

"Yes," she said. "I suppose I may take *your* word." At Maggie's look of surprise, she laughed. "I never expect anything, you know, until I have seen it with my own eyes. If Diana Montcrieff told me she would ride out, I should laugh, and the more I laughed the more she would insist that she *would* come. But she would not, you know, and I would be an idiot to wait for *her*. But I see you are different."

Maggie did not know whether her new friend meant to be flattering or not, but she was inexplicably pleased to be set in a different category from the mincing, flirtatious Miss Montcrieff by this beautiful, blunt creature.

Miss Haversham had turned away to speak to a groom, and in a moment two glorious horses were led out of their stalls. One was an exceedingly fine-looking, rather wild black stallion, which immediately upon seeing his mistress snorted and pawed the ground. Miss Haversham's filly was dapple-gray, very fine about the mouth, and with what looked like a most playful disposition. Maggie made one last protest at being lent such a glorious animal, to which her friend responded with a laugh.

"If you are afraid of her, my dear, by all means stay behind. But I suggest you come along, for there is nothing so grand in all the world as a good ride to hounds."

Maggie instantly remonstrated against being left behind.

If Miss Haversham would hunt, then so would she, and she did dearly love a fast ride over easy country. Her companion smiled at this, and looked over her horse's girth. Suddenly she glanced up, with a curious expression.

"You do not seem to like your cousin very well," she remarked abruptly.

"I hardly know him—I first laid eyes upon him yesterday."

Miss Haversham seemed surprised, but said no more. Maggie, however, had felt an instant affinity for this young woman, and proceeded herself without any encouragement—

"There was a quarrel between our families for many years. My cousin's father disowned my mother, who was his niece, and I have never met any of the Ramblays before. My visit *now* is only a kind of gesture of reconciliation on Lord Ramblay's part, but I do not think he cares much about it."

"I should not be so quick to judge him, if I were you," said Miss Haversham, still intent upon tightening her horse's girth and arranging the stirrups to her liking. "He is not an easy man to know—you may take my word for it. *I* have known him these five years and yet do not feel I am equipped to make him out. But of one thing I am certain —a better man does not exist in England, and though his respect is not easily won, there is no one more loyal afterward."

"I could wish for a little less stiffness, however," responded Maggie lightly, at which Miss Haversham turned to her with a keen look.

"My dear girl, 'lightness' is a cheap virtue. I hope you never have cause to discover that for yourself. For *my* part, I value duty and honor a great deal more highly."

The assembling of the rest of the party just then made further conversation impossible. Maggie would like to have heard more upon the subject of her cousin, but in the ensuing commotion of horses being led from the stables, the yapping of hounds, and cries back and forth between masters and grooms, her curiosity soon gave way to enjoyment. Seated upon the wonderful filly, Maggie was too engrossed in the proceedings to care about anything but the colorful spectacle going forward around her. The gentlemen all wore scarlet and black, and the ladies, seated side-saddle, looked like an array of fashion portraits from France. Whether they hunted or no, they had all the proper garments on, and Maggie thought, with a smile to herself, what a waste it was in yards of fine cloth, to have so many bodies dressed for a pastime they neither indulged in nor cared about. The party began to fall into place behind the master of the hunt, who, sounding his horn for the hounds to be led out, called for the ladies and gentlemen to take their places behind him. Just at this moment, Lord Ramblay, who had been consulting with his groom, rode up beside her.

"Do you accompany us to the start, Cousin?" he asked with a smile. "I see you have been very well mounted indeed."

"Oh, admirably so! But I think I go beyond the starting line—at least, as far as I am able to keep up."

At this Lord Ramblay looked grave. "It is a dangerous sport, Miss Trevor. I should not advise you to undertake it unless you have great confidence in yourself, and in your mount. The men all go extremely fast, and there are one or two fences in the field which have confounded more experienced riders than yourself, and stronger arms."

"I am grateful for your concern, Cousin," responded Maggie with a smile, "but in truth, it does not worry me much. If Miss Haversham is not afraid of them, I do not suppose they can be so very bad. We are of the same height, and I believe I am quite as strong as she."

"Miss Haversham is an astonishing good horsewoman, Cousin—and afraid of nothing. Indeed, I wish most heartily she was *more* afraid, for she takes her fences sometimes in such a way that I wish I was not forced to watch. I should not judge my skill against hers, if I were you."

Now Maggie was a little offended, to be spoken to as if she was a child. What could Miss Haversham, a pampered belle, dare that she could not? Was not she Admiral Trevor's daughter, and had she not inherited, if not his authority in battle, a good deal of his bravery? Thrusting out her chin a little, she replied:

"You have no need to worry about *me*, Cousin. I shall do nothing to injure myself. It is true I have never undertaken a hunt before, but I was raised upon a horse, and believe I have some little skill in the handling of them. I shall just follow what I see the others do, and back away from any jump that looks too high. Rest assured, I have no ambition to be killed."

Lord Ramblay attempted to dissuade her once more, but seeing that his cousin was determined to do as she liked, and that nothing he could say would deter her, he moved away with a resigned look. Had she looked after him, however, Maggie might have seen him ride up to a groom and murmur something. The servant glanced in her direction and nodded. With one last look at his cousin, Lord Ramblay took his place at the head of the hunt, and in a moment they were moving forward.

The starting point for the chase lay at a distance of two miles from the stables, where the formal wooded deer park converged on a vast expanse of wild fields and woods. Here the ladies drew in their mounts and moved off to one side, while the rest of the party gathered behind the master of the hounds, now giving his beasts the scent. Maggie had only time to look out for Miss Haversham, who, returning the look, smiled encouragingly, before the trumpet sounded and, with a great clamor of beating hoofs and a raising of dust behind them, they were off. Maggie had little trouble in keeping her place at first. The exhilaration of the sport, the feel of brisk wind about her face and throat, the powerful rhythm of her filly's pace, all raised her spirits and made her brave. She had a natural seat, and powerful arms, and had always felt comfortable in the saddle. The filly was so swift and smooth that her confidence was raised with every moment, and when she saw that she was going as fast as any of the men, and that the ground they covered was clear of rocks and not unduly rough, the tremor she had felt at first died down. For half an hour they raced along at a full gallop, with the yapping hounds guiding them over the hills and through intermittent wooded patches. The first fence was low, with only a small rivulet behind it. The filly sailed over it as if it had been a mere nothing, and Maggie, relieved to see how fearless her mount was, and how limber, gave up all worry to the enjoyment of the day.

Miss Haversham, meanwhile, had begun slowly to gain upon the others. Her stallion, without any evidence of exertion, now seemed to leave them behind in a cloud of dust. In amazement, Maggie saw her friend head straight toward a ravine which might have been avoided—which,

indeed, lay out of the path they were taking. The ravine
was very deep, its sides nearly vertical, and almost twenty
feet across. The stallion took it without a moment's pause,
and the sight of that tall, proud girl in her scarlet coat
and plumed hat, upon her glorious beast, nearly took
Maggie's breath away. She saw one or two of the men
follow behind, and then young Montcrieff, with a determined look, turned his horse in the same direction. Lord
Ramblay, however, who had been second behind Miss
Haversham, fell off a little and rode close by his cousin.
Without a word, he signaled her to go around the ravine.
Nodding her head, Maggie rode to the right of the jump,
where only a small gully wound between two muddy banks,
and in making her crossing, lost sight of the others. Only
a low cry, when she had reached the opposite bank and
ridden beyond it, made her turn her head.

Eight

SHE HAD ACHIEVED the entrance to a wood, following behind the other gentlemen in the party and their grooms,
when the sound from behind her made her rein in her
filly and turn. At first she could see nothing. Miss Haversham, having made her crossing, had pulled up and was
going back to the ravine. Lord Ramblay, turning at the
same moment, began to gallop full tilt toward the gully.
The sides of the ravine were very steep, and must have
hidden whatever had occurred from view. But by now
several others were turning in the direction of the gulf,
and Montcrieff's groom, together with some other servants,
were gathering at the edge. Turning her beast about, Maggie cantered in the same direction.

There was so much confusion, when she reached the
bank, that she could not at first understand what had
occurred. Lord Ramblay was scrambling down the shore
on foot toward a crumpled figure at the bottom. With a
gasp, Maggie guessed it was Mr. Montcrieff, and from his
immobile, twisted position, thought at first he was dead.
But in a moment the young man gave a groan and raised
his head. Lord Ramblay was now at his side and, lifting
him gently, was demanding if he were very badly hurt.
It was soon discovered that the chief injury was in his
leg, which still lay twisted beneath him, and which he
seemed unable to move. With the aid of his own groom
and the young man's, Lord Ramblay lifted him gently
from the ground and helped him to climb cautiously up
the steep and slippery bank.

The safety of the gentleman having been assured, the
party's attention was now turning to his horse, still lying
motionless upon its side. From the agonized gaze in its
eyes and the pathetic resistance it was giving a groom who
was pulling at the reins in an effort to raise it, it was clear

the beast was in an agony of pain. Heedless of her skirts, Miss Haversham had jumped down from her stallion and rushed down the bank. Having accorded her lover one glance and being assured that his injury was slight, her attention was now turned to the animal. With one quick, angry cry she pushed the groom aside and bent down beside it, feeling with expert, gentle fingers, about its neck and the left shoulder.

"Idiot!" she cried, glaring up at Mr. Montcrieff. "Vain, stupid idiot! You have broken his neck!"

Mr. Montcrieff, leaning between his groom and the Viscount, could only swallow and stammer some incoherent phrase.

"By Jove, Blanche!" he protested lamely, "it's only a horse, you know! You ought to be thinking of me, surely!"

Miss Haversham gave him a withering look.

"Ought I?" she said in tones of heavy sarcasm. "I suppose you are right. I ought to think of you, who have nothing but a sprained ankle for your idiotic conduct, while this poor beast is damaged beyond help. I suppose you will blame the horse for leading you over the jump just where the ground gives way, too!" Miss Haversham gestured in the direction of the place where Mr. Montcrieff had fallen. A section of earth had crumbled beneath the horse's weight, and earth and rocks had collapsed into the ravine.

"Why, what are you talking about?" cried Montcrieff indignantly. "It was just where you took the jump! I only followed you, Blanche."

"Nonsense. I took it three feet away, where I was sure the ground was firm. But you were too occupied with showing off your own skill to pay any heed to where you rode. It is to just that sort of vain, egotistical riding that half the accidents in England are owed. If men would put as much intelligence into their riding as they do arrogance, there would be no need to kill so many innocent animals."

A number of the party had by now assembled on the banks of the ravine, and Maggie saw from their faces that they felt as mortified as she at hearing Mr. Montcrieff thus upbraided in public by his own fiancée. Only one gentleman, coughing, put in—

"Now, now Blanche, you cannot expect us to believe

that *you* knew the bank was weak at that point!"

Miss Haversham stared at the speaker coldly for a moment, and then walked to the place where the ground had given way.

"It has always been my understanding," she said now, in a low, deliberate voice, "that one does not ride blind. See here—pointing with her crop to a piece of turf which had fallen away from the banks, and on which, amid the trampled clots of mud and grass, a hoof mark was plainly visible— "that is where his left foreleg trod. It was the very edge of the bank, and jutted out over the ravine without any support. I would never lead *my* horse over a jump without knowing he had a firm foothold from which to spring."

"I am afraid Blanche is right," said Lord Ramblay, moving closer to the spot where Miss Haversham stood and examining the piece of earth. "It was a false ledge. You ought to have looked more carefully, Montcrieff. But be that as it may, the thing's done. We had all better move along now. I shall take Montcrieff back to the castle, while you finish the hunt." Seeing protestations were about to be raised, the Viscount held up his hand— "No, no, there is no point in giving up the chase. Continue along as you were going before."

Those of the party who still had any ambitions of killing a fox that day began to move off in the direction of the wood where Maggie had first heard Mr. Montcrieff's cry. Hoping to be of some help, Maggie herself stayed behind, turning aside her cousin's urging to join the rest with, "I have some little knowledge of bandages, Cousin, and am an able nurse, if it is needed."

Miss Haversham, meanwhile, had gone back to the horse, and murmuring some directions to her own groom, gave the poor beast one last look before scrambling up the sides of the bank, waving away the proffered hand of a servant. Waiting for Mr. Montcrieff to be helped onto a new horse, Maggie could not help watching the young lady with admiration. Her skirts muddied and torn, her hat sitting awry atop her tangled black waves, her black eyes shining with anger and indignation, she had looked like a young Athena standing at the bottom of the ravine and lecturing her lover. Even as she had felt a twinge of sympathy for the hapless Mr. Montcrieff, Maggie had agreed with Miss Haversham's estimation of the vanity and heedlessness of the young man. It was so rare to see a female who had the courage of her convictions—sufficient courage, in any case, to ignore the sneers and hidden smiles of the others, who had been all too astonished at her outburst to do much more than shuffle their feet and stare at the ground. Miss Haversham, if she had been perhaps a little hard on the gentleman, had plainly a brave heart, and a higher standard of values than her friends, who seemed to care for nothing save their own comfort and pleasure.

The return of the invalid with his host and the two young ladies excited a great interest in the party at the castle. The ladies were all gathered in the morning room, and Maggie was astonished to see that those who had ridden out for the start of the hunt had changed their elaborate riding costumes for equally studied morning frocks. If they had hoped to impress each other with their ringlets and ribbons, they seemed none of them to have succeeded, and from the numbers of yawns Maggie saw smothered behind beringed hands, they did not find much amusement in each other's company. Her own entrance— she had come in on purpose to find Miss Montcrieff—made them raise their heads and wonder what had brought her back so soon. An explanation followed, which brought a communal gasp.

"What!" cried Diana Montcrieff, jumping up from the sofa where she had been playing with a tiny dog. "Is my brother injured? Oh, take me to him at once! I cannot bear to think of it!"

Maggie's assurances that, though suffering from an injured ankle, Mr. Montcrieff had escaped any great harm, were received almost with disappointment by the other ladies.

"Oh, it is only an *ankle*," said one, and another wished to know what all the commotion was about, for nothing greater. But Miss Montcrieff, looking as if she would faint dead away, clung to Maggie's sleeve.

"I hope there is no wound!" she wailed. "For I cannot bear the sight of blood. Indeed, if there is any, I had better not go, for I shall surely be quite miserable."

"There is no blood, and indeed the wound is not very great. I only came to tell you, for I thought you would certainly wish to see with your own eyes how well he is, under the circumstances."

"I suppose Blanche Haversham is with him?" inquired Miss Montcrieff as they walked along the hall toward the apartment where the invalid had been taken. Maggie did not know how much she should tell the young lady of what had transpired between Miss Haversham and her inamorato, but concluding that Miss Montcrieff had better be kept as calm as possible, said only:

"I suppose she is. She returned with us."

In fact, Maggie had no certainty on this point whatever. Miss Haversham had indeed accompanied them back to the castle, but her obstinate silence, and her refusal to ride next to her fiancé, suggested that she wished to have as little as possible to do with him. However, on coming into the sickroom, Maggie was surprised and greatly relieved to see the beautiful young woman, still in her muddied riding habit, bending over the divan on which Montcrieff was lying. Though her expression had not softened much, and though she said not a word, she was administering a poultice to his brow with gentle hands. Mr. Montcrieff, meanwhile, who seemed to suffer more from his lover's criticism than from his fall, was gazing at her with woeful eyes.

"Poor Freddy!" cried his sister when she saw him, rushing up to the divan and falling down upon her knees beside him. "Are you most awfully hurt?"

Miss Haversham said nothing, but smiled to herself as she turned away, giving up the poultice which Miss Montcrieff had seized from her and was now applying to her brother's brow with less than expertise.

Maggie, seeing that the siblings were engrossed in each other—the one with wailing about his awful pain, and the other with making crooning noises in return—turned away to leave the room. She meant to see if a surgeon had been called for, but was detained by Blanche Haversham's voice behind her.

"Wait a moment, Miss Trevor, if you will," she said, hurrying down the hall behind her. "I should like a word with you, if I may."

Surprised, Maggie halted in her path long enough to allow her friend to catch up.

"You are not going to join the other ladies, are you?"

demanded Miss Haversham, with a doubtful look.

"No—only to see if a surgeon has been called."

"Oh, well—Percy has already done that. I believe he went himself to fetch one. I did hope—that is, I hoped we might speak privately for a moment."

Maggie replied that she most certainly did not mind, and followed the other down a corridor and into a tiny sitting room. The walls were lined with books, there was a fire in the grate, and the furnishings, composed of several worn leather armchairs and unmatched incidental tables, gave the place a comfortable and homelike air. Miss Haversham did not sit down at once, but walked toward the shelves, all loaded down with books, and stared up at them for a while without speaking. The books, as Maggie noted with some surprise, were not merely handsomely bound editions, purchased for their look and never read, but rather a motley array of every kind of volume, from history to fiction, with a well-thumbed collection of scientific journals and what seemed like several hundred French and Italian plays and novels.

"I suppose you have read a great many of these?" demanded Miss Haversham at last.

Maggie could only laugh. "Heavens, no! Not above a fraction of them, if even that. Though I *have* some acquaintance with Moliere and Chaucer, have read most of Shakespeare's plays, and one or two histories—but goodness, I doubt I could have done much besides, if I had read all this!"

"Your cousin has, you know," returned Miss Haversham. "I asked him once, and he admitted he had read every one. I believe this is his favorite room, for I discovered him here once by chance. I doubt not he comes here to escape his overbearing mama and have a little quiet."

Now Maggie looked about the place with a keener interest, for the room had so different an air than any other part of the castle she had seen, and it had struck her at once as twice as welcoming as all the gilt and gew-gaws, grand as they were, to be seen about the other apartments. That it should appeal to her cousin, the very incarnation of everything formal and elegant, was startling. And yet it made her think that perhaps he was more human than he seemed. Perhaps he, too, needed to let down his guard from time to time.

"Why," she inquired with a smile, "does my cousin really hold Lady Ramblay in so much awe as Mr. Whiting claims?"

Miss Haversham only snorted in reply.

"Awe! No, nothing like it. I do not believe Percy holds anyone in awe. But he does more than *I* could do, if I had such a mother: He seems to listen to everything she says, refrains from contradicting even her most idiotic remarks, and actually defends her, if she is attacked."

"And is she attacked very often?"

Now Miss Haversham turned to face her friend and smiled. "Everyone is attacked, you know, in Society."

The last word had been uttered with so peculiar an inflection that Maggie could not help smiling back. Miss Haversham did not appear the kind of lady who would put so much emphasis on the term. But her pronunciation of it had made it sound more like a kingdom or a very lofty state than the mere grouping of a set of people.

"Society?" repeated Maggie, still smiling. "You make it sound a very awesome thing."

"Oh! And it is! There is nothing more awesome—or more awful, if you like. It makes and breaks reputations for a whim, and has been sometimes known to kill strong men." At Maggie's look of surprise, she continued: "Oh, to be sure, it is an awesome thing. Only try living outside its rules, if you are one of those poor unfortunates who depends upon it for happiness. *Then* you shall see what importance the raising of an eyebrow can have!"

"Well then—I suppose you are not one of those poor unfortunates, Miss Haversham, for I have not seen you tremble overmuch at shocking your friends!"

"Oh, la! You are an innocent, ain't you?" exclaimed the other, pushing back a lock of raven-colored hair from her brow. "I abide by their rules more than they do themselves!"

At Maggie's expression of amazement, Miss Haversham only smiled and, turning around, walked to the window, where she stood for some moments without speaking. When she did, it was to ask an unexpected question.

"Do you think I was unjust to poor Freddy?" she said quietly.

"Unjust? No, I think every justice was on your side. Indeed, I was amazed—and vastly pleased—to hear what you said. Perhaps you were a little overstern, most especially as it was before his friends—but unjust, never!"

"I am glad to hear you say so," replied Miss Haversham, without turning about, "for I had really feared I might lose you as my friend."

Such an admission, spoken in so quiet a voice, and coming from so unexpected a quarter—from a young lady, in fact, who seemed impervious to any such human needs —could not but flatter Maggie.

"I felt as soon as I saw you," Miss Haversham went on, "that you were different from the others. It was not merely your clothes—forgive me if I speak bluntly—but the way you held your head, and the sensible look in your eyes. I saw at once that we were creatures of the same sort."

"That is very kind of you," interjected Maggie, feeling herself flush, "and I wish it were really true! But while I am admittedly very blunt myself—and some would say, perhaps all *too* sensible—I have, compared to you, led a very plain life. My father is an admiral, you know, and before he was an admiral, he was a captain, and when he married my mother, he was a penniless ensign. I have lived all my life at Portsmouth, amid a hurly-burly crowd of sailors and their ladies. Any refinements I may have gleaned in the two and twenty years I have lived upon the earth have been culled accidentally from books and from the kindness of my father, who has ever made it his purpose in life to try to make me a lady. I have no pretention to seeming other than what I am."

Now Miss Haversham turned about, and with an extraordinary expression in her beautiful dark eyes, said slowly: "Well, then, I was wrong! It seems that in two points at least, we are completely opposed. You have a father, while I have not; and *I have every pretention to seeming what I am not.*"

Nine

MISS HAVERSHAM POSSESSED, besides beauty of a most unordinary kind, the sort of look which is so proud, so forthright, and so dignified, that her whole mien seemed to speak the truth. Her figure was tall and elegant, and stately even in its slenderness. Her shoulders—wider than most women's—were held back in an almost military fashion, and the expression in her remarkable eyes was so candid as to make anyone who looked at them positive that she was incapable of telling a lie. There was a softness about the mouth, too, which many did not notice at first. But those who had had the opportunity of gazing at that face for very long, must have noticed it, and when they did, must have seen there traces of sensibility which did not leap out at first acquaintance with the lady. She was so often silent, and her silence seemed so haughty (though on knowing her better, Maggie decided that the attitude was more one of absolute self-discipline than real haughtiness) that many must have thought her incapable of that sweetness of nature which is a woman's chief attraction. Sweet she most certainly was not. No resemblance did she possess either to a flower or a dainty, unless the flower were one so tall and proud and regal—a calla lily, perhaps—that it grew with as much sober dignity as she, or the dainty so rare and delicate that it could not be gobbled up without a moment's hesitation at wreaking damage on so splendid a creation. And yet there *was* sweetness in her—or rather, softness. It was just this quality that most struck Maggie as she listened, all amazement, to her friend's next words.

Miss Haversham spoke plainly, almost defiantly, but in her attitude there was something almost pleading, and it could not help but touch her friend.

"I asked you a moment ago," Miss Haversham began, staring fixedly at her companion, "if you had read any of

these books—" gesturing at the shelves. "You replied you
had read only a smattering of them—Chaucer, Shakespeare, Moliere—and that your knowledge was acquired
almost by hazard. *My* knowledge of the world has been
acquired in the same fashion—though not, as you have
done, with the help of a devoted father, or in the luxury
of a happy home. All *my* knowledge has been forced upon
me, as a fish must learn to swim and to forage for food
among the tiny growing things in the ocean—in order to
live. I am not, you see, at all what I seem to be."

Miss Haversham paused for a moment, seeming to search
Maggie's eyes for an indication of her thoughts, but seeing
there only encouragement and concern, she turned away
and moved to a window, where she stood for some moments looking out in silence. At last a low laugh issued
from her lips.

"It is not a bad joke," she said, as if to herself. And
then, seeming to remember she was not alone, made a
gesture of her hand in the air.

"This is not my world, although I have learned its rules
so well that I am among the few allowed to disobey them.
In fact, it is just that which let me enter it: The *haute ton*
is in truth a very dull place to live. Any surprising or
novel person—so long as she does not absolutely violate
the first decree of it leaders—is instantly welcomed in for
the sake of diversion. I was just such a one, although not
by intent. At first I did not understand them, and was not
much interested in what they thought of me. That was my
first great stroke. To people who have been obsessed for
so long with their own importance, it was an awakening
to discover one who was not. And then I learned that,
the more cold I was, the less attention I paid them, the
greater value was put on any attention I *did* pay. But I
have gone ahead of myself. I meant to tell you how I came
to inhabit this elevated world into which I was neither
born nor brought up."

Miss Haversham paused again, collecting her thoughts.

"My father was a fish merchant in Carbury, on the
outskirts of London. He was not poor, but neither was he
rich. By dint of hard work and economy, he amassed what
was in our world considered a reasonable fortune. Of
course, by the standards of these people—and by your own,
no doubt—it was penury. When I was just fifteen, both he

and my mother died in an outbreak of cholera. My brother and I were cast upon our own fortunes and the charity of our friends. We had sufficient funds to live modestly, of course, and without any kind of luxury—but still to live. My brother was then nineteen, four years older than myself, and he at once joined the Navy. It was agreed between us that I should stay in London, keeping my father's house, and looking after him when he was on leave. In order to increase our income a little, I also began to take in fine laundry work for ladies. Some of the people I worked for were members of the highest society, even of the court. But of course I had no opportunity to meet them. The laundry was brought in baskets by their servants, and taken away in the same fashion.

"A year passed without much incident. My brother was stationed at Liverpool, and was used to coming home on leave. But he began suddenly to appear less and less frequently. In look and temperament, we are exactly opposed. My brother is as fair as I am dark, and blessed with a gift for drawing others out which has naturally endeared him to all who knew him. His great charm and easy laughter had always been the envy of myself and the pride of our parents. But, as often happens, I think, his charm was allowed to take the place of those inner strengths which may sometimes make life difficult, but which are yet necessary if one is to live with honor. He had begun to make new friends in the Navy, and advancing rapidly through the ranks (for he was as clever as he was charming), must have fallen into the society of those richer than himself, and with less scruples. I did not see him for six months, and save for an occasional request for funds, heard nothing from him. At last, by accident, I heard he had been involved in some mischief and was in debt. I wrote to him, begging him for an explanation, but had no reply.

"In the end, frightened and unsure where to turn, I went myself to Liverpool, and heard, to my distress, what had occurred. The Captain of his vessel told me that my brother had been living above his means for some time. He had befriended some wealthier officers, taken to gambling, and was now seriously in debt. Although he would not at first agree to my coming, I managed to see him myself, and begged him to have a care. He laughed at my distress,

saying the Captain was given to overstatement, and that he
was nowhere nearly so badly off as I had feared. Certainly
I wanted to believe him, and when he assured me that he
would change his ways, I returned to London, much relieved in my heart, and took up my former life.

"For some time things went along as before. Charlie's
letters were more regular, and from all he said, I could
only believe his habits were changed for good. He applied
himself with new vigor to his career, and the proof of this
was that he was soon offered a commission and had been
granted a long leave in London before his next cruise. He
came home only for a few days, in fact, and I was amazed
to see him. He was changed almost beyond recognition:
Where there had been a boy, here was a man, and a
gentleman, besides. His clothes were so elegant I could
hardly believe he had bought them with his wages. But
he assured me that, having given off cards, he could
afford a gentleman's attire at last. In truth, I should *not*
have believed him—but his manner was so merry, he
seemed so happy, and above all, so solicitous of *me*—that
I could not resist him. He was enraged that I should continue to take in ladies' laundry, and bid me give it up as
soon as possible. I protested—for I did not know how we
could live without it—but he convinced me at last that his
wages had increased so much that there was no need for
it any more. In the end I agreed, only opposing his desire
that I should take a larger house, where, as he put it, 'he
should not be ashamed to invite his friends.'

"That idea could not help but hurt me, but I still would
not consent. It was just possible, if his wages had been so
much increased, for me to give up work; but to take on a
higher style of living so soon would have been to invite
eventual penury. And so I agreed to take in no more laundry, but to remain in our old house. Charlie was dissatisfied,
but finally consented to my decision. He went away, leaving
me what I considered a small fortune—twenty pounds, I
believe it was—to improve my wardrobe, with strict instructions to visit a lady in Chalmsford Square, who was
known to be a wizard with a needle. No young girl, on the
eve of her eighteenth birthday, could have resisted such an
order and, much to my regret, I did not.

"Now, as it happened, my reputation had begun to
grow. I was to give up my work just when I was the most

sought after, when ladies and gentlemen of the highest rank were eager for my services. So much so, in fact, that Mr. Brummel—you will have heard of him, no doubt—was curious to see what the uproar was about. He was renowned for his meticulous attention to his dress, and had been known to cast aside forty cravats for the fault of one crease or the tiniest fleck of dust. So meticulous was he, in fact, that before sending his cravats to be laundered, he wished to meet the girl whose hands would touch that sanctified stuff. He came to visit me without any warning, and with barely an introduction, walked in. I was too ignorant to know who he was, and thinking him a most uncouth fellow, ordered him away.

"Perhaps you have heard that Mr. Brummel himself made his reputation at court by outright incivility. The Prince dearly loves to be slandered by that tongue—it is accounted a great compliment to be upbraided by him for some minor point of dress or of conduct. Indeed, I believe there is not a being in the whole of London who would not swell with pride to be insulted by him. And yet—to insult *Brummel*! I believe no one would have the courage to do that! And yet here was I, a mere laundress, daring to order him away! He looked at me, and blinked with his great bulbous, pale eyes, and blinked again, and then put back his head and laughed. I had expected him to be insulted, but to laugh! I really did not know what to make of him."

Miss Haversham paused, turning around for a moment and smiling at her companion. So immersed had Maggie been in the narration that she could only exclaim,

"Pray, do not stop! It is better than any novel I have read! You must tell me the rest."

"Yes, I suppose it is better than a novel," agreed Blanche Haversham, smiling. "And yet it is perfectly true, you know. Indeed, I wish it were not.

"In any case, Brummel—or the "beau" as he is called— made no move to leave. On the contrary. He set about making himself as much at home as possible, first requesting some refreshment—he was appalled that I had not any claret—and then requiring that I show him my work. I told him bluntly that I had no intention of doing so, and that I had given up laundering in any case. He seemed surprised at this, and wondered why. So outrageous was his conduct that in truth I was too astonished to resist him. I told him

my brother had just been granted a commission in the
Navy, and that he wished me to stop all manner of work.
'An officer in the Navy!' he exclaimed. 'Why, then he is
a gentleman!' And if my brother was a gentleman, then I
must be a lady. As I had always been taught to think of
myself as a lady, even if I was not rich, this made me
bridle. I said nothing, but was as cold as possible, and the
colder I was, the more Brummel liked me.

"He began to look at me more closely, actually getting
up and walking around me as if I were a horse. 'Very nice,'
he said. 'Yes, yes, you are quite a beauty, my little laundress. You will do very well indeed.' When I inquired what
he meant, he only laughed and took his seat again. By this
time, as you may well imagine, I was so enraged, so insulted, and yet so fascinated, that I could hardly have said
a word even if I wanted to. I had no intention of flattering
him by letting him see that I was curious what he meant,
but neither did I intend letting him leave without—if not
an apology (for I saw at once he was not a man to admit
he had been uncivil), at the least an explanation. And at
last it did come out—what he meant, that is. He proposed
a scheme to me so outrageous that at first I could only
stare at him. He had long had it in his mind, he said—in
fact, it was the dearest wish of his deformed heart—to play
a trick on that same Society which had turned him from
the grandson of a blacksmith into the greatest lawmaker
in the realm. Just how he was to accomplish this feat had
been a subject of amusement for some time—but he had
not decided just how to go about it until he saw me. Something had reminded him of a story he had once heard, in
which a whole kingdom was deceived by a pauper, and it
had given him the exact inspiration he required.

"You may well inquire why such a rake, a man who
owed everything to Society, should seek his vengeance
upon it, for in truth that is what he intended doing. Brummel's motives are no business of mine. But I should guess,
having seen what I now have of the Great World, that *that*
is exactly what made him hate it. I have often observed—
have not you?—that we are most likely to despise what
has done most for us: It is the way of humankind to resent
bitterly the charitable hands which are held out to us,
which we would rather do without, and yet are prevented

from resisting, either from poverty, or some other dire need of our hearts or minds."

Miss Haversham paused, looking into the air, but in so abstracted a manner that Maggie could not help but think she was really looking into her own heart. And when she added, in so soft a voice that it was barely audible: "I could not have understood *then* what drove him on," her listener was awed at the solemnity in her voice, and at the nearly tragic air which seemed to hang about her, as palpable as a cloak.

But now, as if realizing she had drifted too far away from her subject, Miss Haversham gave herself a shake and smiled in her old arch, almost ironic way.

"But I have left off my tale, and we have not much time. Brummel's scheme was this: He wished to introduce me to Society, to parade me about as his latest 'find,' the new nonpareil of fashion, to show me off to the haughtiest ladies as prettier than they, more cognizant of fashion than they. To my astonished inquiry, What would they say when they discovered I was naught but a fish merchant's daughter? he responded with a laugh—'Never mind, my dear, I shall simply let them guess—and since they are all nearly as stupid as they are vain, they will naturally suppose you are highly born. How else, they will say, could she have learned so much? I shall let them think what they like, and they will certainly prefer to think you are of noble lineage than otherwise.'

"I really did not know what to say, but one thing was certain: I could never do as he asked, and this I told him. He seemed astonished at first that a girl as humble as I should refuse so easy an entrance into a world she could only have dreamed of hitherto. He gaped, and chided me, but at last, on seeing I was firm, merely left me his card and promised me that some day I should change my mind —when, as he put it, I 'grew more sensible.'

"I could not imagine I would ever be 'sensible' enough to wish to be a mere pawn in the game of such a Machiavelli as Beau Brummel, and yet I was intrigued by the idea —much as I abhorred it, I was intrigued, and not a little flattered. The matter, however, did not stay long in my mind. Life was too busy to flatter myself with such absurd ideas as he had put into my head, and soon another matter came to occupy all my attention.

"My brother, as I have said, had received his commission, and seemed to have changed his ways altogether from the frivolity of his younger years. He advanced steadily through the ranks, becoming at last a full captain, and winning for himself an ardent little circle of admirers in the Navy. He had his own vessel, stationed at Liverpool, and between voyages was used to coming to London. He stayed with me only part of the time; the remainder was divided between his friends' houses—as always, he had so many friends he knew not which ones to look up first— but when he was with me, he hardly saw any of them. One or two I did meet, and these I cannot say I liked overmuch. I should have suspected, on seeing them, that his life had not changed so much as I wanted to believe, but rather that his vices had grown in proportion with his rank. But in my company he was such a picture of upright, virtuous manhood, and so gay and companionable besides, that I could not really be blamed for looking no farther. At last, however, an incident did occur which could not be hidden from me.

"One day I received a call from a gentleman I had seen only once, conversing with my brother in the street—a foreign gentleman, very elegantly clad, but with something in his manner I did not like. The gentleman inquired whether I had not a message for him from my brother. No, no, I said—I had none. In fact, I believed him to be on a voyage at the moment, and had not seen him in two months. The fellow refused to believe me, and staring in a very rude way, mumbled something to himself and went off. That evening, as I was preparing for bed, there was a clamoring at the door. I heard the servant girl run to see what was the matter. By the time I had achieved the head of the stairs, I saw that Charlie was standing in the hallway with the foreign gentleman. They were both out of breath, disheveled from riding, Charlie would not tell me what was the matter, and ordered me to be silent when I asked a question. He requested that supper be served them, and said they would both stay the night. A room was readied for the stranger, and when I had seen them fed, I retired myself. On the morrow no more was said about the matter, but Charlie was not himself. Both he and his friend lurked about the house, hardly saying a word to me, and plainly ill at ease. I began to be uneasy myself, but when I demanded to be told what the matter was, he inquired, laughing, why I should think there was anything the matter? Still, neither of them quit the house that day nor the next, and a week passed in this same peculiar way. Then, as suddenly as they had come, they left. It was not until a week had gone by that I discovered what villainy they had been up to that day. It came to my attention in a most extraordinary fashion, by way of the very gentleman they had wronged. I shall not tell you very much about it, save that my brother had involved himself in a despicable plot, involving a lady of high rank and, what is worse, a man whom of all men I believe to have the courage of his convictions."

Listening to this astonishing narration, Maggie had been too much absorbed in her friend's tale to wonder why she had been chosen to hear it. But now, Miss Haversham having walked to the window in silence and remained there for some moments without stirring, she could not help saying—

"But why have you chosen to tell me all this?"

"You must think me very odd," replied Miss Haversham, smiling, "but let us say simply that I have my reasons. I wished, first, not to mislead *you* about my identity. And I wished also to have your help."

"My help! Why, what could *I* do?"

"First, I had better tell you what I set out to say at first, and to do so, I must tell you yet a little more, if you are not already tired of this tale."

At Maggie's protestations to the contrary, Blanche Haversham continued: "Then let me finish quickly, for I think we had better join the others.

"I discovered this intrigue, and at last Charlie himself confessed. I am afraid he did not do so only for his conscience, but because he needed my help. He had done more harm than he intended doing, for in truth he had not meant to be really wicked, but through weakness had been led beyond his first intentions by the influence of more hardened men. He needed money—a great deal of money—and now, having failed to get it as he hoped, he had alienated those very persons who could have helped him most. He knew of Mr. Brummel's visit, for I had recounted it to him as a joke in one of my letters. And now he urged me to take up the scheme for his sake, as it could help him."

"Help him to get money?" demanded Maggie, astonished. "Why, how could it have done that?"

"Not so much money outright, but credit; when you are accounted a regular member of the *ton*, there is no limit to the bills you may run up without once being called upon to pay, until you are so much in debt that the King himself could not pay 'em. I protested at first, of course, but at last allowed myself to be convinced. It was not that I condoned my brother's conduct, but he was all the family I had, and torn between my own beliefs and that loyalty which must sometimes be placed above strict adherence to honesty, I could not refuse him. You must understand, besides, that he is the most persuasive man in all the world. I believe he could make a stone smile, if he liked. Oh! How I wish *now* I had not been so soft!

"But I had made up my mind, and having kept the card as a memento of Brummel's visit, went to call upon him. He was delighted, though not much surprised, and instantly set up the scheme. Before I knew it, I had a new wardrobe entire from the best dressmakers in Bond Street. A house was taken for me in Grove Street, a carriage hired, and I was proclaimed the brightest belle at Almack's. Brummel even changed my name—and yet let it be known that I was not who I claimed to be, saying he had found me on the Continent and that I had a tragic and mysterious past. The two together were enough to fascinate the whole *ton*, and as I saw at once what kind of people made up that world, and liked them not at all, they were the more impressed that I did not tumble before their quizzing glasses. Brummel saw to it that I had dancing lessons, and himself taught me a little French and Italian. He was quite giddy with his own success—the more especially as he had won a pretty sum of money from the Prince, who had bet him the ruse could not be carried off. And in exchange for this deceit, I was to be his very slave. Not a move could I make without his consent; I slept, ate, and paraded about for his pleasure, and the more sullen I became at this arrangement, the better the world liked me. My life became very like that of a bird in a gilded cage—the gilt, no matter how pretty, could not lessen the fact that I was imprisoned. I had the further pain of seeing my brother, who had nearly

lost his commission through his folly, be reinstigated with
my help, and, in the shadow of my conquests, be admitted
to Almack's, where he had nearly as much success as I
had myself. No one knew he was my brother, of course:
It was believed we were old friends, and that he knew my
past. Everyone was clamoring to know about it, but playing
the game to perfection, he teased them endlessly. Thus we
have continued for five years and everyone, save myself,
pleased beyond words. The more the game was played out,
the more enmeshed I became. It had begun for me as the
only means in my command to rescue my brother from
absolute ruin. I believed, in my innocence, that there
would be no more to it. Ah! If I had only known *then* what
I know now! That the world, once it has got you in its
hands, will not let go. It wraps its fingers around you, like
some mysterious beast, and, so gently that one hardly
knows it is there, begins to strangle you."

Once again Miss Haversham paused, and once again
Maggie was struck by the air of tragedy which lingered
over her, and which was increased rather than diminished
by the young woman's obstinate refusal to cower before it.
She had actually smiled as she spoke the last words; the
combination of the smile—so out of place at that moment
—the lady's voice, and a kind of dark amusement in her
brilliant eyes made Maggie shudder.

"Charlie would not, of course, leave off. As soon as he
discovered what had been opened for him by my charade,
he would not hear of my giving it up. And then—and then,
of course, I met Mr. Montcrieff."

Blanche Haversham's voice grew soft, and her face,
hitherto so commanding and proud, softened with it. But
in an instant she gave herself a shake, and hurried on.

"And now we come to the point, why I have tired you
so long with this story. There were only five of us who knew
the truth about me—Brummel, of course, and the Prince,
who considered it the height of entertainment, my brother
Charles and myself, and one other—your cousin, Lord
Ramblay. Oh! do not ask me how *he* knew, for it is not
in my power to divulge that. Indeed, I only tell you now
because it was he who, of all of them, was the only one who
understood my unhappiness, and who, till this day, has offered me the comfort of honesty without once compromis-
ing my position. Even now, when I hope to be betrothed

to Diana's brother and when I could so easily be a great weight on his mind, he has been nothing but kind."

There were a hundred questions Maggie dearly longed to ask, a hundred points she desired to have clarified. What was the role her cousin had played in all of this? Why, of all men, should he have been privy to such a well-kept secret, which had continued now so long? And this new side of his character astounded her. Indeed, she would like to have told Captain Morrison's tale to her friend in order to have a second opinion about it. But there was not time to say another word, for just at that moment footsteps sounded in the hall outside, and in a moment the door was flung open.

"Ah, Miss Haversham—I thought I might find you here," exclaimed Lord Ramblay, and then, catching sight of Maggie, stopped. "Why, Cousin—I did not see you at first. I hope I have not interrupted some private *tête-à-tête?*"

Miss Haversham smiled back at him. "No, no, Lord Ramblay—nothing like it. I have only been showing Miss Trevor your amazing collection of books. She solicited my help in finding her a novel, and I thought you would not mind our venturing in here."

Lord Ramblay looked doubtfully back and forth between the two young ladies, and Maggie could not help but look a little guilty. He seemed not to notice, however, and remarked lightly, "Why, of course I do not mind. Only I am afraid Miss Trevor would have a greater success in finding a novel to her liking in the main library. This is only my little sanctuary, Cousin—and I suppose my own books would not amuse you much. I know how little fond ladies are of histories, and such kinds of dreadful old stories that make no mention of the latest fashions or current gossip."

Even as she protested this abuse of her sex, in as light a tone as the Viscount's, she watched the two others closely. But not a flicker passed between them. No movement, either of their eyes or lips, gave away the secret knowledge they shared. She noticed, too, that while all his other guests addressed her cousin as Percy, Blanche Haversham, who must have been on a still more intimate footing with him, always used his title. And even now the two stood smiling at each other, but without any trace of the complicity that joined them.

Lord Ramblay had been to fetch a surgeon, who was now attending upon young Mr. Montcrieff, but it seemed he desired some assistance. Recollecting what his cousin had said earlier, Lord Ramblay inquired whether Maggie would go to them, or if Miss Haversham would go in her stead. Blanche Haversham was willing; none of that critical coldness she had leveled at her lover earlier was in her eyes *now*. But Maggie mentioned that she had often bound up the lesser wounds of her father's sailors when there had been no doctor nearby, and so it was decided she should go instead. Passing out of the doorway behind the Viscount, she turned to smile at her new friend. The smile was returned, and in that mutual glance was a wealth of understanding, and a little nod, which, on the part of Blanche Haversham, was full of questions. The returning look was more a reassurance than a flood of words could have been. "I understand you," it said clearly, "and I do not judge you. I think you are the most glorious creature in the world!"

Ten

MR. MONTCRIEFF'S WOUNDS were greater than they had
seemed at first. The spraining of an ankle was compounded
by a cut upon the shin, much deeper than it looked. The
cut was in danger of festering, and the surgeon, when he
saw that Maggie knew what she was about, gave her
careful instructions for the patient's care. He was to have
complete quiet and bed-rest, though the proposed journey
to London, if it were conducted quietly and easily, would
not harm him, so long as he went straight away to bed
when he arrived. Miss Montcrieff cried out at this, nearly
smothering her brother in yellow curls and whimpers, and
it was plain that *she* had not the presence of mind to nurse
him. But Miss Haversham, who had watched quietly
throughout the proceedings, now offered to go with her
friend. At this suggestion, young Montcrieff looked infinitely gladdened. His smooth young face, which had
looked very low all morning, brightened instantly. In truth,
it was a splendid suggestion! They should all stay at Grosvenor Square, and when he was recovered, they should
dance the jig together as merrily as she pleased! Miss
Haversham smiled, and said nothing; Maggie was struck
again by the resolution of the young lady, and once more
wondered that she should be in love with such a foolish
character as Montcrieff. It is true he had borne the pain
better than she had expected, and even smiled when the
surgeon had twisted his ankle back into place. That he
was very sweet, and cheerful, and madly devoted to Miss
Haversham, she doubted not; yet he did not possess that
profundity of character which the lady had to such a
degree.

Throughout the proceedings, Lord Ramblay stood
quietly by, and, had Maggie noticed, she might have seen
him gazing at her as she worked with an intensity out of

all proportion to the task. Maggie did not notice, but Miss Montcrieff did; and when the surgeon rose to go, she followed the Viscount resolutely out behind the doctor, and drawing him aside in the passage, mocked at him for being incapable of taking his eyes away from his cousin. Lord Ramblay looked surprised, and said, in a milder tone than the young lady's petulant manner deserved:

"Why, it is no such thing, Diana! I only admire the capable way she undertook the work, which was not pleasant, I imagine. She has a deal more mettle than her bantering manner would make it seem."

"Pooh!" cried Miss Montcrieff, who had been incapable of looking at the wound until it was wrapped up. "Anyone could have done the same! Why, if anyone had asked me, *I* should have bandaged it up! In any case, I only taunt you for looking at your own cousin in such a way. It makes me envious, for you never look at *me* thus!" And Miss Montcrieff tapped him playfully upon the sleeve with her fan. Lord Ramblay, however, did not see the joke.

"Nonsense, my dear Diana. I do nothing but gaze at you admiringly," he said, in a resigned tone, and with a little sigh escaping his lips. "If I looked at you any more than I do, I should have no sight for anything else. Besides, you cannot blame me for taking an interest in my own cousin, whom I have never met before."

But Miss Montcrieff was not so easily satisfied.

"Do you think her beautiful?" she inquired in a critical tone. "*I* do not. She is too tall, and her mouth too wide. And besides, she has got that manner, which is entirely too comical for my taste."

Perhaps a little doubtful as to the meaning his fiancée wished to ascribe to the word "comical," Lord Ramblay smiled. That she had a very laughing manner he would allow, and that it did not suit him completely, also. And yet, if she was not an absolute beauty, she was very handsome, and her handsomeness was made greater still by the bloom of perfect health and the expressiveness of her eyes, which he thought very fine. But aloud he said, "No, she is not beautiful."

The remainder of the party, assembling for dinner, was quickly informed of the events of the morning. The ladies, who had first scoffed at so slight an injury, were now alarmed by Diana Montcrieff's exaggerated depiction of the wound. Lady Ramblay, emerged at last from her apartments, stared down from the head of the table through her raised glass.

"What!" she cried in her commanding tone, which was rather like the blaring of a bugle before a battle. "Why was not I informed of it?"

"There seemed no need, madam," replied her son from the opposite end. "The wound was not half so bad as Diana has painted it, and the surgeon was fetched at once. My cousin helped him very capably, and there seemed no point in disturbing you as well."

Now Lady Ramblay focused her quizzing glass on Maggie. "You helped him, did you? I suppose you held the poultice on his brow?"

Maggie could not help smiling to herself.

"No, madam—nothing like that. I only helped to wrap the bandage around his ankle, and to cleanse the wound."

"Wrap the bandage! My dear child, I hope you did not indeed! Why, what if the wound should fester, or his leg become infected?"

"She did it very well, madam," put in Lord Ramblay, in an effort to stop what looked like an interrogation. But his mother ignored him.

"And where did you learn doctoring, Miss Trevor?"

"I learned what little I know, your ladyship, nearly on my father's knee. It is often the commander of a vessel who must double as ship's surgeon, and when I grew older, I used often to nurse his sailors myself, when they were in port."

"Ah!" muttered Lady Ramblay, but with no evidence of being satisfied. "Sailors are a very dirty lot, do not you think? I wonder you did not contract some rare disease, such as they are always dying of in the tropics."

Maggie smiled more broadly still, but seeing Blanche Haversham smiling encouragement from across the table, endeavored to keep her voice level. "They are no dirtier than other men, madam. Indeed, less so, for they have the constant proximity of water and wind, which are the best natural cleansing forces in the world. They are in general a very healthy group of men. I do not suppose there are any Englishman much better off."

Lady Ramblay seemed to snort, and subsided for a

while. Maggie noticed that Miss Ramblay, who had been sitting quietly near her mama, was deeply flushed. Once more Maggie's heart went out to the young girl. She would draw her out as soon as she could, for a sweeter, prettier, more shy-looking creature she had never seen in her life.

The opportunity came sooner than expected and was initiated by Miss Ramblay herself. Coming up to Maggie as soon as they had quit the dining room, she laid a small flower-like hand upon the other's arm and smiled shyly.

"I have wished most awfully to speak to you since last night," she said. "But I have been all day studying with my tutors. Mama says if I am to go to Town with you, I must apply myself diligently beforehand. But ever since I heard of you, I have been so eager to meet you! And now I see I was not mistaken in my hopes."

More flattered by this artless show of friendship than she would have been by any compliment from the worldly women in the party, Maggie replied warmly that she, too, had been longing to speak to her young cousin. The two walked together into the withdrawing room, where coffee was already being served, and, as if from instinct, Miss Ramblay left her hand in her cousin's. They sat down upon a sofa together, and the younger girl began to quiz her cousin about her life at Portsmouth and about her father, her eyes shining all the while with interest. At last, when there was a pause in the questions, she burst out:

"Why! It does not sound nearly so bad as I thought!" Maggie inferred from this that Miss Ramblay had been made to believe that the Admiral and his daughter were some sort of gypsies, as unlike the people her cousin had been brought up with as fish. She smiled to herself, and said, "No, no—I suppose it does not."

"I am most awfully glad we are to make our come-out together," confided Miss Ramblay.

Maggie was astonished at this, for she had guessed her cousin's age to be not above fifteen or sixteen. Her look and manner, her tiny, frail figure, and most especially the excessive naiveté of her manner, confirmed this idea. And yet, inquiring her age, Maggie discovered her cousin to be eighteen. That eighteen years had passed before those eyes was nearly unbelievable. They must have been so shaded from life, or at the least from real life, as it was lived by nearly all the world, that they had managed to retain that shining, naked innocence which was at once extraordinarily appealing and a little frightening. The notion of those eyes now being exposed to the rude, rough world made Maggie almost flinch. And yet there was a something about the mouth, on further knowing the young lady, which spoke of an innate wisdom—almost a worldliness—completely contrasting to the rest, and which reminded Maggie of some reproductions she had seen of medieval paintings. It was an understanding as timeless and patient as the earth itself. Maggie began to understand now why the child was treated with such protectiveness. That combination of innocence and experience would have pierced any man's heart.

Lady Ramblay billowed up to them like a stately battleship under full sail. She must once have been a handsome woman, Maggie thought, but the regular lines of her face and form had been taxed by an evil disposition and an excess of flesh. Whatever charms had once lurked about that chin and in those eyes, was now hidden beneath a dozen pink folds, and what might have been a jolly old age was marred by a strident manner.

"Well, child!" the Viscountess cried, "I see you are getting acquainted with your cousin! I hope she has not put any peculiar notions in your head about life."

"No, no, Mama!" exclaimed Fanny in protest. "Miss Trevor has only been telling me about her father and the Navy. It is a most fascinating tale!"

"I would imagine so, my dear," replied the Viscountess, pressing her lips together and glaring at Maggie, "but not one, I think, meant for the ears of innocent girls."

Maggie could not help protesting at this that she, too, had once been an innocent girl, and that the living out of her life had not done her much harm. Lady Ramblay merely snorted, and then said, in what appeared to be an effort at condescension:

"I believe we are soon to have a neighbor of yours in the vicarage, Miss Trevor. No doubt you will be glad of a companion from your own *milieu*."

"Oh, if it is Mr. Wayland you are speaking of, madam, I have indeed heard of his coming to you. We are not very intimate friends, but I shall certainly be glad to see him."

"You knew of his coming!" cried the other. "Why, it

was understood between us that his appointment should be secret!"

Maggie smiled in recollection of the Vicar's eagerness to impart to her this delicate matter.

"I do not think there is much that can be kept secret in a small village."

"No, no—I suppose not. Gossip among the lower orders is nearly as prevalent a vice as poverty. It has long been my opinion that the elimination of both would greatly improve this kingdom."

Maggie was unable to contradict her hostess on this point, for while her acquaintance with what she seemed meant to take as the "higher orders" had done little to convince her that gossip was not prevalent among *them*, she could hardly dispute the fact that poverty was not a greatly desirable state. That it should be called a vice, however, had never occurred to her before. The idea made her smile to herself.

Lady Ramblay went on, "Be that as it may, you shall have the pleasure of seeing your old friend on Monday, for that is when he takes up his duties. A most attractive gentleman, I think—most diligent in his attention to the Church. Indeed, I do not believe we shall miss our old Mr. Congreve very sadly, for young Wayland has all the promise to *my* mind of gaining a bishopric some day. It will be among my greatest pleasures to push him along as well as I may, for there is nothing so helpful to a young curate—especially one of Mr. Wayland's modest disposition—as an interested patron."

"It seems Mr. Wayland has done himself a great turn," thought Maggie at hearing these amazing words of praise spoken of the very gentleman she had long considered among the least religious of any she had met, and likewise the most greedy. "I doubt not but he thought more about the lady of the castle, on applying for the post, than any good he might do among the parishioners." Smiling to herself, she decided that no two souls of earth deserved each other more. If Mr. Wayland was a pompous idiot, he might yet learn a lesson or two in gracelessness from his new patron. Lord Ramblay, with his stiff, formal manner, had at least escaped his mother's influence on that one point: If he was too awkward to be thought really agreeable, and even if he had been cruel to his wife, he had at least none of his mother's outright incivility. Rather, his short-comings seemed to veer in the other direction, for even Miss Haversham's tale had not influenced Maggie's opinion of his manner, but rather confirmed it. Captain Morrison's summation of him as a man of duty beyond everything, came to her mind again a moment later, when the gentlemen came in.

Lady Ramblay went off to oversee their coffee, and Miss Ramblay, who had been gazing miserably into her lap on hearing her mother's extraordinary remarks, now lit up with pleasure when she saw her brother approach them.

"Oh, Percy!" she exclaimed, "I have been having *such* a lovely time with Miss Trevor! She has been telling me all about her life. I think it is better than a novel!"

Lord Ramblay smiled indulgently at his young sister and, turning to Maggie with a formal bow, remarked, "I hope Fanny has not been boring *you* unduly with tales of woe about her studies."

"Oh! Nothing like it! Your sister has made me speak only of myself this last half hour. But I understand we are to be together at London, so I shall have ample opportunity to hear about *her*."

"Oh, there is very little to tell," said Miss Ramblay diffidently. "I have not done anything nearly as exciting as you have. My life is perfectly dull in comparison."

"Nonsense, Fanny! You have led a life exactly suited to a young girl of your situation."

There, again, were those words—the same idea, only slightly altered in the expression. Lord Ramblay had not been so uncivil as his mama, and yet there was in his tone the same intimation that Fanny, being what she was, was set apart from the rest of humanity and, in this particular case, from her cousin. It was not an absolute affront, but once more Maggie felt a little like an orphaned relation brought to live with her aristocratic cousins, more for their own satisfaction at doing good than for her own pleasure or health. She received Lord Ramblay's thanks for the part she had played in helping Mr. Montcrieff with rather less grace than she might have done, and a little while later, when a cry went up for music, used as an excuse her love of playing to move away.

Diana Montcrieff was first to play. Hardly an urging was needed to make *her* rise from her chair and go to the instrument; though a great show was made of reluctance. With many little grimaces and protestations, and saying that she should oblige them if some others would do the same, she was seated upon the stool in an instant. She had insisted she should only play one or two tunes, but once established at the pianoforte, could not be coaxed away for an hour. Her playing was so full of false notes, so lacking in feeling as well as technique, that Maggie could hardly comprehend the clamor that went up upon the completion of every song. But at last the young lady rose up, and having inquired of one or two of the others if they would not play, she turned to Maggie.

"Well, then, Miss Trevor, *you* must oblige us! I am sure you know all kinds of lively songs that sailors sing. Pray, give us one or two of those!"

Saying she would do her best, Maggie took her place at the instrument. Though she did indeed know many a naval hymn and ballad, she took an especial pleasure in playing first a particularly difficult sonata she had mastered more from strength of will than anything. Out of the corner of her eye she noticed Lord Ramblay turn away from a group he had been in conversation with and walk a little nearer to the pianoforte. When she had finished the second piece—a livelier tune—he was standing beside her.

"And will you sing with me, Cousin?" she demanded, starting in upon a well-known ballad. She did not expect him to concede; she had really meant to taunt him by the invitation, thinking Lord Ramblay too conscious of his own dignity to risk it upon a song. She was amazed, therefore, when he merely nodded, and commenced.

Lord Ramblay's voice was cause for even more amazement. Though evidently out of practice, it was deep and round and—more astonishing still—made resonant by natural feeling. Whether he had once been trained to sing in this fashion, or had acquired the skill from intuitive understanding, his voice swelled and softened with so much beauty that she nearly ceased playing in order to listen. Indeed, she herself stopped singing after the first verse was done, and on the next, when only the Viscount's voice was heard alone, conversation ceased among the other guests as they drew around to listen.

"By Jove, Ramblay!" cried Mr. Whiting, "I never knew you had such a voice!"

The others joined in the clamor, but Lord Ramblay would not be flattered. It appeared no one had heard him sing before, save Fanny, who coming up beside her cousin inquired softly if her brother did not have a great talent?

"To be sure he does!" exclaimed Maggie with feeling, for the moment forgetting her dislike of him. "I have seldom heard such a voice as that."

Lord Ramblay flushed at this praise as he had not done at that of the others, and denied that his was anything unusual.

"But, Percy—I did not know you ever sang," Miss Montcrieff cried out. "Certainly you have never sung for *me.*"

"I have not sung these five years at least, Diana," he assured her. "Not since—not since——" but the sentence was not finished. Lord Ramblay colored, and changed the subject. "But indeed, it is not *me* you ought to be praising. My cousin's playing is infinitely superior to my accompaniment."

"No, no, it is no such thing," protested Maggie, but felt more pleased than she would admit. "I am very fond of music, it is true—but my talents are not sufficient to do my fondness the justice it deserves."

"You ought not to underrate yourself, Cousin. You have a natural ear for what is right, and great dexterity. If you were to apply yourself diligently, no doubt you should make a fine musician."

This last almost banished Maggie's pleasure at the Viscount's first praise, for it struck so certain a note, a note she could not but admit was true, that she colored. But the conversation went no further, for Miss Montcrieff would have her say. She ardently wished her "dearest Percy" to sing a particular favorite of her own, and her insistence was so great, her pouts so pretty, and her petulance so absolute that there was no denying her. For half an hour the company listened to her every request, and at the end of it, Maggie rose, saying she was too tired to play any more.

Blanche Haversham had not been present since dinner. She had, as Maggie suspected on looking about for her, been sitting with her lover. But as Maggie rose from the pianoforte, she saw the other young lady walk quietly into the room and take a seat in a far corner.

"That was lovely," said she, on Maggie's taking a seat beside her. "I have heard only a little, but what a relief it is to hear something other than Diana's hammering!"

Maggie smiled.

"And how is poor Mr. Montcrieff?"

Miss Haversham made a gesture with her shoulders that might have been a shrug. "He is bored, and tired of being abed. But I think his pain has lessened. He has been very eager to make me think well of him."

"I dare say," replied Maggie, smiling. "I should be so, too, had you berated me as you did him!"

"I should not have embarrassed him so in front of the others. But I cannot bear to see a dumb beast killed through the stupidity of a man. It seems such a profligate kind of act, when only a little thought might have prevented it."

Miss Haversham spoke with great intensity, but without any of that contempt which had been in her eyes when she had stood at the bottom of the ravine, lecturing her fiancé. *Then* there had been a kind of wildness in her look, which had astonished Maggie and even frightened her a little. But now the wildness, if it was part of her friend's true nature, had been tamed again. She was once more a composed young woman, concern for her lover showing in her eyes, but only to a degree acceptable in a drawing room.

"Oh, you need not apologize to *me*," Maggie assured her. "I often think I am fonder of animals than human beings. They are more honest by far, and uninhibited by pride, or vanity, or an excess of ambition."

Miss Haversham smiled her agreement, and then Maggie asked a question that had been perplexing her.

"How is it you learned to ride so well, Miss Haversham? My cousin told me, and I saw with my own eyes, that you handle the reins better than any of the gentlemen. And yet you could not have been much used to hunting in—in——"

"In Carbury?" smiled Miss Haversham. "No, you are quite right. I never was upon a horse before I was taken up by Brummel. But I soon discovered the sport, and now find it gives me more real satisfaction than anything. When I am galloping full tilt after a pack of hounds, with the wind in my face and mud flying into my eyes, it is impossible to think of anything else. Besides, riding well

requires only two things: The first is to understand that
horses, however beautiful, are immensely stupid and will
obey anyone who understands that fact; the second re-
quirement is an absolute indifference to one's own safety.
I have not had much reason to value my own life during
these five years. . . ."

Maggie glanced sharply at her new friend. She would
like to have asked a dozen questions at that moment,
but something in the other's expression made her stop.
She contented herself by saying softly. "I hope you have
not forgotten that you asked for my help, Miss Haversham.
Please believe that I am as eager as possible to do anything
in my power that may be of service to you."

Blanche Haversham smiled.

"Thank you, my dear friend," she said simply. "I shall
tell you very soon what it is, and then you must be absolutely frank with *me*—for I could not ask of you what is
difficult."

Maggie replied that if it was within her power, she
could not think of anything she would *not* do to help
so brave a woman, and so steadfast a one. With this seal of
their friendship, they agreed to call each other by their
Christian names, for while Blanche Haversham was not her
real name, it would have to do for the present. They were
shortly interrupted by Mr. Whitting, who, coming over to
where they sat, drew up a chair and wished to be told all
the details of Mr. Montcrieff's fall that morning.

Eleven

MAGGIE, LYING IN the splendor of her silk and silver bed
that night, had much to occupy her thoughts. As often
happens, she had found her first impressions of Ramblay
Castle and its occupants misleading. Although some fore-
bodings of the coldness she might be received with as she
had driven toward it, had been confirmed in the person of
Lady Ramblay, everywhere else she had found herself
welcomed with kindness. Miss Ramblay was as sweet and
soft as a rose, and the unexpected disclosures of Miss
Haversham, who had at first seemed so distant, so proud,
and so haughty, made her feel she had acquired two good
friends in a single day. Even Lord Ramblay had seemed
to make some offers of friendliness, and while his manner
was such that she supposed she would never feel completely
at ease in his company (for the gentleman himself never
seemed at ease), he had not been anything like the cold,
proud man she had expected. He had certainly made an
effort to be kind; if his kindness was too stiff, and marred
by a perpetual consciousness of his position to be a proper
conduit of affection, his efforts had been noticed and were
appreciated. At first she had doubted his tale, the reason he
had given for having been at Dartmoor, but she began now
to understand that such a man might sometimes stumble
blindly on, in such haste to reach his objective that he did
not notice anyone around him. Since having felt the prick
of his mother's temper, she began also to see how such a
nature might have been formed. The greater mystery by
far was how Miss Ramblay had escaped so well. Maggie
did not approve much the manner in which she had been
raised, and considered it did her little good to be so protected from the world that any contact with it was in
danger of breaking her frail spirit. The forthcoming entrance into Society would no doubt prove whether her

estimation was justified, and Maggie hoped that her own
presence might help to ease the way a little.

But the chief of Maggie's thoughts centered about Miss
Haversham and the extraordinary tale she had related. So
far was it removed from the practical world in which
Maggie herself had been raised, that for a while she had
almost been tempted to think it was made up. But there
was no doubting Blanche Haversham. Hers was a candor
seldom seen among her sex, and her courage was so great
that the tale of how it had been tested had really torn at
Maggie's heart. That so great a creature should have been
abused by a selfish, weak, and dissolute brother! That her
sacrifices for his sake had been taken without any thanks,
but only accepted as his due, while *he* did nothing but
shame her in return! She wondered if she would meet the
man, and then, remembering her friend's remark about
how her brother made use of her position to advance his
own, supposed they might meet in London. How she
would dearly love to berate him herself, for the villainous
character he had shown!

The tale of Brummel's jest amazed Maggie as much as it
shocked her. She would have been amused as well, no
doubt, had it not affected her friend's whole life. But the
tale only strengthened Maggie's mounting suspicion that
the whole existence of these people—this privileged little
group of men and women—was utterly jaded. Accustomed
to having every whim satisfied, having never to struggle
against the real perils and dangers of the world, their lives
centered inexorably about the business of entertaining
themselves. If, in order to fill up their empty days and
nights, they sometimes encroached upon the happiness of
others, they hardly noticed. It seemed they cared not what
lengths they went to for amusement. No—a sillier, vainer,
or more selfish group, nor one so given, however unwittingly, to unconscious cruelty, she had never seen. She
had once hoped to find among them attainments of intellect
and culture greater than her own, minds more discerning
and educated; now she could only wonder at her innocence. To have thought that *here* she could share her love
of books and music, could discuss at long and pleasurable
length the poems of Tennyson and Milton, could learn
simply from a proximity of subtler tastes and more educated minds!

If Maggie was as grateful to Miss Haversham for her elucidation of the lives of the nobility as for her offer of friendship, she was the more perplexed by the lady's tale. There were still a dozen points she wished clarified and, had she not felt herself selected by some random and improbable chance—an acute loneliness, perhaps, coming to the peak just at that moment—to have heard the tale told at all, she would have voiced them. But as it was, she felt she must remain silent until Miss Haversham herself chose to tell her more. What, for instance, could have been the reason for her cousin's knowing of the secret when the mystery had been kept so carefully for three years? The question aroused in Maggie a whole series of speculations about that gentleman, which had been only hinted at by Captain Morrison's tale. Remembering Miss Haversham's words that morning at breakfast—"He strikes me as a man with a great secret," her imagination began to work upon the subject. With only the slenderest evidence to go upon—the strange mix-up in Dartmoor, his awkward excuse for it, the occasional strained expression which came over him from time to time, a worried look, a furrowed brow, an air almost of private agony, carefully suppressed—her imagination did its work. The vast and echoing castle, silent now, contributed to her mental wanderings and made them the more ominous. It was not until the early hours of the morning that Maggie fell into a deep and troubled sleep.

If she had hoped to hear more of Miss Haversham's tale the next day, Maggie was destined to be frustrated. On Sunday there was no hunting, but church and preparations for chapel took up all the morning. A violent rain storm made going on foot impossible, and a quarrel immediately rose up among the ladies on the point of who should ride in which carriage. Their own traveling chaises were unfit for so short a journey, but the notion of being thrust up into a brougham in muddy weather pleased no one. At last they were arranged as much according to their tastes as possible, some having determined at the last moment to stay at home instead of risking their slippers. Maggie, who cared not where she rode, but hoped to remain as close as possible to Miss Haversham, was disappointed to learn that

the latter would not go at all, for Mr. Montcrieff would not
hear of her leaving his side.

The retiring Vicar, Mr. Congreve, delivered an excep-
tionally long and tedious sermon in token of his leaving,
which everyone ignored in favor of talking among themselves. Mr. Congreve was not much better than his replacement. If he was older and less enraptured with his own
voice than Mr. Wayland, he was very little wiser, and a
great deal more corpulent. His whole manner spoke of
that complacent belief in his own worth which is the first
hint that a person has no worth at all. He droned along
for forty minutes with about as much interest in the ideas
he espoused as Lord Ramblay's guests, who all were more
fascinated by their own remarks than his.

A luncheon was laid out when they returned, and Mr.
Montcrieff, so much improved that he had left his bed,
walked in to greet them, leaning upon Miss Haversham's
arm. His happy expression declared that his sins had been
forgiven and Miss Haversham's good favor restored. In
her eyes was a softness Maggie had never seen before. Mr.
Montcrieff would not let his beloved leave his side for a
moment, and only an occasional, apologetic glance from
her friend told Maggie that she was sorry they could not
continue their *tête-à-tête*.

Cards were the order of the afternoon. Maggie, declin-
ing to make a hand at whist, retreated to a sofa with a
novel, where she was soon discovered by Lord Ramblay,
who had likewise no taste for games that day.

"My mother tells me we are to have the advantage of
an acquaintance of yours to do our honors at church from
next Sunday," he began, drawing up a chair.

Putting down her book, Maggie inquired if he had not
met Mr. Wayland himself?

"No, and from what I have heard, it is my own loss
that I have not. I have been away much of late on business, and my mother had all the obligation upon her shoulders of engaging the new Vicar. And yet I hear he is a great
friend of yours—I believe we have been most fortunate in
finding him."

The compliment was not lost upon Maggie, and she
flushed. The blush was not all from pleasure, however;
she dearly wished to clear herself of any connection with
the Vicar in her cousin's eyes. Why the desire was so great,

she could not tell, but the thought of *his* contempt when he met the clergyman, supposing them to be great intimates, made her flesh tingle with chagrin.

"I beg you to reserve your judgment of the gentleman till you have met him yourself," she said. "He is not a great intimate of mine, although I know him well enough. Indeed, I only narrowly escaped a *most* intimate connection with him some weeks since."

Lord Ramblay's brow shot up. "Ah! I beg your pardon; I did not wish to embark upon a subject that might be painful to you."

Now Maggie was twice mortified. Clearly her cousin had mistaken her remarks, supposing that *her* affections had been rejected. With a flush she exclaimed: "Oh, no, it is nothing like that, I assure you! I meant that Mr. Wayland had done me the honor to make me an offer, which I was forced to refuse."

"It is none of my business what your reasons were, Cousin, but from what I understand, Wayland would make an admirable match. My mother seems certain he is destined some day for a bishopric, and is in other wise a personable young man."

"Even were that the case in my own view, sir," replied Maggie, "I should have done the same. I cannot love a man only because he is destined someday for a high office or some consequential position, any more than I can love him for the color of his eyes or the size of his feet. Those may, if there is already some great feeling present, increase the temptation, but where there is nothing but disdain, even contempt, they will certainly not take the place of deeper motives."

"You dislike him violently, I see," said Lord Ramblay, smiling.

"No, I do not dislike him violently; I only know him to be a vain, pedantic, and sycophantic man, more fitted for the life of a dandy than of a clergyman. Were he born to a higher level of society, no doubt he should have preferred the former life himself. As it is, his pocket can only afford a religious existence, which has, besides, the advantage of allowing him a great use of his voice, a property of which he is very fond."

Lord Ramblay looked for a moment as if he would laugh out loud, but evidently remembering his own position, thought better of it. The resulting expression was almost prim, which made Maggie, in her turn, smile.

"Forgive me if I have vilified your new curate's character, Cousin," she said hurriedly. "Indeed, I am probably tempted to exaggerate his faults because of his overcertainty of gaining my affections. There is nothing so calculated to raise a woman's ill opinion as a man's complacent assurance of inspiring a favorable one."

"That is a fact I shall bear well in mind, Miss Trevor," replied Lord Ramblay, with a little mock bow of his head. "Heaven preserve *my* inspiring anything like the opinion you have of the unfortunate Mr. Wayland."

Maggie cocked her head a little to one side and replied, archly, "Oh, there is very little danger of *that*, Cousin. My opinion is already formed of *you*—or, if not absolutely formed, at least molded enough to prevent its being changed much."

Now it was Lord Ramblay's turn to look startled.

"And what is the verdict, Cousin? I hope I am not to be called 'vain, pedantic, and sycophantic'!"

"No, you are none of those. But I shall not tell you what you *are*—for I am certain you have not sufficient self-mockery to like me afterward."

Lord Ramblay gazed at her a moment in silence. But his eyes were full of doubts, questions, and not a little mortification. This last pleased Maggie very well, for it was the first time she had beheld her cousin without that complacent self-assurance she found so irritating.

"Self-mockery?" he inquired, doubtfully. "Is that a great virtue in your eyes?"

"Oh, to be sure! I count it even higher on the scale of human virtue than a general mockery of humanity, which is certainly a necessary quality for anyone."

"And do you count it higher than *simple* virtues? Such as honesty, or courage, or duty?"

"Higher than the last, at any rate: for where there is only duty, without any feeling behind it, there is very little. It is like a cake all made of air bubbles, and will collapse as easily the moment you try to eat it."

Lord Ramblay stared at his cousin for a moment before replying. His look was full of doubts and questions at first, but soon resolved itself into the ironic expression, so difficult to see beneath, which was his usual mask.

"I see we think differently, Cousin," he said gravely, "and I am very sorry for it. In my own view, there is nothing so worth striving toward as a dutiful way of life. Without duty, and without honor, we are little better than animals, ruled always by our basest passions, and incapable of any higher kind of existence than eating and drinking and seeking warmth."

Maggie could make no reply at first, for which she was thoroughly irritated at herself. Lord Ramblay always seemed to speak so convincingly that it was difficult to argue with him. She inevitably found herself feeling like a child before a disappointed tutor, though she believed these high-sounding words in fact defended nothing more than his own reluctance to be defeated in an argument. She said at length, with a little triumphant sparkle in her eye: "I cannot argue with you, Cousin—to do so would make me seem to defend base conduct and dishonorable deeds, together with sloth, greed, and selfishness. I assure you I do not; but I still am firmly resolved in my opinion. You shall not convince me that to be civilized, one cannot also be amiable and friendly, nor that laughter in any way decreases a man's honor."

And with these words, Maggie rose up from her seat, and casting her book down, walked from the room. Lord Ramblay stared after her for some minutes with a frown upon his face. It was not so much a frown of anger, however, as one of uncertainty, which in a man so accustomed to being listened to, was a peculiar sensation indeed.

Twelve

MAGGIE HAD BEEN disappointed by her failure to speak privately with Miss Haversham all the day on Sunday, and the departure of the guests being set for early on the following day, she had not much hopes of another *tête-à-tête* before her friend left Essex. Determined to try to get her alone, however, she rose early on Monday, and by eight o'clock was dressed and going down the stairs. She saw at once that Blanche Haversham was occupied variously by her patient and the patient's sister, endeavoring to satisfy the demands of one, and fending off the ineffectual assistance of the other. But Blanche had the matter equally in her own mind, and glanced up at Maggie as she came into the breakfast room as if to say—"Only wait a little, if you will. I shall soon have done here, and then we shall be alone for a moment."

Time passed, however, without an opening, and the carriages were driven up before the door. Ladies and gentlemen, exclaiming at some forgotten item or rushing back and forth to say their farewells, were soon disposed within, and the last of the guests were filing out of the doorway when Miss Haversham at last drew Maggie aside.

"Shall you be in London soon?" she inquired softly, with a gloved hand upon the other's arm.

"Within a week, I believe—but that depends upon Lady Ramblay's mood!" responded Maggie.

"Oh, indeed—never mind about her, my dear. I think her bite is not half so painful as her bark. Only try to ignore her as much as possible, and continue to be as civil as you have been. Shall you stay in Grosvenor Square? Good—for my house is in Grove Street, just off Berkeley Square. We shall see each other often. As to that other matter——"

But Miss Haversham broke off and glanced at Lord

Ramblay, who was bidding his guests good-bye some distance from where they stood.

"Never mind, my dear friend. I shall tell you more about it when we are at leisure in Town. And, Maggie——"

"Yes?"

"Have a care of your cousin. I believe he is not as happy as he deserves to be."

And with these astonishing words, spoken in a confidential murmur, Blanche Haversham smiled and turned away, and in a moment was out the door. Maggie stood perfectly still staring after her in amazement.

The departure of the hunting party left the castle empty and echoing with the sounds of their laughter. The prospect of spending the next week alone with her cousins in that vast building did little to cheer Maggie, who wandered disconsolately from room to room in search of some occupation. No one was about, for Lady Ramblay was still in her room, her daughter upstairs with her tutors, and the Viscount, when his guests had left, retired immediately to his study saying he had work to do. He had not gone, however, before hinting that Maggie might do well to spend an hour or two practicing her music. This hint was not lost upon her, and indeed the truth of the matter was that her cousin's very perception annoyed her. There is nothing so calculated to raise our antagonism as a person who knows our faults, especially if that person be of the opposite sex and very handsome.

With a little flush of anger, therefore, she spent half an hour in pursuit of every *other* occupation she could think of. But the lower rooms of the castle, without any other occupants, proved barren of amusements, and after toying for a little with a novel, she finally threw it down and with a resigned look went into the music room. There she labored for an hour diligently, but at last she could bear it no more. Her natural energy and usual manner of living had made her require constant occupation. She was not one to sit idly by the hour gazing into space, and even the most interesting diversion wearied her after an hour or two. The day was very crisp and fine. She glanced repeatedly out of the windows, longing for a walk or some other exercise. At length, determining upon an exploration of the grounds, she ran up to her apartments to fetch a

cloak and bonnet. Very soon she was striding down a path
that led between two banks of hedge.

The brisk air, the smells of earth and grass, the brilliant
colorations of the leaves, had soon done their work upon
the young lady. Almost at once she felt refreshed, her
cheeks were lit with color, and her eyes sparkling from
exercise. Maggie had naturally a long stride and, her
attention divided equally between an admiration of the
natural beauties around her and her private thoughts, she
had soon covered half a mile. The path now was giving
way to an avenue. Leaving the garden proper behind, she
struck out along this route into a kind of wood. From the
great height of the trees, and the rougher terrain on either
side the avenue, she assumed this must have been part
of the ancient forest. The combination of serenity and
great age of the place struck her as doubly pleasing for the
careful attention it received. Here and there were gardeners
laboring near the tree trunks, weeding out any minor
growths and shrubs. The ground was perfectly covered
with pine needles, and every leaf was plucked up as it
fell from above.

Absorbing the tranquil luxury of so much beauty and
order, she was soon lost in her own thoughts and did not
notice much where she walked. Miss Haversham's words
to her that morning had continued to turn in her mind
without any comprehension. "Have a care for your cousin,"
she had said. Why a care for *him*? What could she have
meant, indeed? And what on earth could *she*, a mere
cousin, do to improve his spirits? Miss Montcrieff had
better be looked to for that! And yet what had Miss
Haversham meant by saying he was not as happy as he
deserved to be? What more did he deserve, beside the
luxury of this place, with all the devotion and respect
of his family, rank, place, and great wealth?

It was true she had seen an occasional expression come
over Lord Ramblay's face which had struck her as a great
sadness. But these moments were always instantly covered
over by his usual formality and that cold civility with
which he was used to address everyone. It struck Maggie
all at once that his sadness might be the result of penitence
over his marriage. Perhaps after all he had felt remorse
for his heartless treatment of the young lady who had been
his wife. That such might be the case, made her like him a

little better. Even had he been really cruel, even had he
felt nothing more than a pride of possession for her, if
he *now* repented of his conduct, it proved he was not
altogether without a heart.

Turning the matter over in her mind, she stepped off
the avenue and into the woods. Here the smells of leaves
and pine needles were stronger, and here the atmosphere
of great age and history lingered in the branches of the
trees as palpably as a fog. Absorbing everything, but without
any conscious knowledge of it, she began to reconstruct
what that marriage must have been like. Captain Morrison
had said the lady was exquisitely beautiful. Aside from
this, Maggie had hardly any knowledge about her. That
she had been very young, very innocent, and in awe of
Lord Ramblay, she had been told, and that she was a
stranger to England, having been brought up all her life
in the West Indian Islands. Such a kind of creature might
well have been the foil for an arrogant man's pride. How
could she defend herself against his superior mind, greater
experience, and worldly view of life? No, no—surely she
would have stood too much in awe of him to ever question
his interminable orders, his strict code of conduct, his un-
equal idea of how they should live. Yes, it was all clear
now—she would have gone willingly wherever he required
her, and kept silent even as he dashed about on a ceaseless
round of pleasure with his friends. Confined to the country, to loneliness and heartache, she would have awaited
his infrequent returns eagerly, hoping for a little of that
tenderness and love which he had never shown her.

The picture was forming itself very clearly in Maggie's
mind as she looked up and, glancing through the trees,
noticed the outline of a small building. It seemed to be a
sort of gazebo or summer house, constructed in the midst
of the forest. Still lost in her reverie, she wandered toward
the shape, and at last came into a little clearing of trees.
There she stood for a moment, entranced by the charming
picture before her. The gazebo—for it was one of those
constructions that had been in vogue some few years before, with a Chinese roof and supporting columns, but
without any walls—stood up upon a platform, several
feet above the ground. A flight of steps led up to it on
three sides, and the light and shade falling upon it lent it
an almost fairy-like appearance. In the middle of the little

house was a crumbling stone statue of the goddess Diana, lifting her bow as if to shoot an arrow into the overhanging bows of trees. On four sides were small stone benches. The appearance of the place was very delightful, and yet Maggie was struck by some oddity about it. It had the air of a place no longer in use, though it was obviously of recent construction. The paint on the slender columns was peeling off, the steps were crumbling a little, and the roof appeared to have sagged under the weight of rain. Yet here she was standing in a really ancient wood, so well tended that it was immaculate. Why should not the little pavilion have the benefit of an equal degree of care?

Pondering this, Maggie walked closer and ascended the steps. She stood for a while wondering why it was not in use any longer, until a thought struck her, and she sat down upon one of the benches. To be sure! It was here that her cousin would come with his lady, on his infrequent visits to the castle. Here they would walk, conversing about the time they had been parted, and here the innocent Lady Ramblay would hope every moment for a tender embrace. Suddenly something caught Maggie's eye: a shining object under the bench across from which she now sat. Leaning down to pick it up, she saw at once what it was. She held in her hand a tiny pair of scissors, of the kind kept by ladies in their reticules for needlework. It was all made of silver, with inlay of gold and mother of pearl, a most enchanting little instrument. Turning it over, she descried upon the side the tiny initials, ALR. Indeed, it must have belonged to Lady Ramblay!

Maggie remembered all at once the tapestries hanging all over the lower part of the castle. What better occupation could there be for a wife confined to the solitude of the country, without the benefit of her husband's company, than such labor? The picture was now fleshing itself out, and all at once Maggie had a vision of a scene, enacted in this very place, some years before.

Lord Ramblay would have returned from one of his long visits to town. Lady Ramblay, having patiently waited for him, would joyfully greet him. He would be cold, indifferent, to all her longing looks and silent pleas. Together they would walk through the park to the summer house, where Lord Ramblay would make some cold inquiries of how she had passed the time since last he saw her.

The stoical replies (for in Maggie's mind Lady Ramblay was as steadfast of heart as she was fragile of appearance) would bring forth a nod or two. Lady Ramblay would then make some eager inquiries of her husband. How were their friends, what had he done, had he been amused? It would be more and more apparent that they had nothing to say to each other, until finally Lady Ramblay—who had been working silently upon her tapestry—could bear it no longer. She would throw down her scissors, in a rare outburst of emotion, and begin to weep. Whereupon, the hard-hearted Lord Ramblay would—why, what would he do? Certainly he would lecture her, perhaps even strike her! The thought brought an angry flush to Maggie's cheek. She would like to have struck him back, to defend his defenseless lady. She was just considering what *she* would have done in such a case, when the sound of step nearby made her jump.

Whirling around, she was just in time to see a man's figure advancing through the trees. With the sudden realization that she still held the scissors in her hand, she just had time to drop them in the pocket of her cloak when Lord Ramblay spoke.

It must be said in Maggie's defense that she felt exceeding foolish upon staring down into that face. So eminently sensible, so exceeding amiable an expression did Lord Ramblay wear that she instantly regretted the vividness of her imagination. And when he expressed his astonishment at finding her there, without any trace of the guilt appropriate in a man whose great secret has just been found out, she was doubly ashamed of herself.

"Why, Cousin!" exclaimed he, "you have found out my favorite hiding place! It is admirably suited to quiet contemplation, is it not?"

Maggie blushed and agreed that it was.

"But, Lord Ramblay, I hope I have not intruded upon it."

"Quite the contrary. I only come here now and again to be alone and think."

"Then I am afraid I have prevented your doing so today."

Lord Ramblay smiled as he ascended the stairs.

"Think nothing of it, Miss Trevor. I am not so much

in need of solitude as of escape from my work. Today I have been laboring at the accounts with my steward, who is a most demanding fellow and impatient with mistakes. I had infinitely rather sit here with you for a while than anything."

"But I am sure you only say so to be civil," said Maggie, beginning to stand up. "I will just continue my walk and leave you alone in your sanctuary."

Now Lord Ramblay reached out a hand to prevent her going and declared that no sanctuary was so perfect that it could not be improved upon by the company of an intelligent woman. Maggie was well pleased with this compliment, and took her seat again.

"It is a delightful little building," said she, glancing around her. "What a pity it is not better cared for! It could not be very old——"

"No, it is not. It was built only six years ago, for my wife. I was married at one time, you know."

Lord Ramblay had turned away a little, and his expression was unreadable.

"Yes, I have heard," murmured Maggie. "I am very sorry for you; for I know your wife died very young."

"Oh! Do not be sorry for me, Cousin! Heaven, everyone is sorry for me!"

Had it been Maggie's imagination, or had he spoken angrily? In an effort to ease the situation, she replied, "I am sorry, then, if I have made you think of it again."

Lord Ramblay had stood up, and walking toward a railing, stared out into the trees for a moment. But suddenly his expression changed, as if he had determined to forget the subject, and with a determined cheerfulness, he said, "Pity is not of much use to anyone, Cousin. And in any case, there is nothing to be sorry for. I was married barely three years, and my wife, who was ever of a fragile constitution, was carried away by a lung fever. Such is life. But tell me, how is your father?"

Lord Ramblay inquired civilly into the Admiral's health and happiness, and seemed to hear Maggie's replies with very real interest.

"I am glad to hear that your father is so well," said he, after a little, "for I have found it is often the case with very active men, who have been used to taking a great part in life, to be discontented with retirement. They grow irritable and depressed, dwelling in the past and bitterly resenting their diminishing strength."

"Well, then you need have no fear," laughed Maggie, "for such is not the case with Papa, I can assure you! Irritable he sometimes may be, but only because he detests country amusements. But save for his writing, no man could dwell less in the past. As to bitterness and resentment, he bitterly opposes every sort of foolishness, and resents those who would make him join in theirs!"

"I am glad to hear you say so," smiled Lord Ramblay. "And yet I believe there is *one* part of his past he cannot forget so easily as you claim."

Maggie understood where her cousin was leading, and said quickly, "I think you are wrong, sir! My father is certainly stubborn in some things, but he is very quick to forgive and forget, once he has set his mind to it."

"Ah—once he has set his mind to it," murmured Lord Ramblay, thinking of the letter he had written four years before which had never been answered. "And perhaps that requires a great while."

"No longer than it requires some others!" responded Maggie archly.

Her cousin gave her a puzzled glance, and would have protested had not Maggie, who had suddenly remembered her first reason for disliking the Viscount, already risen from her bench and proposed returning to the castle.

Neither spoke during their return. Maggie had been brought up against her initial prejudice, and angered by the Viscount's insinuation that it had been her own father who had put off the reparation of their quarrel, she was determined to say nothing more. The thought of her father's face when he had told her of the invitation from the Ramblays, of his great earnestness in wishing her to accept, and of his own letter, made her turn her head away from Lord Ramblay in dislike as they walked.

As to the gentleman, he was too much confused by this young lady to know what he *could* say. His solicitude for the Admiral had been genuine and, had not he been reproved by Miss Trevor, he would shortly have made some allusion to his first letter. He had long been troubled by her father's silence, and wished to know what had inspired it. The letter had been, in his own estimation, everything it should have been. It had striven to bridge the gap imposed

by a family feud, and yet had not unjustly blamed his own
father. It had regretted certain qualities of stubbornness
and intractability in the older man's judgment without deni-
grating his real family loyalty. Yet he had received no reply
for four years, until that peculiar missive from the Admiral
had arrived. This last had been such a reversal of mood
that it instantly raised his suspicions. Had Lord Ramblay
been less eager to end the quarrel, he might have ignored
it, upon seeing that its purpose was nothing more than to
advance the daughter's situation. Indeed, had not his
mother urged him to ignore it, just as Admiral Trevor had
ignored *his* letter? The letter had made Lady Ramblay
sneer and exclaim at its vulgarity. It had made her swear
she would never like Miss Trevor, and had convinced her
that both the Admiral and his daughter were nothing but
social-climbing hypocrites. Lord Ramblay himself had felt
some hesitancy, but at last he had replied, offering the invitation to go to Town with them. If he had wondered what
sort of young woman would appear and had at first determined to be no more than civil in his treatment of her, he
had been amazed by his first glimpse of Maggie Trevor.
Her very brusqueness pleased him, so far was it removed
from the insipidity of the ladies he had known. Her arch,
pert manner, while annoying sometimes, often delighted
him, and the candor of her eyes, which never stooped to
the kind of maidenly flutterings and other tricks so often
resorted to by tonnish women, never ceased to cause a
flutter in his heart. Here indeed was a woman worthy of
the name, here indeed was a woman to be reckoned with.
He could not help believing that her excessive bluntness
and all-knowing air might be cured by the right masculine
teacher, and when they were a little curbed, she would be
the most delightful creature in the world. She had courage
and resolution—that he had seen when she had been helping the surgeon to tend young Montcrieff. Her mind was
quick and agile and, if she was not an absolute beauty, her
handsomeness was of a kind almost more pleasing than
perfection. She was tall and walked well, and her features
were enhanced by such radiant health and good humor that
it was impossible to see her without smiling.

Lord Ramblay could not guess what had angered Maggie, but he had patience enough even for *her* moods. Determining to outlast her vexation, he walked silently beside

her. A glance at that pert face, now lifted in disdain, made him smile. Her anger had made her flush, and lifted her chin in so delightful a fashion that he would not have disturbed the mood for all the world.

As they came within view of the castle, Maggie stopped and gazed ahead of her.

"I hope you approve the architect's work?" inquired Lord Ramblay after a moment.

Feeling herself teased, Maggie did not reply. Nodding her head, she remarked, "I have not seen it from this view before. I see now where my own bedchamber is—" pointing to the northern wing—"but what is in the other wing? I do not believe I have been there."

"It is all closed up," replied Lord Ramblay, beginning to walk on. "We have not used it since my wife died. There are some memories better left untapped."

Maggie glanced at her companion. His face was set, and the pleasant smile had given way to a frigid look. It passed over her mind, just as they reached the steps, that perhaps she had not exaggerated her idea of what had passed between the Viscount and his wife.

Thirteen

MR. WAYLAND ARRIVED at the vicarage and in due course made his visit to Ramblay Castle. In actual fact, he had not been in the little house above an hour, had barely glanced at his chapel and tried out his new pulpit before sending for a clean cravat and striking out across the park. Had he a wife and family he should have waited to be called upon by the lady of the castle and her son, but as it was, there was no custom to stand upon. Glancing into the mirror to assure himself his pate was shining and several strands of hair well plastered over the balding place, he took up his hat and stick and set forth.

Maggie was summoned from her apartment shortly after her return to receive the curate with the Viscountess. She found them already established in the morning room, and from the posture of one and the gratified expression of the other, guessed Mr. Wayland's work was already well begun. She was not far off the mark, for upon walking toward them she heard the curate remark—

"I am exactly of your persuasion, ma'am. There is little opportunity in such a place for a clergyman to exercise his best powers. Where there are no people of discrimination, the greatest orator upon earth shall not move them."

"Quite," agreed Lady Ramblay, plucking at the fur of a Pekingese beside her, "but are there not one or two families you could address yourself to? Admiral Trevor——"

"Ah, yes, my good friend Trevor," the curate cut her off, waving a thin hand in a gesture of dismissal, "*he* is not so bad as the rest. Still, he is a Navy man; I could not hope for such delicacy from *him* as from a great lady like yourself."

Lady Ramblay accepted this tribute with a stately wag of her head, and Wayland leered back at her happily.

It was just at this moment that the Viscountess looked up, and seeing Maggie, beckoned her toward them. The young lady was in such a tumult of suppressed laughter, delight at the sight of these two salving each other's vanity, and a hope of drawing forth more along the same lines, that she nearly threw her arms about the clergyman.

Mr. Wayland must have felt some awkwardness at seeing her, even though he had already heard of her presence at the castle from his patroness; and yet so enthralled was he by his own wooing of the great lady that he looked really happy to see her as he stood up, and bending his oily head, attempted to bestow a kiss upon her hand.

"Here is your good friend's daughter now," pronounced Lady Ramblay, smiling with great condescension at her relative. "Mr. Wayland has just been telling me about his old parish."

"Indeed? I hope you have not painted it too drearily, Mr. Wayland. A small country village will never bear comparison to such a vicarage as this, amid the noblest houses in the nation."

Mr. Wayland now had the grace to flush and lower his eyes a little.

"I hope I have never been ungrateful, Miss Trevor," said he. "A man of the cloth can never be too humble, nor thankful for whatever little blessings the Lord chooses to bestow upon his servant. And yet, it is at just such times as these that I am reminded of those memorable lines— 'Blessed are the meek, for they shall inherit the Earth.' Surely *I* have been rewarded for my long years of service— my meekness, if you like—in the personage of this great lady."

Mr. Wayland had contrived to speak so as to ingratiate himself with the Viscountess while simultaneously making amends to Maggie for whatever she might have heard him say before he was aware of her presence. This he managed by many little twistings of his torso back and forth, leering alternately at one and then the other. Maggie was too overcome to say anything. She was forced to turn away with the pretense of finding a seat in order to hide her smiles.

A little silence ensued, while Maggie and the Vicar sat down and Lady Ramblay stroked her pet.

"Since you are such old friends," she said at last, "I

suppose you have a great deal to talk about. You may do so at another time. I am sure," she added, in what she must have considered the very height of gracious condescension, "my niece will be glad of a companion while she is here, Mr. Wayland. I am afraid she has not had much to occupy her since she came, though she has made herself very useful with poultices and the like."

"Poultices!" exclaimed Mr. Wayland in amazement, and Maggie should have cried out likewise had she dared, for she could not remember having been so *much* occupied in all her life.

"I believe her ladyship refers to a most insignificant event, when I was able to assist the surgeon to bind up a gentleman's wound after a hunting accident," explained Maggie.

"Oh, to be sure, my dear—you ought really to be a surgeon yourself! It is a pity such kind of occupations are not open to ladies of a certain type. A great pity, I have always thought, that they should be limited to governess-ships."

Wayland stared back and forth between the ladies, blinking. He was unsure if he had heard aright, and a sudden fear of antagonizing one by ingratiating the other loomed up in his bosom. After a quite speedy calculation, however, he determined that it could do no harm to oil both seas. If, as it appeared, there was a quarrel between them, it would be safer than to unload all his guns on one target. He had oft, in any case, observed to anyone who would listen that the aristocracy behaved very differently from ordinary mortals. The usual laws of decorum did not hold to them, but were enlivened the more for the rest of humanity, by their more interesting ways. After a moment, he observed:

"I am sure I should be honored, Miss Trevor, if you would accompany me on a tour of the park sometime. I have been admiring it all the morning—it must be among the most glorious of its type in England."

It was clear from Lady Ramblay's expression that he had struck the right note this time, and unwilling to give it up, he pursued it to its very limits. There followed a stream of superlatives, of "magnificent beauties," "heights of elegance," "perfection of form and flowers," which might have awed another audience. As it was, however, Maggie was too much accustomed to the clergyman's manner to be astonished, and Lady Ramblay too content with this volley of admiration to wish to see beyond the exterior of the idolator. Her several chins beat a happy little jig in time to the nodding of her head, and when she was most pleased, she absently plucked away at the fur of her pet until Maggie thought the creature should have none left upon its head.

Having disposed of the subject of parks—parks in general, their limitations and recommendations, other parks glimpsed by the Vicar, or read about, and, in particular, of course, Ramblay Park—Mr. Wayland moved on to the subject of domestic residences. There was first the vicarage to be praised, and held up favorably against the one he had had at Sussex (though this, in truth, was a hypocrisy, for Wayland, while he had not had time to observe much about his new home, had yet noted the absence of a maid's pantry and the paucity of bedchambers) and then the castle itself was held up for his eager admiration. He had not seen much of it to be sure—only the southern vista on his way across the park and that part of the castle he had glimpsed as he was shown into the morning room—and yet he had such a multitude of compliments for it that a stranger might have supposed he was speaking of Windsor. Lady Ramblay attended to all this with a look of increasing approbation upon her face, and when at last she was allowed a moment to speak, exclaimed—

"Why, I did not anticipate such a connoisseur of furnishings and architecture as you have proved yourself to be, Mr. Wayland! It has always been my experience that clergymen are generally ignorant of such things. Pray tell me, are you as ardent an admirer of *all* of Halsey's buildings?"

In point of fact, Mr. Wayland had never heard of Robert Halsey, the architect who had been commissioned to expand the original castle fifty years before. It had been on the tip of his tongue to suppose the place was built by one of the Adamses (for in truth it held a great resemblance in simplicity and harmonious balance to those famed brothers), but now he blinked once or twice and nodded his head emphatically.

"Why, yes!" cried he, hoping to make up for his lack of honesty with the enthusiasm of the lie. "I have ever held him to be among the greatest artists we have had!" Whereupon Lady Ramblay commenced to interrogate him upon the finer points of several other of his castles, parks, and abbeys, and Wayland was thrown upon the mercy of his wits to respond.

As luck would have it, just at this point, while the Vicar was showing himself as ignorant of the general principles of architecture as he was uninterested in them, the Viscount returned from his walk and, hearing voices from the hall, came in. He stood for a moment silently in the doorway before letting his presence be known, regarding the little party assembled within. He had not meant to keep his presence hidden—the expression on his face attested to the fact that he had need of that moment to collect his wits, which a recent discovery had momentarily disarmed—but the moment afforded him a chance to see very nearly what Maggie had seen a little while before. Like her, he was struck instantly with the obsequious posture and expressions of the clergyman, and, like her, was torn between revulsion and amusement by them. But the sight of the Vicar endeavoring to salvage himself from the turn the conversation had taken could not hold his attention long. The Viscount's eyes wandered to the place where his cousin sat, her eyes cast down into her lap and a smile struggling to subdue itself about the corners of her mouth. The sight rendered him incapable of further irritation (for it must be hinted that Lord Ramblay had only recently been given cause for grave irritation, almost anger) and made him smile. Just at this moment Maggie looked up. She saw her cousin's bemused look and started. But in the instant before her eyes darted back to her hands, with a flush creeping up her cheeks, a glance had been exchanged between them so full of meaning, of mutual understanding —in short, the interplay of quick minds on common ground, amused and amazed by the same idea—that she was incapable of looking up again for a full minute. This was ample time for Lord Ramblay to recover himself, to cough, and to walk into the room.

Mr. Wayland jumped up at once, smiling all over his face. But there was no sign in Lord Ramblay's expression, as the clergyman was presented to him and made a series of bows and expostulations of joy, that he had seen anything to make him disapprove the fellow.

In the time Lord Ramblay had stood at the door, he had heard Mr. Wayland show himself to be a fool—not only innocent of any knowledge of architects and their trade, but so eager to please the Viscountess that he cared not whether he spoke the truth or a lie, if only it would please her. Now, with the gravest expression of interest upon his face, Lord Ramblay expressed his desire to continue the conversation he had interrupted and, taking a seat, took up his mother's interrogation. Lady Ramblay knew precious little more than the Vicar, though her knowledge of names and places was a little more extensive. But her son had interested himself from an early age in the art of buildings, and his questions were more difficult to answer. Mr. Wayland, had he a grain of sense, should now have thrown up his hands and admitted his own ignorance honestly. But his vanity was such that he would not give an inch, and in attempting to salvage himself from his present miserable position, he walked further and further into the trap.

Mr. Wayland, however, did not know there was a trap. Indeed, he never suspected that Lord Ramblay was listening to his replies with anything but the gravest approval, and this gave the Vicar so much courage that he at last ventured into a long eulogistic speech upon the merits of a certain castle in Dorset which Lord Ramblay had mentioned as among Halsey's finest buildings. The castle did not exist—had never been built or dreamed of—but of this fact Mr. Wayland remained in happy ignorance as he poured forth praise upon the interesting entrance, the curious circular wings, the noble and lofty central construction. Lord Ramblay led him further and further along, as a cat might lead a mouse before it at last determines to pounce. Maggie watched the game with mounting amusement, but soon a fear that Lord Ramblay's inevitable pounce might really kill the poor wretched Vicar made her fearful. She saw in the game a cruelty reminiscent almost of the scene she had so foolishly envisioned that very morning, sitting in the gazebo. But Lord Ramblay, evidently concluding that the game was itself sufficient amusement, did not take advantage of his victim. He stood up, instead, after a quarter of an hour, and with a little sideways smile at Maggie, said,

"I have been most happy to make your acquaintance, Mr. Wayland. My mother warned me we were to have a most *unusual* replacement for old Mr. Congreve. I see now what she meant."

Mr. Wayland bowed almost to the ground and said, with a smirk, "I suppose you are not used to thinking of the clergy as well versed in matters of culture and art, your lordship. It will be my very great privilege and honor to prove to you that such is not the case. It is possible, you see, to attend to heavenly matters without forsaking the most lofty mortal concerns."

Smiling very broadly, Lord Ramblay expressed his eagerness to probe the Vicar's mind upon other matters, and to discover what his knowledge of Heaven must be like, if it was greater than his expertise in other fields. He retired quickly, saying he had work to do, and in that moment, Maggie liked him better than she had ever done since seeing his face for the first time at Dartmoor.

There are two sides, at least, to every question, and Maggie's mind just now was divided almost equally between a desire to dislike her cousin and to think well of him. His manner toward herself had been consistently generous since she had come to Ramblay Castle and, if he still retained a trace of that frigidity in his mien and voice which reminded her of Captain Morrison's description, she was disinclined to believe he was capable of outright cruelty. She could not be unconscious, either, of his admiration for herself, and as her vanity was no less than that of any other young woman, it inclined her to think the more of him. She had caught his eyes wandering toward her often in the last few days, and the curious smile in them when he caught her own glance was impossible to misinterpret. Yet there were too many difficulties with him to be sure of his thoughts. Where another man's admiration might be bold and clear as an open stretch of sea, Lord Ramblay's admiration was mixed—first, with censure, and second, with doubt. His eyes were too often brooding and dark for her to be certain of his thoughts and feelings. There wandered into his expression, just at those moments when she was most at ease with him, a look which made her almost shudder. It was not anger, and neither was it misery, and yet it had elements of both, combined with a fierceness Maggie had never witnessed even in her own father's look before. Whatever occupied his thoughts at those moments carried him away from the present into some dark, brooding world of his own. It was a mystery Maggie would have given much to clarify, but which became the more perplexing as time went on.

Mr. Wayland stayed another quarter of an hour, until Lady Ramblay, growing restless, began to tap her hand upon the satin pillow and glance toward the door. Wayland had not much subtlety in his own nature, and a smaller hint would certainly not have sufficed him, but when he saw his patroness begin to cough and look annoyed, he rose to his feet and made his excuses. Before he left he secured Maggie's promise of accompanying him on an exploration of the park and the castle on the following day. It was proposed the Vicar should collect Miss Trevor beforehand for their walk. If anyone had suggested to Maggie a month before that she might one day eagerly anticipate an hour of Mr. Wayland's company, she should have put back her head and laughed. But by the following day she had reason to be eager, not simply for the company of an old acquaintance. . . .

Fourteen

THAT AFTERNOON WAS passed very unremarkably by the
young lady. Left once again to her own devices—for Lady
Ramblay retired at once to her apartments, pausing only to
commend her young relative on her choice of intimates—
she attempted to fasten her attention on Mrs. Radcliffe's
latest work. But the novel was too full of unlikely charac-
ters, and the plot hinged upon an idea which, though unnatural in the extreme, was yet too closely linked to some
thoughts Maggie had entertained herself of late to offer
leisurely amusement. Throwing down the volume at last,
she wandered about the lower rooms of the castle in the
hope of glimpsing a portrait of the late Lady Ramblay.
But no portrait was to be found that could conceivably be
a likeness of the deceased Viscountess. One or two pictures
hanging in the gallery did represent females, but they were
clad in garments that had gone out of fashion fifty years
before, and bore more resemblance in face and form to
the present dowager than to a young and lovely tragic
heroine. It struck her now as doubly curious that there
should be no sign of her cousin's late wife, for, not only
was there no likeness of her anywhere, but, save for the
one instance that morning in the gazebo, no mention had
been made of her—or even of the fact that Lord Ramblay
had ever had a wife. In the evening she determined to
draw out Fanny Ramblay upon the subject and, succeeding in getting her attention shortly after dinner, drew her
a little away from the others with the pretense of asking
her the history of a tapestry. Miss Ramblay at first was all
happy conciliation at being selected above the others for
such a duty, and willingly followed her cousin into the
gallery where the tapestry hung. A history was promptly
rendered up—with many little apologies for the informant's
ignorance—and did not differ much from the one Lord

Ramblay had given her of the hunting scene on her first evening in the castle. It was an ancient artifact, worked in Flanders two centuries before, and represented a scene at court. Maggie next moved to a much smaller tapestry, hanging beside it, which had aroused her curiosity that afternoon.

"I am in the greatest awe of such kind of skill," she said, conscious that she was leading her cousin on, and feeling a trifle guilty for the fact. "Imagine! To have spent most of one's life upon such a work! I have no patience of the kind—and yet it would be vastly pleasing to know that after I had died, some testimony should still remain of my life."

Fanny murmured her agreement with great earnestness, and would have walked on had not Maggie stopped her.

"Now this—I can perhaps imagine finishing one of this size, had I the skill. Yet even this must have taken ten years to make."

"Oh! Nothing of the kind!" exclaimed Fanny ingenuously. But then an expression of horror came over her face, and she stopped.

"Why! Did not it take so long? Five years, perhaps?"

"I believe," said Fanny, with a restrained look, "it took the lady only a year or two to work."

Maggie gave the young girl a sharp look.

"Oh! That is extraordinary. Then you must have known her."

Clearly Miss Ramblay was in an agony of indecision. If there was one lady to whom she would readily have imparted a secret, it was her cousin Maggie. In only four days she had made of the young woman a kind of heroine and, besides everything else, really trusted her implicitly. But here was a secret which it was not her privilege to share with any living soul. Indeed, the secret had been kept from *her* for so long—and should have continued thus, had not she stumbled upon the evidence—that it was not her own. That fact had been well rubbed into her little head, with many assurances that to whisper a word of it would be to defame her family forever. Miserably she stared at Maggie Trevor, who seemed to be holding her eyes incapable of looking away, and whose own candid, intelligent look made her wonder how it could harm anyone to confide in her cousin. In actual fact, she was unsure of the parameters

of the word "family"—was not Miss Trevor of their own
blood? Would not she understand what discretion was
needed? And yet something made her hold back—a memory of her brother's eyes as he had explained it to her, with
oh! so many painful silences and unhappy looks.

"Well, I can see you will not answer me," said Maggie
at length, beginning to turn away.

At this, Fanny's hand shot out and caught the other's
sleeve. "Oh, it is not that I *shall* not, Cousin! Only—
only——"

Maggie watched the young girl, with a dreadful feeling
of shame at having made the young girl suffer so. "Never
mind. I shall not ask you any more."

And now Miss Ramblay burst out: "Then I *shall* tell you
—it was worked by my brother's wife, by Anna. I should
have told you at once, for I loved her dearly, but we are
not meant to speak of her."

Now Maggie was really ashamed of having made the
younger girl speak out against her wishes, but her guilt was
not so strong as the sensation of triumph which now rose
up in her bosom. Here, if she had needed any proof of foul
play, was evidence indeed that things had not been as they
should between Lord Ramblay and his lady. She longed
to draw her cousin out further upon the subject, but Fanny
Ramblay had turned away with burning cheeks and a
pleading look, which spoke more clearly than any words
could have, her urgent desire to be allowed to remain
silent. As if to apologize for it, she stole a little hand into
the crook of her cousin's arm, and as they walked back
into the drawing room where the others were sitting, leaned
against her more closely than ever. Moved by this little
display, Maggie put her arm around the girl's slender
shoulders and hugged her.

"Never mind, my dear cousin. I see I have made you
speak of what you had rather not. I shall not inquire further, if it will make you any easier." Fanny's grateful look
was reply enough.

Maggie was half tempted, when they came back into the
drawing room, to go up to Lord Ramblay, who sat in a
corner with a book, and make some mention of the scissors
she had found. She was certain now that the news would
disturb him, and if it did, then she would have a stronger
foundation for her suspicions than ever. Only one aston-

ished or uneasy look would have convinced her that he harbored some guilty feeling about his marriage. That, in truth, was all she wanted.

If the reader is a little amazed that a young lady with so much sense and such a strong feeling of right as Maggie Trevor should be determined to cause her own cousin unease, even distress—a man who had, in truth, done nothing to harm herself—it may be explained by the fact that, for two or three days, she had been incapable of looking at him with equanimity. That she mistook a quickening of her pulse and a giddy sensation of not knowing quite where to look when he spoke to her for acute dislike, was not altogether incredible. Maggie had never in her life felt the need to look away from a gentleman's eyes. She was by nature spirited, practical, and self-assured. It had never occurred to her that such kinds of trepidations as she felt in her cousin's presence might be a sign of something besides doubting *his* worth. And the more uneasy she felt on seeing him gaze at her as if he could read the very essence of her spirit, the more determined she was to find some crookedness in his own.

Maggie was prevented from speaking to Lord Ramblay by the entrance of a footman, who, approaching his master, leaned down and spoke into his ear. Lord Ramblay flushed and looked angry, making some inquiry of the servant. The reply made him jump up and, flinging down his book, stride out of the room. Maggie watched him go in some amazement. When she glanced at Miss Ramblay, she saw she was pretending not to have seen anything wrong.

Lady Ramblay had put down her needlework, and called out to the servant. There followed a quiet exchange between them, with the Viscountess's expression growing rapidly more angry. Now she, too, stood up and sailed from the room like a man-of-war going into battle. She paused in her progress to order her daughter to bed, and would no doubt have ordered Maggie there as well had not a glance at the young lady's set countenance made her think again.

Maggie was left alone now to wonder what had occurred to upset the family so. Her first thought was that some mishap had occurred in the kitchen—a forgetful kitchen maid had let the fire spread out of the grate—but upon inquiring of a servant going past if there was anything amiss

belowstairs, she heard that nothing untoward was afoot.
For an hour she contrived to entertain herself, expecting
any minute the return of either Lord Ramblay or his
mother. But neither came, and the silence of the house
belied there was anything amiss. At last she heard a foot-
step in the hallway and jumping up, went to see who it
was. The comfortable figure of Mrs. Black, the housekeeper, was the last she had expected to see.

"Ah, miss!" exclaimed that woman, coming into the
room. "I feared you had stayed here waiting for his lordship. But you had better go to bed, for indeed, he shan't
be calm any more tonight."

"Why, what is the matter?" cried Maggie. "I hope there
is nothing wrong!"

"Oh, indeed, indeed," clucked the good woman, "it is
only the poor child again. His surgeon has given him a tonic
which won't stay down, and the poor creature is half dead
with retching."

Maggie demanded in some amazement whom the housekeeper referred to, at which Mrs. Black looked surprised.

"Why, it is the little master, of course, Master James—
oh! I had forgot. His lordship did not wish to trouble any of
the guests about it, and so I suppose nothing was said to
you. Poor child, he has been that miserable for a fortnight.
No one can do anything for him, and naturally he cannot
tell us what is the matter. Poor child!" And the woman
shook her head in dismay.

"Why, do you mean to say," exclaimed Maggie, walking
nearer to the housekeeper, "that my cousin has a child?"

"What! You did not know it?"

"I was ignorant of the fact that he had even been married
until several days ago, Mrs. Black."

Now the woman seemed to recollect something, and
nodded.

"There, I had quite forgot! Your mama was cast right
out of the family, was she not? Well, my dear, it is a subject no doubt best left unspoken of. Such things seldom
do anyone any good to remember. It was an ill-fated match
from the start—I always thought so, anyways—what with
her ladyship being from another kind of life altogether.
Such kinds of marriages do no one any good, and the proof
is in the pudding, as they say. Look at poor Master James,
who cannot speak a word. A terrible tragedy, I always say,

when a poor innocent child must pay for the sins of its parents. And now his lordship, bless him, must live out the tragedy every day of his life, though *I* contend 'twas no fault of his!"

Maggie stared at the woman for a full minute. She could hardly bring herself to believe her ears, for the idea of Lord Ramblay's possessing a child was too much of a shock for her to digest in a moment.

"Do you mean to say, Mrs. Black, that the child is ill?"

The housekeeper nodded her head gravely.

"Ill either in body or in soul, miss. The child has not uttered a word since his mother's death."

"What! And is there no treatment for him? Surely, if he *has* a tongue, there must be a way to coax him into using it!"

"Tut, miss—with all due respect—it is my opinion that mortals have no business mixing their hands in such matters. If it is God's will, the child will speak. I have said as much often and often to his lordship. But *he*, poor man, cannot accept it. Not a week goes by but he has got some new surgeon or other down from London. This one, now—the one who has just disgraced himself—was said to be the greatest wizard in England. Our own Regent swears by him, and nothing would do for his lordship but he must have him here to attend Master James. But I fear it is all in vain, and always shall be. 'Pon my word, the Lord does sometimes give us rough roads to travel. It is all I can do to hold my tongue when I think of that poor innocent baby paying for his own mother's sins."

Maggie glanced sharply at her companion. "His *mother's* sins!"

But if Mrs. Black was sometimes given to gossiping, she knew also how to hold her tongue. With the sudden consciousness of having poured forth more than she ought, she now pressed her lips together sternly.

"Tut! You ought not to make me talk so, miss. I always hold no good has ever come of gossiping. Besides, it is not *my* business, I am sure, and never was. I should not have said so much indeed, were it not that the sight of that dear man being made more miserable every day makes my blood fair boil. *I* cannot speak out, miss—I am naught but a servant, though Ramblay Castle has been my home these thirty years—but *you* perhaps could!"

"What!" cried Maggie in surprise. But the thought made her smile to herself, and she explained, "I am afraid, Mrs. Black, that you overestimate my powers over my cousin. Though we *are* cousins, I am nothing but a stranger to him—and I fear that if I made any mention of this subject, he should lose what little esteem he may now have of me." But a sudden idea made her add, "Besides, if I *were* to speak to him, what could I say?"

Mrs. Black stared back at the young lady in perplexity, shaking her head a little. "Ah, well, I suppose you are right." The woman said nothing for a moment, and then, as if on a sudden impulse, burst out with surprising passion, "What the little fellow needs, miss, is a mother! Not a vain piece of muslin like that Miss Montcrieff, the Viscountess is always urging the master to marry, but a *real* woman— like yourself, miss. I fancy you could do both of them more good than all the surgeons in Christendom. A little of your laughter would cheer up this great empty place a deal, too. Lud, it has been five years at least since I have seen his lordship smile so happily as he has done in these past days!"

Mrs. Black recovered her composure almost instantly after this astonishing outburst had escaped her lips, and with a sheepish look, implored the young lady to retire for the night before she could be allowed to listen to any more nonsense. Maggie would dearly have loved to continue the conversation, but she did as she was bid. It was not until the early hours of the morning, however, when the sky had lightened to a pewter color and the rays of a full moon lay across her coverlet, that she could still her racing thoughts sufficiently to drift into an uneasy slumber. The morning was well advanced when she awoke, her head still full of strange, disturbing dreams—a young woman laboring at a tapestry which never was completed, the miserable sobbing of a child, and over all, the unreadable eyes of Lord Ramblay staring back at her.

She gave herself a brisk shake, lecturing herself as she dressed and the maid arranged her hair. But she had half formed the intention of confronting her cousin as soon as she could by the time she had reached the breakfast room. Just what she would say, or how she could broach the subject, was not absolutely clear to her, but one thing was certain: She could no longer remain in the dark on so many points. If she was a cousin, and was to be treated as such, then she deserved to be undeceived. She felt increasingly resentful of the mysteries all around her, and of the absurd attempts being made to keep her in ignorance of them—for she felt, in the heat of the moment, that it was a kind of plot formed by all the Ramblays precisely to baffle her. Try as she might to persuade herself otherwise, the same feeling of ill-usage crept up in her bosom. The news, received almost the instant she sat down to breakfast, that her cousin was called away on urgent business to London, only served to aggravate her further. That there should continue to be such secrecy about the real motives for Lord Ramblay's journey angered her more than she could bear. Well did she know what had caused the Viscount's sudden departure—no doubt he had driven the offending surgeon back to London himself, under the guise of having business to conduct. Suddenly she remembered the strange little man in black who had been with Lord Ramblay that day in Dartmoor, and the realization that this must have been the famous surgeon on his way to the castle brought her up.

After breakfast she went in search of Mrs. Black, in the hope of finding out more about the little boy. The woman, whether because she wished to avoid her out of a fear of speaking more than she ought, or because she was really occupied, could not be found, and Maggie was left more restless and perplexed than ever. All at once she remembered the appointed walk with Mr. Wayland; the prospect afforded her more pleasure than she ever before would have thought possible. Might she not, with a companion, and both with the excuse of having never seen the place before, be pardoned for exploring the house and grounds? She wished fervently to have a glimpse of the tragic product of her cousin's marriage, and not only because the story had touched her deeply: Some part of her kept going back to the image she had had in her sleep of the sorrowful little boy. She clung to the idea that the sight of him might explain everything. She hoped to have such a glimpse that afternoon.

Mr. Wayland was to come at two o'clock to fetch her. The hours from nine till noon were an interminable wasteland. At length she sat down with the idea of writing to her father, but three separate attempts were cast into the waste basket. She had tried at first to explain to him what in her own mind was unclear. In the end she settled on a briefer note:

"My dearest Papa, So much has happened since last I saw you that I hardly know where to begin in a narration of the strange and perplexing events which have taken place here. In truth, I hardly know any more what to believe of what is told me, and what to regard with a greater degree of incredulity. Your sensible Maggie has at last met her match—indeed, you would smile if you knew what a knot my poor brain has been in these past days.

"The journey itself was safe enough, but marred by an incident which I shall explain to you later. I was helped by a very amiable kind of gentleman—a Captain Morrison, whose ship is under repair at Portsmouth. He spoke of you in very glowing terms, and says you have met him. If so, I think you will agree he is an excellent fellow. To me he was all kindness and helpfulness, and I look forward to meeting him again in Town.

"As to Ramblay Castle, and the family here—I hardly know what to tell you, for I hardly know any more what is true. Save for the Viscountess, who has taken an inexplicable aversion to me and never tires of giving out every kind of incivility, I have been treated with great kindness. Fanny Ramblay is a sweet child, though she seems too much in awe of everyone to have a mind of her own. I hope that when we are in London she will be less under the influence of her mama—who in truth is an overbearing, and imperious creature—and will learn that everyone in the world is not set to frighten her. As to my cousin, Lord Ramblay, he has been as kind as possible for a man who seems incapable of complete easiness; were it not for the tone of his letter to you, and a tale I heard from Captain Morrison, I should be almost tempted to like him. Did you know that he had been married? His lady was from the West Indies, and died two years after they were man and wife. She is a great mystery, for no one will speak of her and there are no portraits of her anywhere. She left a child, however, whom I have not seen, nor heard spoken of by any of the family. I have been told the little boy is mute since his mother's death, and perhaps this is the cause for my cousin's strange silences and moodiness. It would be a natural cause for grief, but so much strangeness and mystery surrounds the story that I am half tempted (do not laugh) to think there is more to it.

"The castle and grounds are very grand—you would be amazed to see your own Maggie reposing amid such luxury. I have been on a hunt, and been commended for my great dexterity with bandages, when one of the gentlemen fell into a ravine. My hope of hearing great music and great conversation has not been satisfied yet, but I hope I shall have better luck in London, where we remove next week. I confess I am longing to go, for it is so quiet here a good deal of the time, and everyone is occupied with their own interests. However, I have one companion, whom you shall be astonished to hear is a great comfort to me. Pray, sir, do not smile too much when I tell you that your old friend Mr. Wayland has made himself more welcome in my eyes than I ever dreamed possible. He is not much changed, and smirks more than ever (if that is possible), and yet he is a fellow human being. I begin to think sometimes my cousins are not quite mortal, or at least are driven by desires very different from my own.

"I must go now to meet this same distinguished Personage—we are to have a tour of the park, and I am in hopes of glimpsing the poor little boy I mentioned. Pray send my regards to everyone, and reserve for yourself the fondest embrace from your own devoted daughter—Maggie."

The letter folded up and inscribed with the address, and commended to the care of a footman, Maggie went to change her morning frock for a more suitable walking costume. There was then only an hour left to await the arrival of the Vicar, and this she passed in great restlessness pacing up and down the morning room.

Fifteen

MR. WAYLAND WAS much surprised to find Maggie awaiting him with such an eager look upon her face. In truth, he had been a little apprehensive about meeting the young lady alone again without the benefit of a third party. His first encounter with her since their painful parting in Sussex had been much eased by his interest in his new patroness. So enthralled had he been with the business of winning *her* good opinion, that the addition of Admiral Trevor's daughter had been but as a minor annoyance. He had endeavored to suppress the last traces of his irritation with her in the belief that a proven intimacy with a cousin might improve the Viscountess's view of him. The subsequent suspicion, which had risen to the surface of his brain like a cast fly to the shimmering surface of a pond, that all was not as it might have been between the two ladies, had only concerned him in so far as it might pose a threat to his ambitions. He had accepted Lady Ramblay's command (for indeed, it had been very like a command) to walk with Miss Trevor without thinking about it. But a day had made him ponder the idea more deeply, and now he was much annoyed with himself for being forced into a situation which could only mortify him. Miss Trevor had no doubt changed very little, and she was not likely to be much more charming company today than she had been at their last interview. It was with very grave misgivings, therefore, that the Vicar set out after his first night in Essex expecting to see his arrival greeted with a sullen or a laughing look.

His amazement was the greater, therefore, when, instead of seeing before him a reluctant face and downcast eyes, he was met by a smiling, grateful countenance and the assurance that she had been all the morning looking forward to their meeting.

What meaning could the Vicar ascribe to this? He thought at first she meant to tease him, and prepared his own bitter reply. But they had not covered half the southern lawn before his doubts began to give way to incredulity, and incredulity to a newly kindled hope. Maggie was so glad of company, to be sure—even the company of Mr. Wayland—that she fairly rattled away in the happiest of spirits, and actually forgot for the moment to censure his every word and look. Mr. Wayland's vanity was such that he instantly interpreted this new character to be a repentance of her former actions. Before they had circled half the inner gardens, before they had traversed the third of five rose gardens, or even come within sight of the kitchen gardens (which, from a fondness for brussels sprouts and endive, he was very eager to glimpse) he had begun to envision the happiest of futures. It was clear to him, clear as daylight, that Miss Trevor was attempting in her own way to make amends for her unfortunate words upon the former occasion. Then he had seen in her only an Admiral's daughter, with twenty thousand pounds; *now* he saw a Viscount's cousin. What had looked then like a possible advantage, *now* seemed an absolute assurance of success. It was with the most complacent expression in the world, therefore, that he now began to peruse what more and more seemed to him to be his destiny. A sideways glance out of the corner of his eye showed him the pretty picture of a girl remorseful and endeavoring as well as the powers of her mind would allow her to win his good opinion again. Mr. Wayland could be stern, but had he in his power the sternness to reject so obviously genuine a plea? No, he could not; and though he determined to allow her a little more time to pay for her sins, he was equally decided upon renewing the proposal at the first possible moment. A vision of the life before them sprouted up in his mind, and the elegant surroundings in which they now walked added fuel to his dreams. The bishopric he had once envisioned was now elevated to a state office, combining the prestige of the cloth with the dignity of political power. He could see it all before him now—weekends at his cousin the Viscount's, where they would be honored guests, aside from being on intimate terms with everyone; the idea of being welcomed at Windsor was not far from his thoughts, when he was interrupted by a tug upon his sleeve.

"Mr. Wayland! I believe you have not attended to anything I have said!"

The Vicar blinked, and objected to this accusation.

"On the contrary, my dear Miss Trevor, I have attended with great keenness. If I am perhaps a little distracted this morning, it is only the beauty of the day and of yourself which has put me in a sort of trance. Besides, you know," he added, with a sudden consciousness of his dignity, "I have much to occupy my thoughts. There are so many duties to be attended to when one takes up a new post, and I should consider myself deleterious were I not *somewhat* distracted this morning."

"Of course," consented Maggie, who did not wish to disrupt her companion's apparent good humor. Despite her own chattiness, she had been consciously leading them around the castle to a path which ran between flower beds and into a little orchard. The grouping of the trees was such that it masked an interior courtyard, just giving off from the wing of the castle. This was the wing which Lord Ramblay had told her was not used any more, but here she was forced to believe must be where the little boy lived. It was in the hope of glimpsing some sign of him that she now steered her companion in that direction, keeping up as rapid a flow of conversation as she could.

"To be sure, you must be exceedingly busy, Mr. Wayland," she now remarked. "And you must not think I am not grateful for your generosity in offering to keep me company this afternoon. My cousins have their own affairs to occupy them; since Lord Ramblay's hunting party left, I have been much alone, and not a little at a loss for how to amuse myself."

"Come, come, my dear Miss Trevor!" exclaimed the Vicar in a reproachful tone. "A young lady as resourceful as yourself ought never to feel lonely. Where there are so many beauties, both natural and man-made, to occupy your eyes and mind, I find it difficult to believe you could ever be at a loss for what to do. And when you have seen everything, there is Lord Ramblay's library to amuse you. I am sure a man of such fine sensibility as your cousin has, must have at his disposal a vast collection of books."

Maggie admitted this was true, but added, "Still, Mr.

Wayland, I confess that another matter has occupied me more since I have been at Essex than even the greatest treasury of books. I suppose you know that Lord Ramblay was once married?"

Mr. Wayland had in fact heard something of the kind. He had had the benefit, that very morning, of hearing his housekeeper—a woman very fond of gossip, and pleased to have a fresh ear into which to pour her news—elucidate for him the whole history of the family at Ramblay. He had listened with more attention than he was accustomed to give to anyone else's words, for well did he know the value of a certain familiarity with one's employers' lives. The story had been most absorbing, and he was now very pleased with himself for being able to speak upon the subject with authority.

"A very tragic marriage, too, Miss Trevor, if I am not mistaken. Where there is a great difference in birth, there is nearly always a tragic ending. I am sure that had not Lady Ramblay died when she did, an even more unhappy resolution might have been reached. I know her ladyship did not approve of the match. It was against all her better judgment that her son was married to begin with, and now I suppose he must admit his mother was not mistaken, for I am told—" Mr. Wayland had the happy gift of making a piece of gossip take on the proportions of a generally held view, related to him by a great authority— "that he *now* intends marrying the young lady his mother had always hoped would be her daughter. A great lady of noble family, I believe."

Twice Maggie had been told—first by Mrs. Black and now by Mr. Wayland—that her cousin had not chosen Miss Montcrieff himself, but was in fact complying to his mother's wishes in paying court to her. The news interested her more than she would admit, and nearly obscured the amusement she felt at hearing Diana Montcrieff described as a "great lady." Her own opinion of her cousin's betrothed more nearly matched Mrs. Black's—"a vain piece of muslin."

Aloud, however, she said, "Yes, yes, Mr. Wayland—but did you know a child was born while Lady Ramblay lived? I suppose you must, for indeed it appears that *I* am the only one who has never been told very much. The child is mute, and has been since his mama's death."

The Vicar pursed his lips, attempting to remember what his housekeeper had said upon the subject. He was a little shocked at Miss Trevor's manner, which seemed to him to lack that solemn respect for her betters that he considered she should exhibit when speaking of them.

"The child is mute, you say—very true, very true. A tragic instance of our Savior's justice. And yet I am informed Lord Ramblay will not accept the boy's fate, but persists in commissioning specialists in the art of medicine from all over Europe to try and cure the child. I suppose he cannot resign himself to the fact that God's will is done."

"And would you?" cried Maggie. "Would you watch a child suffer all his life? In *that* respect, I confess I am completely of my cousin's mind——"

But Maggie cut herself short before she had time to continue. She had nearly burst out, with the immediate passion of her nature, what had been in her mind since she had learned of the existence of the child. But whatever ill she might suspect of her cousin, she would not let a stranger know of it. Mr. Wayland, however, was more interested in pursuing his own idea than in listening to Maggie.'s.

"Allow me to say, Miss Trevor—for indeed, I think my position gives me a little more credence than another man might have—that where the Lord has chosen to show his anger, no mortal can dissuade him from it. It is true that some miracles have been acknowledged, even since the time of Christ, but in our enlightened age we must not expect such kinds of supernatural tricks. I believe Lord Ramblay is mistaken in pursuing the matter so far. And I think I shall make it among my first efforts here to try to persuade him of the fact."

Maggie would have warned against such a tactic. The idea of her cousin, already convinced of the Vicar's foolishness, listening to any such advice brought a smile to her lips, and yet she did not like to think of even Mr. Wayland inviting the kind of cutting criticism she believed such a deed would bring down upon him. She was saved from an argument with Mr. Wayland, however, by a sudden noise ahead of them. They had by now entered the little wood, which consisted of no more than two dozen slender trees. The view into the courtyard was nearly unobstructed. Through the branches Maggie could discern a rectangular patch of lawn, in the center of which, lying in the midst of a patch of dark green shadow, was a small fountain in the shape of a zephyr. Save for the splashing of water on marble and the faint rustle of dry leaves, there was no other sound. Something in the unnatural quiet of the place, actually heightened by these sounds, had struck her as peculiarly eerie. The sound of a door opening, and being closed quietly again, came like a clap of thunder in the stillness.

Mr. Wayland had stopped speaking when he felt Maggie's gloved hand upon his arm. For a moment he did not see what made her purse her lips in a silencing gesture, but then he, too, perceived the two figures. A woman perhaps forty years of age, dressed in a dark cloak and bonnet, appeared first. She walked a little way into the courtyard, and then turned about, holding out her hand as if beckoning.

"Come, James," she called, and Maggie immediately took a liking to the low, melodious sound of her voice. "Come along then, pet. There now, why haven't you brought along your ball? Oh, deary me—I hope you are not going to sulk all afternoon. The horrid surgeon has gone away, and shan't come back. Come along now, child!"

The woman's voice was gentle, but contained a note of briskness, as in one much accustomed to dealing with children. She stood patiently holding out her hand in exactly the same attitude for a full minute before the small figure of a little boy, who could not have been more than five or six years old, stepped reluctantly into the courtyard. Maggie had half expected to see a twisted little body, or some other obvious sign of long illness. But the little boy walked perfectly upright, and if he was a trifle thin, if the color in his cheeks was paler than it ought to be, he seemed at first like any ordinary little boy. He walked slowly up to the woman, who must be his nurse, and slipped his hand into her own without a sound.

"Why! There is the child now!" cried Mr. Wayland, in a voice which nearly made Maggie jump. She had hoped to remain silently watching a little longer, and now was dismayed to see that the nurse, too, had heard him. She turned around abruptly, the color draining from her cheeks, and peered through the orchard.

"Who is there?" she called, in a voice that struck Maggie as almost fearful. But without waiting for a reply, she leaned down and picked up the child hurriedly, holding him to her as if some harm might come to him.

"Why, what a strange way of going!" declared Mr. Wayland upon seeing this, and, taking two long strides forward, called out: "Fear nothing, my good woman! I am the new Vicar here, Mr. Wayland, and I am with the child's cousin."

This news apparently did so little to calm the nurse's apprehension that she only clung harder to the little boy, and even seemed in two minds about staying where she was or running back into the castle. But Maggie, fearing to lose this opportunity of speaking to the woman, had run ahead of Mr. Wayland and in an instant was standing next to her.

"Oh, please do not run away!" she exclaimed, reaching out a hand. "I have been so eager to meet my little cousin!"

The nurse stared doubtfully back. A glance at Mr. Wayland, standing with his immensely long legs astride as if he were in fear of being toppled by an unknown enemy, a self-important expression upon his simpering face, gave her little consolation. The child, too, had been so frightened by his booming voice that his head was instantly buried in the nurse's shoulder. But Maggie's open, smiling countenance, and the great earnestness with which she had spoken, seemed to do its work at last.

"I am sorry, miss," the nurse said hesitantly. "I did not know who you were. I am not meant to let the child see anyone, you see—but, if you are a cousin, I suppose there can be no harm in it."

"Of course there is not!" boomed Mr. Wayland. "What could be more natural? The child must learn to speak to his relatives—"

But even Mr. Wayland must have noticed the look of horror which now came over the woman's face, and he stopped, conscious of having offended her.

Maggie smiled kindly at the nurse, and laying a gentle hand upon the child's head, inquired why he could not see anyone.

"It is my master's wish," replied the woman simply, with a little shrug of her shoulders that Maggie took to mean that the woman could not question an order from so high an authority. "His lordship believes the child is too easily frightened, and while the surgeons are here, doesn't like their work being interrupted. For myself, I think it is unnatural to keep a child away from people. It will only increase his fear, and then he shall never be able to live happily."

"Well, Master James must not be frightened of *me*," said Maggie, stroking the little head, which was all covered with dark waves like his father's. "For I have not even seen his face, but already I love him. And besides, I have come to play with him. You shan't dislike me for that, shall you?"

While Maggie spoke, the child had begun to raise his head, ever so slowly, and now stole a look into the young lady's eyes. The effort nearly overcame him, for he looked away again at once, but another second made him look again, and now he stared at her as if she was an apparition.

"Shall you dislike me for wishing to play with you, James?" she repeated, but the child showed no sign of hearing her. His eyes were huge and dark and limpid, and at first held no expression at all. His features were delicate and so fragile that Maggie realized at once he must resemble his mother, though there was a something about the small mouth and chin that reminded her of her cousin. Maggie kept up her chatter for some minutes, in the hope of seeing some hint of trust appear in his face. At last she was rewarded, for the tiniest smile in the world curled up the corners of his mouth, and he began to lose the look of a ghost. The solemnity of that little face tugged at her heart. Save for the tininess of the features and the look of wonder which was now apparent in his eyes, he might have lived upon the earth for half a century instead of half a decade.

"Shall you come and throw a ball with me?" inquired Maggie, stepping back a pace or two. The child made no sign of understanding, and at first Maggie supposed he might be deaf as well as mute. But now the nurse, whose initial uneasiness seemed to have left her, unwrapped his arms from about her neck and lowered him to the ground. He stood a moment, hesitating, and a hand reached out to grasp his nurse's skirt. A gentle push from her was needed to make him move forward, and this he performed with a great air of apprehension.

Maggie was at last able to get the little boy to smile, however timorously, and after some urging had coaxed him into a game with a stick and a pebble. As she played, she questioned the child's nurse.

"How long have the surgeons been coming?" she began, glancing into the child's face to see if he understood them. Master James gave no sign of listening—his attention was all focused upon the game—but when he heard the word "surgeon," his back stiffened a little, and though he did not look up, his face was set.

"Ah, miss, ever so long. The child learned to talk when he was hardly more than an infant, so we know it could not be that he was really mute. But the day his poor mama died he closed his lips and has not made a sound since—not even a whimper. He did not cry nor laugh like other children, and his lordship, who will never leave off blaming himself, began to search the whole of England for a physician who would cure him. There have been a dozen surgeons here these past few months alone—for Lord Ramblay has not resigned himself to the fact, but seems every day more tormented. He is like a man possessed, sometimes, miss."

"And has there been any hope held out by these surgeons?"

The nurse shook her head sadly.

"They will have their potions, miss, and their fancy curatives—but each one goes away more puzzled than the last, and I believe little James, rather than getting stronger, has slipped farther into his silence. Last evening, miss——"

"Yes, yes, I know!" Maggie cut her off, fearing to frighten the little boy any further by invoking the memory of his most recent experience with a doctor, which seemed to have been so painful. "I know my cousin was greatly annoyed with the man——"

"Annoyed!" gasped the nurse, her eyes widening. "Why, I thought surely he would murder him, when he saw what the fool had done! I have never witnessed my master in such a fury before, miss, save for that one time——"

But the woman cut herself short as if she had spoken too freely, and pressing her lips together, glanced at the child. Maggie glanced in that direction, too, unsure whether the woman had stopped because of the child or herself. Seeing the little boy's head bent in concentration upon his game, she attempted to encourage the nurse into further speech, but with no success.

Mr. Wayland was by now shifting his weight impatiently, and thinking he was about to start up on one of his lectures, Maggie leaned down to say good-bye to James. The little boy lifted his head and, when she touched his cheek and ran her fingers through his locks, smiled up at her with a glowing, happy look. It was a different child altogether from the one she had seen half an hour before clinging to his nurse's hem, who now stood up and waved good-bye. He was no stouter, to be sure, and there still lingered in his look a sense of having seen more than his years ought to have showed him—and yet he had begun to resemble a child. It was clear to Maggie, as she thanked the nurse and started off again with Mr. Wayland, that half an hour of play had done the little boy great good. The nurse seemed to think the same, but when Maggie inquired if she could not come back for another visit, looked doubtful and hesitated before replying, "Well, miss—I had rather not have my master know I have gone against his orders. But I must not tell a lie——"

"Why, of course you must not," declared Maggie. "I shall bear all the blame, and tell my cousin myself that I have seen his son."

Sixteen

MAGGIE HAD EVERY intention of doing so. She meant, besides simply informing Lord Ramblay that she had seen the child, and spoken to him, to let him know her own ideas about his treatment. She had never had a child of her own, but being fond of children in general, had observed their ways and considered herself amply prepared to give such an opinion. It was clear as daylight to her that the little boy, rather than improving from this surfeit of surgeons from London, had become so terrified of them that no medicine in the world would have had the power to cure him. Where the mind is closed, she had often observed, the body will not heal itself. Half an hour with James had sufficed to show her that the boy's greatest need was for naturalness. How could Lord Ramblay expect him to behave like a child, if he was not treated like one? To keep him closeted up in a suite of musty rooms, with only a nurse and a string of doctors for company, was as much like prophesying his eventual misery as anything she could imagine. How could the child *not* behave like a little old man, if he was treated as one? The warmth of her nature, and the impetuous tenderness she had felt for the child worked in her all the rest of that day, until by evening what had begun as a conviction of his basic health, had grown into outrage at her cousin's treatment of him. A dearth of any other distraction—for Mr. Wayland had soon gone away to attend to his own affairs—compounded the intensity of her feelings. By dinner time she had worked herself into such a tumult of emotion that she nearly broke her own promise to herself by mentioning her visit to the Viscountess and Fanny. Fortunately she did not, for Lady Ramblay already held such a low opinion of her that this new proof of the prodigal cousin's impertinence would surely have justified all her dislike. But after dinner, when the others had gone to bed, Maggie sat up in her own apartment arguing silently with herself. At last she could no longer resist temptation. Ever since she had noticed the second wing of the castle—and still more after Lord Ramblay had mentioned that it was closed off—she had suspected it contained the answer to her perplexity. So much strangeness and secrecy surrounded her cousin's marriage that she could not believe there had not been some grave wrong attached to it. And now the sum total of the hints she had received—Captain Morrison's tale, the nurse's mention of his anger, Blanche Haversham's strange warning, and above all, Lord Ramblay's own secretiveness—convinced her of the fact. If she had needed further proof, little James's condition provided it, for how could she explain his sudden muteness upon his mother's death had not he been witness to some awful incident? Such an injury, evidently to both mind and body, must have been caused by a sight more terrible than she could imagine. The last traces of Maggie's hesitancy were now laid to rest. With the courage of a really outraged spirit, she determined to find her answer in that silent wing of the castle.

The ladies had retired for bed soon after dinner. Maggie waited until the castle was silent and all the candles extinguished, and then, taking up a candle from the mantlepiece and throwing her cloak about her shoulders for warmth, she opened her own door and stepped out onto the landing.

Maggie's bedchamber was situated at the end of a short corridor, one of several like it running off the main hallway, on the third floor of the castle. To reach the western side of the mansion, it was necessary to descend a flight of stairs, traverse the ancient apartments, and ascend again. To achieve the chief stairway, she must pass by Lady Ramblay's apartments, which lay directly at their head. But there was a rear passage she had seen the servants use, and she guessed this might lead to her objective with a greater chance of going unobserved. Opening the door as quietly as she could, she listened for a moment. There was no sound whatever save for the ticking of a great clock in the passageway and the natural creaking of an old house. Holding her breath, she slipped through the door and trod lightly down a flight of steps.

   She was now in a sort of passageway bounded on both
sides by closed doors. She supposed some of these must
conceal linen closets and the like, and that the stairs leading downward on the left must descend into the kitchens.
Coming to the head of the stairway, she paused a moment
and listened again. The sound of a low laugh coming from
below made her start, but the succeeding murmur of voices
assured her that she had only overheard part of a conversation between a footman and a maid—no doubt they had
taken advantage of the others' slumber to steal a flirtatious
kiss. Maggie smiled to herself and passed along.
   The passageway ended in another door, this one larger
than the others; she hoped it hid another flight of steps.
Holding her breath, she turned the knob; the door opened
silently—it must be used often, she concluded. She had
feared that any stairway leading into that forbidden part
of the castle might be locked, but the joints were well oiled,
and not even a creak sounded to give away her presence
when she opened it.
   She was now standing before a wider flight of steps than
those she had just passed. They lay in pitch-black darkness,
without even the faint flickering of candlelight reflected on
the ceiling of the other passageway. Holding her candle up
before her and raising her skirt, she commenced the climb.
Her heart was pounding wildly now, and though she kept
repeating to herself that she was not really doing any
harm, she could not shake off a feeling of guilt. To be
observed now, sneaking about the castle in the dark, would
assure the hatred of her cousins. Well did she know what
a risk she had taken in essaying this exploration, and the
thought of what her cousin's expression might be like if
he ever learned of it, was enough to make her increase
her caution. But another moment reminded her of the
insults she had already received from their hands—the Viscountess's treatment of her, Lord Ramblay's letter to her
father, the posting house at Dartmoor—and her heart grew
brave again.
   Maggie was afraid she might have chosen the wrong way
of going. The stairway might as easily lead to the servants'
chambers as to the closed-off wing of the castle, but having
come thus far, she could not turn back until she had seen
for herself. In truth, she did hesitate for another reason,
too—a sudden memory of Lord Ramblay's face when he

had been at his most amiable, and of that unhappy look that often crossed his face, made her instantly doubt that he was capable of any cruelty. But now she was so torn between a desire to think well of him and the great doubt that could not help but linger in her bosom, and all this was so much confused by her own emotions, which it seemed to her had never been so tangled up, that she really felt she *must* know the truth. With heart in hand, therefore, and a great feeling of guilt in her bosom, she continued up the stairs and saw, with some relief, that she had not emerged into the maids' rooms, but rather into a hallway exactly like the one on the other side of the castle.

From having several times been confused by the muddle of passages and doors near her own apartment, she had learned to find her way even in the dark. Still, she proceeded with caution, her candle held well in front of her, and her skirt still looped up to keep from tripping. This wing did not, as she thought it might, smell of must and disuse. There were no cobwebs anywhere that she could discern, the Turkey carpet under her slippers was as fine and clean as the one in the opposite hallway, and the doors on either side of her stood open. She peered into the first, and from a stream of moonlight coming in at the window, made out the shape of an ordinary room's furnishings—a sitting room, from the look of it, quite unextraordinary in any respect save that the chairs and sofas were covered up, as they might have been to prevent damage from dust while the house was closed up for a season. Pictures hung on either wall, and as she passed, Maggie held her candle aloft to glance at them. They were exactly like those hanging belowstairs in the drawing rooms and galleries. Here were a multitude of faces, old and young, in every sort of costume, and glaring dourly down upon her with the expression of disdain which nearly every rendering of an ancestor accords the observer. But one likeness struck her, only from glancing at it as she passed, and now she stepped back again to look more closely. The eyes and face and hair were almost exactly her own, and with a tremor, she realized she was staring up at the face of her own mother. The young woman returned her look with an artless, humorous glance. In the gently curved lips and smiling eyes, Maggie saw her own features reflected, and even more, her own spirit. Hitherto Maggie had only seen likenesses of her

parent made after she had become Mrs. Trevor, and the
years had done much to subdue the restlessness and passion
of that glance. Maggie was struck by this quality, and stood
for a moment staring with a sudden understanding of the
woman who had been able to sacrifice her own family so
easily for the affections of a young naval officer. A sudden
feeling of kinship overcame Maggie, as if they had been
sisters rather than mother and daughter. She felt instantly
assured that Mrs. Trevor, had she been alive now, would
have sympathized with her own plight. The idea gave her
new resolution, and whispering a little farewell, she passed
the portrait by.

Maggie was now in a smaller corridor, almost exactly
like the one off her own bedchamber. Turning into it, she
had been frozen momentarily by a glimmer of light coming
from under a closed door. For a second she held in her
breath, waiting, but there was not a sound. She supposed
this must be where the child and his nurse lived—the light
was faint enough to have been a single candle, kept alight
to prevent his fearing the dark. Hesitating for a moment,
she retraced her steps and walked a little farther down the
main hallway to another corridor.

Almost at once she was struck by the difference of this
passage from the others. Where before the doors had all
stood open, here they were tightly shut. But even greater
than this difference was the feeling in the air. It was as
though a dozen souls were all breathing quietly; the very
atmosphere was charged with life—or, as she thought in
a moment, with a little shudder—death. Maggie stood for
several minutes together without moving, aware of a coldness which had begun to grip her heart, unable to stir from
the overpowering sensation of fear which overcame her.
It was only the greatest resolution in the world that made
her move forward at last, instead of turning and retracing
her steps, as she longed to do. Speaking sternly to herself
all the while, she stepped forward and rested a hand upon
the knob of the first door.

Almost to her chagrin, the knob turned easily enough.
Swinging the door open, she stood for a moment speechless
before what she saw. She did not know at first whether to
laugh or cry—for the flickering of the candle showed her
not some untold horror, as she had expected, no trace of
ghosts nor bloody sheets, but rather five neat shelves, all

heaped with housekeeping articles. On the uppermost was a pile of folded curtains, beside which rested two warming bricks and a flat iron. Coverlets and band boxes, an array of various ribbons and strings for securing them, a lady's traveling case, and two or three lap rugs made up the rest. So erect had Maggie been with apprehension, so taut with fear, that this mundane little spectacle almost made her burst into an hysterical laugh. She needed a moment to recover her wits, and made herself stare at the contents of the cupboard several moments longer before saying to herself, with a little frown,

"What an idiot you are, my dear, to be sure! What, had you expected to find the bloody dagger, dried up, no doubt, but still with traces of the murderous deed upon it? Well, and this is no more than you deserve—indeed, you ought to be laughed out of countenance for your imagination!" For in truth Maggie's mind had wandered in the last hour to thoughts of the most dreadful and lurid kind, which the silence and darkness, the echoing vastness of the castle, had only intensified.

With a great feeling of mortification and shame, she turned away, reaching out her hand to swing the door closed. A sudden feeling of weariness had overcome her all at once, and her senses, which had all been alive as a cat's in the last hour, grew numbed. Stifling a yawn, she hardly heard a little thud beside her.

She saw at once that an object had fallen off the shelf, and reaching down, saw with a little intake of breath that it was a miniature portrait. A second sufficed to hold the candle near enough to make it out. Out of the little gilt frame, embossed with pearls, stared up at her the face of a small child. Maggie just had time to recognize a younger version of the child she had seen that afternoon, before a voice sounded behind her.

Seventeen

"WHAT THE DEVIL?!"

Lord Ramblay stood stock-still in the passageway, his candle held aloft to illuminate the stooping figure before him. For several moments it did not budge, evidently from terror. He coughed, and essayed another tack.

"If I may be so bold, may I inquire what you are doing, Cousin?"

Maggie had hardly dared breathe at first. An initial rush of terror at being discovered thus had made her heart beat wildly, and when her thoughts were clear enough to recognize the sardonic tones of the Viscount, she was not much relieved. For a moment, she remained frozen as she was, half stooped over the miniature portrait on the rug, her thoughts rushing crazily along in the effort to seize upon some excuse for her strange behavior. At length, however, realizing that no excuse on earth could salvage her from her present embarrassment, she stood up slowly, and with a mortified expression, turned to face her cousin.

"I—I had not expected you to return so soon, Lord Ramblay!" she commenced rather lamely.

In the flickering candlelight, she could see the Viscount's lips curl into a contemptuous smile.

"I dare say you did not," was pronounced in tones of the heaviest sarcasm. "But I am rather more interested in your present employment than in your calculations of the time of my return. If it is not asking too much, perhaps you would not mind explaining what you are doing?"

"What—what I am doing, Cousin?"

"I see your hearing has not suffered greatly. I hope your tongue is equally unimpaired."

"Ah!" Maggie emitted a little sigh of absolute defeat. There was no point in caviling, she saw at once. Lord Ramblay's expression mirrored his absolute contempt of her, and in truth she could not much blame him. With a self-denigrating smile, she straightened her shoulders and stared straight into his eyes.

"There is certainly no point in trying to convince you that I meant no harm, Lord Ramblay. You will no doubt only think the worse of me for trying to defend myself."

"Defend yourself?" repeated the Viscount, the lines of his mouth beginning to show a trace of real amusement. "Why, what should you defend yourself against? It is no crime to go in search of a warming brick, which I assume is what you are after. Only, I should have thought it a great deal easier simply to ring for a maid, who would have brought it to you gladly—and warm, besides. I myself am not very fond of cold bricks in my bed, but perhaps our tastes are different. Oh! I see by your look that is not the case. Remind me, if you will, Cousin, to reprimand the servant in question. I am sure it has always been the custom of this house to provide guests with every article of comfort they may require, that they may be saved the trouble of ransacking the place in the middle of the night."

Now Maggie's cheeks were perfectly scarlet, and her throat constricted with anger at this cruel baiting. All desire for caution, all capacity for calm flew out the window, as she cried out—

"Pray, Cousin—if you wish to torture me, why do not you have done with it? You know perfectly well I was not searching for a brick, nor any other article for my *own* comfort! I came in search of—of——"

"Of?" repeated Lord Ramblay helpfully.

But here Maggie was rather at a loss. She did not know herself exactly what she had hoped to find. Certainly she could not accuse him, without any evidence, of what she had so long suspected, and yet neither could she allow him to punish her like this when *he* was the one who ought to be interrogated. In an agony of humiliation and doubt, she stood her ground and eyed him warily.

Lord Ramblay waited patiently for a reply, but, when he saw what difficulty his cousin was put to for one, he remarked softly, "Of something, certainly. I have no idea what you were in hopes of finding here, Miss Trevor, and yet I have a notion of what you *might* find, if you persisted. Shall I tell you what it is?"

Maggie nodded dumbly, uncertain if she was still the

target of his wit or if he intended to be serious. Lord
Ramblay's face, so far as she could see, was perfectly grave,
but then she had long ago lost any faith in the outward
movements of his features as an accurate indicator of his
real sentiments.

"You might—and, as I have just heard, already *have*
found—one small child, incapable of speaking. That is very
sad, is it not? A child of six years old, who cannot—and
may very likely never—speak, laugh, even cry?"

"Very, very sad, your lordship," murmured Maggie,
feeling more humble than she had ever done in two and
twenty years.

"Oh! I am glad to hear you say so, ma'am. It was my
unhappy belief that you considered it the height of naturalness."

"What!" cried Maggie, unable to believe what she was
hearing. "However could you think so?"

"Because," replied Lord Ramblay in a flat voice, which
struck the listener as twice as awful as the heaviest irony,
"I have just come from seeing my son. In truth, my early
return—which seems to have inconvenienced you so much
—was precisely on account of him. I was called back from
London by the news that he had taken a turn for the
worse. His nurse—a woman with a kind heart, if lacking
something in sense—was at first too wracked with sobbing
to tell me what had happened. But at last I was able to
coax out of her an explanation. It seems my son suffered
a dreadful shock today, and feeling she had been in part
responsible, she was loath to tell me of it. She had failed
in her chief duty, which is to see that the child is not
disturbed, that he has the benefit of absolute quiet, and is
not frightened or excited by anyone. Miss Trevor, I do
not know if I can expect you to understand my position;
that child has been the center of my existence for the
past five years. At huge expense, and at the cost of any
trace of peace I have remaining in my life, I have been at
pains to ensure that he has the best medical care to be
found in Europe. The most distinguished physicians from
this kingdom and others have attended him, and now, in
one ignorant moment, just when we believed a little progress was being made, you have ruined all of it! Do not
mistake me—I am convinced you meant no real harm.
But you have wrought it just the same. Out of a blind and

ignorant belief that you knew better than anyone, you have forced your way into a situation that you can have no understanding of."

Maggie could only gape in disbelief. Never in all her life had she felt more mortified, more chagrined, more humbled before another human being. She could not believe the child had really suffered from seeing her—and yet here was the proof, put in such certain terms that no power of rhetoric could have disputed it. What had she done? Merely smiled at the child, petted him, played a game with him—and yet here was his father, accusing her of the most vile kind of cruelty!

Lord Ramblay stared at her for a moment in disgust, and then, with a quick intake of breath, turned to go. He had almost covered half the distance of the passageway before Maggie found her voice.

"Pray listen to me a moment, sir! It is true I did not mean any harm—oh, how true! I only meant to help him. But, if I have done any damage, pray let me help to cure it!"

"There is nothing you could do *now*, Miss Trevor," was pronounced with the most awful iciness. "I believe you have done quite enough."

There was nothing Maggie could reply to this, but an awful rage, partly at herself and partly from the belief that her cousin's accusations were false, made her exclaim,

"That is true, Lord Ramblay. But what is my crime, in comparison to yours? I only played with your son for half an hour, and as gently as you can imagine. But what have *you* done to put him in this state in the first place? What must he have seen, to be incapable of speaking? What must he see every night, when he sleeps, that has made him unable to laugh like other children?"

Maggie could hardly believe she had said so much, but saw her cousin's back stiffen suddenly with a feeling of satisfaction. In a very different tone, a tone which showed her she had struck home at last, he said.

"That can be no concern of yours, Cousin. You have already meddled where ignorance and an impassioned spirit, without the benefit of either experience or wisdom, have led you. I could not prevent you doing so *then*, but I had rather be damned to eternity than let you pry into my affairs any further."

And with this, the Viscount turned on his heels and would have strode off, had not he been detained once more.

"I—I shall leave in the morning, your lordship," declared Maggie, driven by anger and humiliation. "I cannot stay any longer where my presence is so distasteful."

"As it happens, I have already arranged for your departure. You are to go earlier than planned to London with my mother and sister. I cannot let you go back to your father until my promise to him has been fulfilled. I shall not see you again, however—my son's condition demands my presence here."

Maggie had no time to argue, for her cousin had passed through a door and closed it behind him before she had time to speak.

Eighteen

WHATEVER PLEASURE MAGGIE might have taken from her first glimpse of London was marred utterly by the quarrel with Lord Ramblay. Not a peaceful night was passed in that first fortnight. Her head was wracked and her heart burdened by the thought of what she might have done to her cousin's little boy, and the fact that the damage had been all unwitting could not ease her conscience. She had not even the comfort of knowing the extent of the injury, for no word was received from Essex, and neither the dowager Viscountess nor her daughter seemed aware that Maggie had had any part in the child's illness. No doubt from some sense of honor, Lord Ramblay had kept the fact from them, and for this Maggie was doubly grateful, and doubly humbled. No mention at all was made of the little boy, in fact—Maggie realized she might never have heard of his existence had it not been for her stumbling intervention.

For one thing, at least, she had cause to be grateful. Had Lady Ramblay any more reason to hate her, her life should have been even less bearable than it presently was. The Viscountess's instinctive dislike was sufficient to torment the young lady as it was; any real proof of her relative's worthlessness might have brought out untold horrors. Maggie would have welcomed even that, however; to be punished by anyone else, tormented by a force other than her own guilt and shame, might have been a relief. Even without this knowledge, Lady Ramblay took a thorough delight in reprimanding her at every turn. Maggie's dress, Maggie's dancing, her conduct in and out of Society, her musical ability and conversation, were all held up against the higher standard of Diana Montcrieff. Maggie was forced to smile to herself at the ignorance that must have driven the Viscountess's abuse, for it was clear she feared Maggie might be a threat to her plans to see Miss Montcrieff become her daughter. Maggie could not know how solidly that fear was founded, for she had not been privy to one or two conversations between mother and son, in which Lady Ramblay had accused the gentleman of admiring his cousin more than his betrothed. Lord Ramblay had only half-heartedly defended himself against these charges, and now his mother was more than ever set against Miss Trevor. But even Lord Ramblay's admitted admiration for his cousin, even his frank opinion that Maggie's eyes were finer than Miss Montcrieff's, that she had a head upon her shoulders while the other did not, and even the most flagrant, though subtle disobedience to his mama, in finding in his cousin something so delicious and intoxicating that he did not often close his eyes without thinking of her, could not make up for the argument they had had that evening, nor for the bitter contempt which had been born in the nobleman's mind against that young lady, and which he was certain nothing could ever alter.

Maggie could not have known how much her cousin had admired her *before,* and so she could not have guessed what a radical change had come over him since. She was only aware that she had lost forever the good opinion of a man whose respect was worth having, and as her own mind turned under the scrupulous eye of her conscience, she began more and more to regret the fact. It was a very grave young lady who now walked, sometimes for hour upon end, in Hyde Park, oblivious to the parade of fashionable horses and chariots about her. Most deeply did she lament the willfulness that had led her into doing harm to an innocent child, and to imagining all kinds of evil of his father. For Maggie was more and more convinced that Lord Ramblay was incapable of the kind of villainy she had begun to imagine. Whatever his other faults—and she did not deny that he did have some awful ones—he was too much of a man of duty to be capable of any outright cruelty. His anger had really offended her, but the more she thought of it, the more inclined she was to sympathize with him. Should not *she* have treated anyone who harmed her child with a similar contempt? It was clear her cousin had had reason on his side, and clearer still that she had harmed him terribly. That wrong grew daily in her own mind, until her greatest ambition became to somehow make it up. She knew not how this could be managed, but that she should, someday, atone for her rash action, was a certainty.

London, meanwhile, with its cavalcade of glittering men and women, its balls and breakfasts, dinners and card parties, passed before her almost like a dream. She went obediently wherever she was invited, but without any real joy. The wonder she felt on looking up at the noble arches of St. James's or walking down John Nash's visionary sweep of avenues to Windsor Castle, was overshadowed by a constant sense of guilt and dread that she might have caused some real injury. She heard the music of Brahms and Mozart performed by the most expert fingers in Europe, attended Sheridan's new play, and even was a guest at one of Lady Devonshire's salons, where the most brilliant conversationalists of the day disposed of reputations with a single flick of a witty tongue. The constant round of balls struck her as dull and rigid; what amusement could be had at a dance, where no one thought of anything but the business of their friends? The gentlemen all seemed vain, foolish, and ignorant, while the ladies were only vain. She derived some pleasure, it is true, from seeing Fanny Ramblay made much of by an ardent circle of admirers, but for the admiration she saw reflected in men's eyes for *her,* she cared not a fig.

Maggie would have given much to have had the benefit of Miss Haversham's friendship at this time. To her, she felt, she might easily have confessed her troubles and depended upon the other's good sense and kindness for advice. But upon arriving at Grosvenor Square, she found a letter waiting for her. Blanche Haversham had gone to Scotland for a fortnight, to visit Mr. Montcrieff's parents, the Earl and Countess of Linley. "Congratulate me, my dear friend," she wrote, "for it seems I have been approved by the Earl. Is not that a great thing? And yet I dare not think of it too much, for it only serves to remind me how soon I must make my confession, and then I dare not hope for any charity. I do not think Monty himself will mind, for he is surely the dearest, kindest man upon earth, but for his father, I believe my birth and rank will weigh heavily, and a connection with my brother will not strike anyone as beneficial. However, let us not think of such things *now.* I shall see you within a fortnight, and then perhaps shall have need of that *help I once mentioned to you.*"

The letter served to remind Maggie that there were other troubles in the world besides her own. She wished Miss Haversham all the happiness in the world, and thought the lady would have it, if there was any justice. She wondered once again what kind of help she could offer. With no knowledge of this world, in which Miss Haversham moved so easily (though at such a cost to her own peace of mind), and now without the benefit of her own cousin's support, Maggie could not see how she could be of any service to her friend. And yet she wished most heartily to do anything she could. Indeed, the resolution had been formed in the first day of quitting Essex that heretofore she should help anyone she could, that she should be altogether a kinder, calmer, and less impetuous being.

Nearly a fortnight after Lady Ramblay had opened up her house in Town, the first of the regular subscription balls at Almack's was held. Maggie had long looked forward to seeing this famed landmark of the fashionable world, and though her taste for balls and society in general had been somewhat diminished of late, she dressed with greater care than usual on this Wednesday evening. Her preparations were not all for the dowager patronesses of the cotillion, either; since that fateful day upon the road to Essex, she had eagerly anticipated meeting Captain Morrison again. With a little flush of shame at being so easily swayed from the path of strict virtue and puritanical conduct she had set for herself, she glanced into the glass, on the way out of her apartment, at a handsome young woman, prettily dressed, and with her eyes radiant with happy anticipation.

The assembly rooms were already full by the time Lady Ramblay and her charges ascended the marble steps into the central foyer. A stream of tonnish men and women passed them by, the ladies resplendent in satin and French silk, the men as proud as peacocks in waistcoats of every hue, or the newer style of stark black and white. Lady Ramblay instantly saw an acquaintance and moved off, leaving the young ladies to fend for themselves amid a crowd of young people. Miss Ramblay seemed to know them all, and her great pleasure at being surrounded in a moment by an admiring group of officers made Maggie smile. But there was only one officer who interested *her*, and at length she began to fear he had not come. Captain Morrison had promised her the first set of country dances, but was it not very likely he had forgotten? The idea that he might even have forgotten *her* was too dreadful to think about. She was just beginning to give up all hope of seeing him when her eye lit on the figure of a tall, fair gentleman standing with his back to her. She could not mistake those shoulders, nor that happy, unconscious way of standing, with one foot linked about the other ankle. Though she could not see his face, and had only known him for about two hours altogether, her heart leaped up at the sight. The gentleman was deep in conversation with another man, a slighter, darker gentleman whom Maggie took at once to be a foreigner, an Italian perhaps. This last gentleman was standing facing in her direction, and as he talked, he kept glancing up, as if looking for someone. His eyes swept over the crowd in which Maggie and her cousin were standing and seemed to catch on Fanny Ramblay. There followed more conversation, and at last the Italian seemed to be nodding in her own direction. Now the fair gentleman turned around, and Maggie saw at once that she had not been mistaken. His glance met her own instantly, and his face lit up in a smile. In another moment he was by her side, bowing and smiling and hoping she had not forgotten that he had claimed her hand for the first set.

Maggie made no effort to hide her pleasure. Captain Morrison, she saw at once, was just as amiable, just as delightfully unconscious as he had struck her upon their first meeting. She went willingly ahead of him into the ballroom, and for the first time since she had been in the capital, felt completely at ease and at home, even amid this gala array of the cream of society. Captain Morrison was obviously happy to see her. His admiration was so evident, and his gaiety so genuine, that her own recent troubles seemed to fall away from her simply from being near him. With a laugh, he inquired how she liked the Great World and all its citizens? Were not they a very haphazard lot? Lady Jersey passed by just then, and he murmured, "There goes one of our most consequential ladies, Miss Trevor. Does not she exactly resemble a prune?" And Maggie could not control her mirth at this fitting description.

The music soon struck up, and having waited for the Princess Lieven and her husband, the Russian Ambassador, to take their places at the head of the line, the younger people followed suit. When they stood opposite each other, Captain Morrison wondered how she had found Ramblay Castle.

"Very grand, and very lonely," she replied, smiling.

"And your cousin? Was my description of him justified?"

"If you mean, is he a man of duty above all, yes; but he was very kind to me, until I angered him. I wish most heartily now I had not been so quick to judge him."

Captain Morrison was all eagerness to know what she meant, but Maggie could not tell him the whole history, feeling that to do so would entail divulging the same secret which had been kept from her so long. She said at last,

"I thought Lord Ramblay was driven only from a love of duty, as you yourself made me believe; but now I have an idea that he is more passionate than he seems, that he has deeper feelings than his cold exterior would suggest. In truth, I had the misfortune to see that passion revealed in a show of temper before I quit Essex, and unhappily, I cannot believe it was unjustified."

Captain Morrison stared at her a moment. "I have had a taste of Ramblay's temper, too. I suppose you know nothing about that?"

"Only what you yourself have told me, and in truth, *your* account of my cousin is the only reason I have to believe he is anything other than thoroughly honorable. It was partly on account of taking your opinion of him too much to heart that I angered him."

"What! I hope you did not make any mention of *me*!"

"Certainly not; you asked me not to mention our meeting." Maggie noticed his look of relief, and continued, "But I *did* begin to imagine, from your tale of his marriage, that he was capable of all kinds of cruel things and, in the desire to prove what my imagination had let me fabricate, I made a thorough idiot of myself."

"I hope you did not. Indeed, I cannot believe you are *capable* of making an idiot of yourself, Miss Trevor. But allow me to say, if it will not offend your natural loyalty to your cousin, that Lord Ramblay has a knack for making others seem foolish, if it will help to preserve his *own* dignity. He has precious little regard for human weakness.

I told you about his wife—but no doubt you have heard another version of the story from *him*."

Maggie denied the fact, adding that so little mention had been made of either the marriage or the last Viscountess that she had begun to think there was some mystery attached to the business. "And, to my great shame, I actually imagined there might have been some really evil act committed!"

Captain Morrison stared at her without replying. "And no one *else* gave you reason to think otherwise?"

Surprised, Maggie shook her head. "No! But, sir, I cannot believe, having seen what I have of Lord Ramblay, and having some other testimony of his character to go upon—" here Maggie was thinking of Miss Haversham— "that he could be capable of anything really cruel. Perhaps a natural coolness of temperament, perhaps even the unconscious cruelty of aloofness, distance, from his wife; but more than that, I cannot conceive!"

The officer smiled. "You are very warm in his defense, Miss Trevor. And yet you say he was very angry at you. How do you forgive his temper so readily—for I must tell you that I have seen how violent that temper can be. *I* could not forget it so easily as you seem to have done. And I cannot believe that you deserved it any more than I did."

The movements of the dance now drew them apart, and in the minutes it required to go down the line, curtsy to an elderly gentleman who smiled broadly back, and return to her partner, Maggie had made up her mind to tell the Captain the whole story of her encounter with little James. Whatever reason he might have to think ill of Lord Ramblay (and she surmised his dislike must arise chiefly out of resentment at the treatment of his friend, the late Viscountess), she could not let him believe that her cousin had been unfair in losing his temper against *her*. If Lord Ramblay never spoke to her again, she must yet have the satisfaction of knowing that her own conscience was clear upon the point of her honesty. Let him think what he might of *her*, she would defend *him*, even when his treatment of her was a reasonable justification for bitterness.

But Captain Morrison's thoughts seemed to be elsewhere when next she saw him. His eyes kept wandering to a corner of the ballroom, and Maggie, following his gaze, was amazed to see Fanny Ramblay smiling into the face of the very gentleman Morrison had been speaking to earlier. The little fellow was bending over Miss Ramblay's hand and evidently complimenting her, for the young girl's cheeks were flushed pink and there was a look of immense gratification upon her face.

"Why!" exclaimed Maggie, "I see that my cousin Fanny is talking to your friend—I did not know they were acquainted."

Captain Morrison nodded and smiled, still staring at the couple.

"I do not think they were, until this very moment. But Orsini has been admiring her since he set eyes upon her, and I see he has not lost any time in introducing himself."

"Is he an old friend of yours?" inquired Maggie doubtfully, for she did not like the look of the little fellow particularly. Though handsome, his eyes were very black and darting, and his tongue seemed to flick out of the corner of his mouth as he spoke, much like a lizard.

"He is one of my greatest intimates," replied the officer.

"In that case," said Maggie in relief, "I suppose he is a respectable gentleman. I know that Italians are not— are not meant to be. What I mean to say is, my cousin is so very innocent that she does not have the least conception of caution with gentlemen, and if he might take advantage of a trusting nature——"

Maggie had spoken in some confusion, and now Captain Morrison cut her off with a laugh. "What you mean to ask, Miss Trevor, is if Count Orsini is a famous fortune hunter? Upon my word, ma'am, I protest! I admit he *does* rather have the look of a snake, but a better fellow I have never known, nor a more gentle one. His family is as old as Caesar, and nearly as rich. Italians have a most unfortunate reputation in our delightful country, but I promise you Orsini bears no resemblance to the old prototype of the poverty-stricken nobleman in constant search of innocent heiresses. Quite the contrary. I think his own fortune is five times that of Miss Ramblay's portion. She could do far worse than to marry him, and a dance or two —which is certainly all he desires—will not harm her."

Much relieved, and feeling rather foolish, Maggie allowed herself to be teased a moment longer. The music subsiding soon afterward, and Captain Morrison led her to an alcove where some chairs were arranged, saying he would go off in search of refreshment. Maggie watched him disappear through the crowd with a smile. In truth, there was no looking at that face and form without one; Captain Morrison could have charmed a snake from out of the very grass. Certainly he had done his work upon *her*. Maggie had not been in his company five minutes when she had begun to feel the unhappy thoughts of the last week roll off her shoulders. The merriment in his eyes denied every other trouble, and yet Maggie was very sensible of a more serious side to his character, and this combination of sense, feeling, and gaiety was more appealing to her than all the titles and fortunes of Europe. She thought he liked her own mind quite as well—his admiration was clearly written in his eyes, and she believed he admired her as much for her soul as for her beauty. It was just this kind of admiration she had always looked for in a man. She had always thought that when she should find herself attracted to a gentleman in such a way, she should have found her husband. It was with no less a serious idea than this that she now determined to be absolutely open with him. She would lay the whole truth before him, and trust his judgment. If he could persuade her that Lord Ramblay was still in the wrong, after what she told him, she should herself admit it. If, on the other hand, he concurred that she had been guilty, she should waste not a moment in trying to make up for her actions.

Looking up from her reverie, Maggie's eye lit upon the figure of Diana Montcrieff making her way toward the dance floor on Mr. Whiting's arm. They paused in their progress to speak to Fanny Ramblay, who still stood with the Italian count. She saw Miss Montcrieff's head go back in a laugh, and the Italian stare at her admiringly before bending down to kiss her hand. This kissing of hands seemed to please the ladies greatly, though it was in poor taste to do so when the ladies were neither married nor of royal blood, and once again a little flicker of uneasiness swept over Maggie. She quelled it instantly, but no matter how she tried, she could not like the appearance of the Count, who looked as oily as a fish, and about as slippery.

Now Captain Morrison, bearing two goblets of champagne, appeared in the entrance to the ballroom, and catching sight of the group around Miss Ramblay, made his way over to them. There followed a little interchange, and Maggie could see that the officer was trying to bow without spilling the contents of the goblets, and that something he had said struck everyone as very amusing. Maggie began to grow impatient. It seemed to her the conversation was going on too long, and the keen interest Captain Morrison was paying her cousin began to irritate her. Miss Montcrieff and Mr. Whiting now moved off, but still Captain Morrison lingered with his friend and the young lady, whose glowing cheeks and radiant eyes spoke eloquently of her pleasure in these two gentlemen's company. Maggie scolded herself for this unreasonable tremor of jealousy. Had not Fanny as much right to Captain Morrison's attention as herself? And had not she, from youth and inexperience, even more reason to be flattered by it?

Maggie managed, by such kinds of arguments, to quiet her annoyance, but the very fact that she *was* annoyed only confirmed her feelings for the naval officer. And now she saw him turn toward her again and begin to make his way in her direction. His first words, upon reaching her side were,

"I have just been with your cousin, Miss Ramblay, and seen with my own eyes what is going on between her and Count Orsini. If I am not much mistaken, they are equally torn between a desire to gaze into each other's eyes and a desire to dance. Such is their dilemma that I do not suppose they shall accomplish either. Miss Ramblay cannot bear to look very long into Orsini's eyes, and Orsini looks too dumbstruck to dance."

Maggie said, with a little sideways smile: "Is not my cousin a pretty girl?"

"Exceeding pretty!" exclaimed Captain Morrison, grinning back. "A prettier creature I never beheld. However," continued he, in a confidential murmur, "she is not my type at all. My own idea of female beauty tends more to height and color, and a quick wit. And for those qualifications, there is only one lady here to fill 'em—one lady, I think, perhaps in all of England."

Captain Morrison spoke these words with such a nice mixture of lightness and sincerity that Maggie was won over at once, and on the spot forgave him for biding so long away from her.

"I meant to tell you," said Maggie after a moment, "what

made my cousin so angry with me. It has made me miserable this whole past week, but I am determined to take your opinion, whether or not it was my fault."

Captain Morrison seemed very pleased with this, and regarded her with great earnestness while she told the tale of what had happened in Essex. Briefly she narrated how her initial prejudice against the Viscount had affected her opinion of him, of how she had been surprised, after the incident upon the highway, and still more from hearing Morrison's summation of her cousin's marriage, at finding Lord Ramblay kinder than she had supposed he would be and, moreover, hearing him again and again defend her before his mother. She recounted how there were no pictures of the late Lady Ramblay anywhere in the castle, and how no one ever spoke of her, save that one time in the gazebo, when Lord Ramblay himself had opened the subject, only to close it again so quickly and so angrily, and how this had made her wonder. She told him, and with no little embarrassment, of the morbid picture she had concocted in her own mind of a really venomous hatred on his side, which she had begun to think might have led up either to an outright murder, or the moral equivalent of one.

"I am ashamed to say I really did suppose, for a moment, that they were all trying to conceal some horrible kind of deed. How unnatural it was, to be sure, that none of them ever mentioned her by name! It seemed to me they wished to forget her existence, to erase it from their minds. There were so many hints to that effect: Fanny herself confessed she was forbidden to speak of the subject! And then, Lord Ramblay behaved in altogether so mysterious a way. He was forever looking strangely off into the air, forever disappearing, and then appearing at odd moments. He would be perfectly open, and then suddenly his countenance would close up in the angriest way imaginable!"

Maggie paused for a moment, hoping she had painted the scene convincingly enough, for she hated the idea of seeming foolish in Captain Morrison's eyes. But the gentleman, rather than smile, as she had supposed he would, was staring at her intently.

"I can well understand how you might have come to suppose such a thing, Miss Trevor. Of course, it is inconceivable that such a man—even a cold man—could, in this day and age, commit so foul a sin against his own wife. Inconceivable. And yet—and yet—there *does* seem to be so much evidence, that is, so many contradictions between his behavior and what we know of their marriage. However," he added, in a brisker voice, "I am sure you now have proof that nothing of the kind could have taken place."

Maggie would like to have been able to confirm this, but in fact, aside from her own belief, she had no absolute proof. The certainty she had felt all week—in fact, ever since the moment of opening the cupboard door that night and facing the array of housekeeping objects that had seemed to mock at her excess of imagination—suddenly gave way before the inquiring glance of her interrogator.

"Why—no, I have not," she was forced to say at last, her eyes wide. And suddenly the memory, which had for the whole week perplexed her, of Lord Ramblay's defensive attitude when she had accused *him* of bringing on James's illness, came back to her. "That can be no concern of yours," he had said angrily, "you have already interfered where you had no right to be." At the time, his anger had seemed a natural outgrowth of the rage he had felt against her for interfering with his son, but now his extreme defensiveness began to have a new significance.

Captain Morrison was smiling at her encouragingly. "Well, I am sure there must be some good reason for all this mystery, though it *does* seem odd. However, I did not mean to interrupt your tale."

And Maggie, recovering from her momentary loss of assurance, continued her narration. She told him about how she had discovered the existence of a son, and of the child's inability to speak. Here, too, was another mystery—for she had yet to comprehend why the child had not been spoken of, even if the mother had not. It was clear Lord Ramblay was devoted to his son, even if his idea of love was to surround the boy with surgeons and keep him closeted away in a deserted wing of the castle. The thought appeared to strike Captain Morrison at the same time.

"How strange!" he murmured, glancing at her. "Surely there must have been some reason for this elaborate mystery! That Lord Ramblay should dislike speaking of his marriage, I can conceive, for he must surely feel some guilt upon the matter of his treatment of Anna. But to hide the little boy away——"

"It is just how it strikes me!" exclaimed Maggie, staring up at the officer. "Indeed, I thought at first the child must have witnessed some act, some dreadful scene, which had made him mute—it was to try to prove it, one way or another, that I went myself—but I am going too far ahead."

And then Maggie explained how she had first seen the child, how she had introduced herself to his nurse, and played with him, quite innocently and gently, for no more than half an hour. That the child had responded, and benefited from the little time they had had together, she was almost positive. She had been so convinced of the fact, indeed, that she had been on the point of suggesting to her cousin that so much elaborate medical attention might more simply, and more effectively, be replaced by a normal life. If the child could not speak, at least he ought to be allowed to play and laugh like other children! Maggie's passionate defense of this view brought a smile to Captain Morrison's lips, and he nodded most emphatically in agreement.

"But I had still to assure myself that his illness was not a result of a great shock. How idiotic you must think me when I tell you that I actually crept out of my room late that night, while my cousin was still away from the castle, and stole about the closed-up wing, exactly as if I had been a thief!"

"And did you find anything?" the Captain demanded quickly.

"Nothing. I saw that the rooms were open and the furniture covered up, and when at last I came upon some apartments that *were* closed off, and flung open a door—discovered nothing more than a cupboard full of boxes and flat irons! And just when I had learned my lesson, when I was on the point of slipping back to my own room, Lord Ramblay discovered me!"

Captain Morrison's eyes had narrowed.

"By God—and I suppose you were made to feel your shame! I do not envy anyone discovered lurking about Lord Ramblay's house!"

Maggie smiled in self-condemnation.

"And you may imagine what irony I was then subjected to! Still, I should have borne *that* perfectly well, had not my cousin then informed me that his son had suffered a great relapse from having seen me that afternoon. He seemed to think I had frightened the child out of his wits, rather than played an innocent game with him!"

No words could express Captain Morrison's incredulity at this piece of news. How could she have been accused so vilely, so falsely! How could so gentle a woman, with nothing but the best intentions, ever harm a child!

"That is what *I* thought," replied Maggie ruefully. "But you see, there is no doubt of it. The nurse herself was uneasy at my speaking to him, and as I learned, was so wracked with guilt for having let me that she could barely tell her master. Indeed, it is astonishing to me that the child, after looking so well when I left him, should have taken so sudden a turn for the worse."

Captain Morrison said nothing for a while, but the expression on his face made it clear how puzzled he was by all of this. At last, he opened his mouth as if to speak, but shut it again, thinking better of it.

"I can see you have some idea upon the subject, sir," murmured Maggie. "I wish you would tell me what you think—for in truth, I have not rested since that night. Do you think I was to blame? I cannot really believe it, and yet neither can I argue the evidence. I suppose no very grave injury was done, or I should have heard of it—but I shall never forgive myself for rushing in where I had no business being!"

A moment passed before Captain Morrison spoke, and when he did, it was with a very measured tone, as if he weighed each word. "What *I* think, Miss Trevor, is that this is a very peculiar business. I no more believe you injured that child than that my name is Smith. I should not wonder that your cousin—if you will pardon me—was not endeavoring to prevent your continued search that night, and only seized upon the nearest excuse at hand to frighten you away. Indeed, the more I think of it, from all you have said, the more convinced I am that that is the only satisfactory explanation for his vile accusation."

Maggie stared at him, aghast, hardly daring to breathe.

Nineteen

COUNT ORSINI HAD made a very great impression upon Miss Ramblay. Considerably older and more polished than any of the young men whose admiration she was becoming accustomed to, his attentions had been the crowning glory of an otherwise triumphant introduction at Almack's. The young lady returned to Grosvenor Square that night with a starry look in her eyes—which was not lost upon her cousin—and before the two retired, slipped into Maggie's room.

"Wish me joy, my dear, good friend!" she exclaimed, with such innocent rapture that Maggie could not help smiling, "for I do really think I am in love!" There followed a minute description of her meeting with the Count, who, too impatient to wait for a formal introduction, had presented himself. He had not attempted to hide his admiration for her, and Fanny, whose nature was about as artless as it was possible to be, considered his Continental manner the very apex of elegance and sophistication. That so worldly a gentleman should have seen anything to admire in a dull creature like herself was almost beyond her belief. It was no mystery to Maggie, however. One glance at that downy-soft complexion, now lit up with amazement and pleasure, those radiant, candid eyes, and that slender child's figure told *her* what any man must instantly see and love. But Fanny would not believe she deserved anything; no, no—surely she was the luckiest creature in the world!

Count Orsini had evidently understood his own good fortune in encountering so rare a gem as Miss Ramblay, for he had lost no time in idle flirtation, but arranged for a second meeting on the very next day. He and Fanny were to ride together in Regent's Park. To satisfy form and custom—for Orsini was nothing if not meticulous in his attention to etiquette—they were to be accompanied by Maggie

and Captain Morrison. This latter gentleman had himself
made a most favorable impression upon Fanny and, with
many little smiles of complicity, she hinted that if *she* was
the luckiest girl in the world, then Maggie was only a little
less so. The arrangement suited everyone very well, for
Maggie was nearly as eager to make the Count's acquaintance as she was to see his friend, and Fanny dearly wished
for the approval of her cousin in her choice of suitors.

Maggie had not hoped to see Captain Morrison again so
soon, for he had once more expressed his hesitancy to call
at Grosvenor Square, even if Lord Ramblay himself was
not in residence. They had left it between them, at the end
of the cotillion, that they should contrive to meet as soon
as possible. It was likely they should see each other very
soon, for Captain Morrison was a great favorite with the
hostesses of the *ton,* and Maggie, being Lady Ramblay's
guest and cousin, was naturally included in every invitation.
That they should meet again as soon as possible, however,
was by both of them agreed upon. They had separated that
evening with so many meaningful looks and such a heartfelt pressing of hands that even without any words to confirm it, Maggie was certain of the officer's feelings. Their
conversation upon the subject of her cousin, moreover, had
raised again all her former doubts, which were now more
strong than they had ever been before. Indeed, their mutual
suspicions and fears had formed a stronger bond between
them than even that natural attraction which had been
present from the start. As often happens, having such a
common ground to work upon, gave all their conversations
and looks direction, which two young people, so little
acquainted, might have lacked otherwise.

Fanny Ramblay was afraid her mother might oppose
their riding out together with two gentlemen, though Count
Orsini had told her it was the most commonly done thing
in the world. But the young lady knew how strict her parent
could be, and she had ever been warned against receiving
the attentions of gentlemen her mother and brother had
not approved. She was so set upon going, however, and the
idea of disappointing her suitor was so awful, that she
actually veered out of her usual path of strict obedience
so far as to neglect telling the Viscountess she intended
going. She did not lie, indeed—but she was conscious of

dishonesty nonetheless. Lady Ramblay's habit of staying abed all morning made the going easy, and until they had come home again, her mother had no idea of what the girl had done.

It was by then too late to make any real opposition, and Fanny's feelings had reason to be more fixed than ever. Count Orsini was even better in the daylight than he had been at the cotillion. Whatever little tremors of doubt she had had on lying in bed that night that his chivalry, his kindness, and his admiration were a product of her imagination, were laid to rest that next morning. Count Orsini was everything kind, everything wonderful. With what tenderness did he arrange her skirts about the girth so that they should not be caught up and trip her while she rode! With what intentness did he listen to her, and what wonder was in his eyes on finding so many common ideas in their thinking! It was true he was much older than she, and yet he seemed to delight in hearing her speak, though she was convinced that everything she said must make her seem foolish in comparison with the great ladies he had known. Count Orsini made her believe she was a woman, and the most lovely woman in all the world. How could she resist him?

After the first quarter of an hour, Miss Ramblay and her suitor rode ahead of the other two. Captain Morrison, with a smile, held back his horse to allow it, and Maggie instantly followed suit. She had seen enough of the Italian to relieve her doubts of the previous evening. In broad daylight, and at a closer range, she saw that he was astonishingly handsome, though small and wiry, and with the kind of quick black eyes that are sometimes described as darting. But his manner was everything it should be, and if his chivalry might, beside the brusqueness of an Englishman, have been considered as a trifle excessive, it was very pleasing nonetheless. Maggie liked him better than she had hoped she would, and liked him still more from seeing the glow in her cousin's cheek.

Satisfied upon this point, which had worried her a little before, Maggie could now turn her attention completely to the Captain. They rode for a little without speaking seriously, only admiring together the fine day and the handsome equipages they saw about them. Captain Morrison knew all the history of the place, and regaled her for a while with tales of the Prince's penury, which had held up the completion of the park, between battles in Parliament and battles with the King, for nearly ten years. He was acquainted with everyone they passed, and Maggie was not a little pleased to see how many of the horses and carriages stopped to allow their riders to speak to him. His manner was always light and amiable. Those who stopped went away with smiles upon their faces, and glanced with great interest at the lady beside him, whom Captain Morrison never failed to introduce as the daughter of the great Admiral Trevor. Maggie's delight in his company seemed to grow stronger with every minute.

But at last the subject which had been uppermost in both their minds since their meeting at Almack's was touched upon. Captain Morrison seemed to steer away from mentioning Lord Ramblay himself out of a regard for his companion. But some mention was made of the castle, and of the house party which had been ending when Maggie arrived. She had not had, on the previous evening, opportunity to tell him about it, and now she related the story of the hunt, and mentioned her great admiration for Miss Haversham.

"What!" cried Captain Morrison, "Blanche Haversham was there!" He seemed amazed, and Maggie wondered if he knew her well.

"Oh, everyone knows Miss Haversham," was Morrison's reply. But there was a look of annoyance on his face for a moment. "She is our national mystery. No one knows where she comes from, or who her family is, but there is a general agreement that she is descended from some one or other of the royal houses—the illegitimate daughter of one of the Dukes, perhaps. There has even been a rumor that she is the Regent's daughter by Mrs. Fitzherbert. And what do you think of her?"

Maggie replied that she admired the lady immensely, recounting how she had behaved after Mr. Montcrieff's accident. "At first I was amazed and a little chagrined at hearing her scold him so openly, before all his friends. But there is such a quality of heroism about her—she is like a young Diana, with her bow stretched tight against the enemy. I could not help admiring how she stood her ground, before all that simpering group of men and women! Besides, I think she was absolutely right—*I* cannot bear to see a poor animal put out, only from the stupidity of the rider."

Captain Morrison laughed at this. "Ah—that is Blanche Haversham through and through! She has not a trace of cowardice in her. But this Montcrieff fellow, what do you think of him?"

Maggie hesitated. She was almost tempted to confide Miss Haversham's secret to him, but a moment's consideration made her stop, for in truth it was not her privilege to divulge such a confidence. Miss Haversham had a right to her mystery, even if it meant withholding something from Captain Morrison. She said at last, "Why, I think him perfectly sweet and amiable, if not quite what Miss Haversham deserves. Yet she seems absolutely devoted to him—it is a most perplexing couple!"

"*I* think him the most absurd little fool in the world!" declared Morrison, with such strength of feeling that Maggie looked at him, surprised. But he continued in explanation, "Our national mystery has a right to a better match than *that*. Why, she could have any man in the whole kingdom if she liked! The Duke of Suffolk is wildly in love with her, and Lord Ernsgate, who is my idea of a really famous Corinthian (and with a vast fortune besides), has made it plain he would cut off his right arm for her! But I hope this little dressing down she gave Montcrieff in the field squelched his passion."

"Nothing like it," smiled Maggie. "On the contrary, when they had made up their quarrel, they were like a pair of lovebirds. And I have heard—" Maggie did not mention the letter she had had, for fear of suggesting that she knew more about Miss Haversham than she implied— "that they are now gone to Scotland, to get the Earl's blessing."

"What! I cannot credit it! The little fool!" Captain Morrison looked quite angry, but seeing his companion glance at him in amazement, smiled and said, "Don't think me idiotic, Miss Trevor. It is only that I am one of Miss Haversham's greatest admirers. And those of us who think highly of her all disapprove this association with young Montcrieff. Why, it is like casting a diamond into the Thames! What will become of our glorious, proud Diana when she is nothing but Mrs. Montcrieff? Even when he comes into the title, he will not have half the fortune required to keep any kind of establishment in Town, besides his drafty old Abbey. Blanche Haversham will fade out of sight and mind. She will become as dull and respectable as dishwater. One must preserve one's national resources, you know—and certainly Miss Haversham is one of ours!"

"But perhaps," interjected Maggie gently, "she will be happy. There is *that* to think of—and I do not imagine national mysteries, for all their style and prominence, derive much contentment from their lives."

Captain Morrison grunted. It was clear they had at last hit upon a subject they did not agree upon, but Maggie, thinking of how much else they had in common, allowed him this one difference from herself. She liked his wit and levity too much to want to dampen it.

Lady Ramblay was in a fury when the two young ladies returned. The sight of the Viscountess stomping up and down the morning room, with her lace cap a little askew upon her head and her impressive bosom heaving, was enough to frighten anyone. She commenced the moment they came in.

"And where have *you* been all the morning!" she cried, glaring from one to the other.

Fanny stammered and went red, for she had not imagined her mother could have known anything about their ride until she was told. She had planned to make the admission herself, and now that her feelings were so firmly fixed she had resolved upon doing so as soon as possible.

Maggie, seeing her young cousin's agitation, stepped into the breach. "We have been riding in Regent's Park, your ladyship," said she with a rather stubborn look, for she could not abide the Viscountess's presumption in addressing her as if she were no more than a child of three. "I did not see how you could object, since we were accompanied by two gentlemen of very high repute."

Lady Ramblay snorted. "Riding in the park! Riding in the park, and with two *gentlemen of high repute*, besides! Miss, you may go to your room till I call for you," she commanded Fanny.

The young girl, who had turned perfectly ashen, made a feeble objection, but was summarily silenced by a wave of the Viscountess's bejeweled hand. With an agonizing glance back at her cousin, she obeyed, creeping from the room like a scolded puppy.

The Viscountess now stood, her feet planted firmly apart, glaring at the remaining young lady, who glared back in kind. Maggie had borne Lady Ramblay's incivility to herself without a word; she had been criticized, mocked at, abused, in a manner which few women could have borne, and yet she had made no objection. But when she saw Fanny Ramblay—sweet, timid, gentle Fanny—scolded for nothing more than riding in the park, she could not bear it any longer. All the wrath and resentment which had been building up in her for nearly a month now came to a head, and it was with a look of unrestrained contempt that she now listened to her hostess's enraged accusations.

"So, Miss Trevor!" she commenced. "You have taken it upon yourself to decide what I might or might not object to! Presumptuous chit! I offer you the hospitality of my house, and much more, the opportunity to move in the best circles of the *ton*—against all my better judgment, I might add—and how do you thank me? By presuming to know what is proper conduct for my daughter! By encouraging her to disobey me, by enticing her into the most scandalous kind of conduct! Two gentlemen of high repute! I should like to know what you consider prepares you to make such a judgment! Perhaps it is considered very fitting behavior for sailors' daughters to ride about the country with strange men, but I assure you that for the daughter and sister of a Viscount, it is most certainly not! What have you to say for yourself?"

Maggie had a great deal to say for herself, and a great deal to say *against* Lady Ramblay. So stifled was she by rage that she could not speak at once. She let the older woman wait for a moment or two, growing more scarlet with every second.

"I shall tell you what I think, Lady Ramblay," she said at last, as calmly as she could. "I think that I have never witnessed more incivility in my life than I have had to bear from you. You have made it the purpose of your life to torment me. I do not know what has made me deserve such treatment, but I am certain of one thing—I shall not bear it any longer. I only came to visit you to please my father, but even to please *him*, I shall not stay another moment! You may think it a great honor to be introduced about to all the *ton*, but I assure you, I have never met such a group of preening, worthless people in all my life!

I should much prefer the company of an uncouth boatswain to all your aristocratic friends! At least I have met *one* gentleman in all of London whom I consider worthy of my respect—and he is not a viscount, nor a peer of any kind, but a mere ship's captain, like my father. They are both sailors, ma'am—whom you no doubt consider too lowly to bother about. But they are both gentlemen, and I am a lady! I do not go riding about the countryside with strange men—nor would I ever encourage Fanny to do likewise. We were accompanied today by this same officer, whom I know my father would approve, and his great friend, Count Orsini. I believe he is in love with your daughter, and she with him. I had hoped to see her emerge at last from the awful timidity she has been driven into by your overprotection of her, but I am afraid I shall not. In truth, I pity her from my heart, for the destiny you and Lord Ramblay have no doubt arranged for her. But indeed I cannot stay in this house another day!"

"*In*solent girl!"

Lady Ramblay was so overcome that she could do no more than tremble and repeat this same phrase over and over. Her mouth was working all the time, but with no other sound issuing out of it, and her eyes were nearly popping out of her head.

"*In*solent girl!"

"You may call me what you like, your ladyship!" cried Maggie. "I do not care what you think of me. Indeed, how could I? What care I for the opinion of people who think nothing of others? Why should I desire the approval of those who care not whom they harm, so long as *they* are comfortable, and have five kinds of hothouse fruit at every meal? Why should I make myself miserable because you do not like me? It killed one other young woman, I know— if there was not a fouler act committed—but I shall not let it cause *me* a day of torment!"

A kind of groan, or gurgle, escaped the Viscountess's lips on hearing this speech, and she fell back into a chair, which luckily, was just behind her.

"Heaven preserve us!" she moaned, fanning herself with her hand. "What have we come to when one of our own family dares speak in such a way? Insolent, insolent girl! To think I actually approved your entrance into this house! Indeed, I ought to have followed my own inkling and never have listened to Percival! I told him—indeed, I did tell him, we should regret the day we ever saw your face! I knew when your father did not reply to Percy's first letter that you were all a pack of stubborn, insolent upstarts!"

Lady Ramblay seemed to have exhausted herself with this speech, and she lay back, fanning herself with a limp-wristed movement, for several moments. Maggie watched her with contempt, hardly hearing her words, and sensible only of the vast incivility of the Viscountess, and her injustice, not only to herself, but to her own daughter. When she saw that Lady Ramblay's energy was all spent, she collected herself enough to retort:

"It is clear from what you have said, your ladyship, that you would be as glad of my departure as I would. I would be grateful if you would lend me your chaise to Dartmoor —from there I shall take stages to Sussex, so as not to be forced into any further humiliation at your hands. Good day, Lady Ramblay—and good-bye!"

And with these words, Maggie turned on her heel and sailed out the door. Without any clear understanding of what she was doing, but in that sort of white rage that sometimes can replace clear thinking, she ran up to her apartment and, ringing for her maid, commenced throwing her gowns upon the bed. It was only after she had completely emptied one closet and had started upon another that she commenced to shake uncontrollably. The gall! The absolute, unmitigated rudeness of that woman! To be accused of corrupting Fanny, whom she loved as much as a sister! To be called a chit, as if she were no better than a slovenly wretch from Newgate! To hear her father called such vile names, and herself denounced as even worse! She had thought it bad enough when Lord Ramblay had called her down, but at least *he* had had a motive! But this— surely this was more than any reasonable body could bear! Lord, how she wished her father had been here to defend her! Lady Ramblay should not have dared speak to *him* in such a fashion! And if she had, how sorry she would have been soon afterward!

And with these kinds of thoughts, which in truth were less like thoughts than a tangle of outraged pride, dignity, and confused phrases, Maggie oversaw the packing of her several trunks and band boxes. Evidently too terrified by her mistress's mood to make any comment, Maggie's maid did as she was told, even leaving off the wrapping up the finest gowns in silver paper, and tossing everything into boxes and valises helter-skelter. At last she did inquire timidly if her mistress did not wish to wait to collect those new gowns which were being made for her in Bond Street?

Maggie stared at her for a moment as if she did not understand.

"The gowns you ordered made, miss—from the French woman in Bond Street? Do not you think you had better collect them?"

"Pshaw!" cried Maggie. "Where we are going, my girl, I shan't need anything finer than what I have. I wonder what was ever in my head to think I could live such a life, away from all I know and love? Indeed, Marie, you had better remind me, if I ever take on such airs again, what has taken place in this house!"

Marie had no idea what had taken place between Lady Ramblay and her mistress, but there was a great buzzing belowstairs, and she knew there had been a quarrel between them. This was a cause for some disagreement among the staff, and not a little entertainment. Though the butler declared himself all on the side of Lady Ramblay, and the housekeeper would not take part in the debate, most of the servants agreed that Miss Trevor must have had right on her side. Lady Ramblay was an impossible mistress. She was forever giving orders and then contradicting them, so that no one ever knew what she really wanted. She was demanding and disagreeable, and in general, had it not been for their devotion to her son and daughter, there was hardly one among them who would have remained in her employ. Marie had heard some of this from whispered conversations, and she knew the chaise had been ordered for her mistress.

Very soon a knock came on the door, and a maid informed her that the conveyance was ready. Maggie had only to write a quick note to Captain Morrison, explaining why she was going away and hoping to receive him in the near future at Sussex. Entrusting the note to the care of a footman, she slipped down the hall to Fanny's room to say her adieux. These were naturally very difficult, and Fanny could not bring herself to understand why her cousin was going away. But at last she began to comprehend and, with a miserable expression, wished her mama had not been so uncivil to her friend.

"I wish, indeed, that you could know each other better!" she exclaimed, flinging her arms about her cousin, "for then you would surely see that she is not half so bad as she *seems*. It is only that since Papa died, she has not had much to occupy her, and she grows cross very easily.".

Maggie was touched by this display of filial loyalty, but she could only think that Fanny had much too generous an opinion of her mother. If this little speech had not in any way changed Maggie's opinion of the Viscountess, it had served to increase her affection for her daughter. With many fond words, they parted at last, and just as Maggie turned to go out the door, the younger girl cried eagerly,

"At least, I know we shall see each other before long, for when we are both married, you know——" with a shy little glance—— "we shall visit each other as often as we please!"

Maggie smiled in reply. But she had not the heart to say anything; the idea of Lady Ramblay and her son ever approving a match based solely upon love was inconceivable.

Within five minutes Maggie's trunks had been loaded onto the chaise and she and her maid were disposed inside. Her exit had been much eased by finding that the Viscountess had retired to her own apartment. With only one last glance at the mansion she had occupied for barely more than a fortnight, she gave the order to drive on.

Twenty

THE WAY OUT of London to the Great North Road lay through Grosvenor Street to Berkeley Square, and thence, to Picadilly Circus and Regent Street. Sitting back in the carriage, and lost in her own thoughts, Maggie barely noticed where she was being driven. But the traffic was heavy at this time of day, which was the beginning of the afternoon promenade, and the chaise progressed by stops and starts through the little maze of streets. They were held up time and time again by ladies drawing up in their little landaus to converse, or the lengthier disputes of young blades behind the reins of phaetons and curricles. At last, impatient to be out of the city which had been the scene of so much humiliation, Maggie leaned forward in her seat to discover why they had not moved forward in nearly twenty minutes. She had difficulty discerning the trouble, but a volley of cries rising above the general din of newsmen and cabbies, the clip-clop of horses' hooves and commotion of iron wheels over cobblestones, told her that some accident or other had occurred. With a resigned sigh, she began to lean back again, when two figures perched up in a very pretty little azure landau caught her eye. The landau, which was driven by a lady, was making its way along the opposite side of Berkeley Street, its progress made easier by its diminutive size and the single gray that drew it. Maggie craned forward again to see if her eyes had played her a trick, but she saw at once, on the vehicle's coming closer, that it was indeed Blanche Haversham who drove it. Recognition of the lady was made difficult by the large feather bonnet and veil pulled over her eyes, but there was no mistaking the gentleman. Captain Morrison, in the same riding clothes he had worn that morning, was sitting next to her!

The landau was now exactly opposite the Ramblay

chaise, but separated by a horse and wagon and several gentlemen on horseback. Maggie attempted to get the attention of her friends by a knock on the carriage window, but saw at once that there was too much noise in the street to be heard. Her first thought had been to jump out of the chaise and make her way toward them, for there were no two people in London that she wished more to see. Her chief regret, in leaving so abruptly, had been that she would not see Miss Haversham again; she had no such fears of Captain Morrison, but to tell him in person why she was going away so suddenly, to have one last glimpse of his face, would have been everything desirable. Maggie thought of jumping out of the carriage, and actually had her hand on the latch when something made her stop.

Miss Haversham was turned toward the Captain, making her expression invisible to Maggie, but the young lady saw, from a gesture of the other's hand and a movement of her head, that she was speaking. The officer was listening with an exceedingly sullen look; it was plain he did not much like what was being said. Now an angry expression came over his face, making his brow grow red, and he raised his gloved hand in an impatient gesture, with a sharp response. Now Miss Haversham's hand lifted to her cheek, and she turned her head away, allowing Maggie to see an expression of horror through the thin veil. Another exchange followed, which, from the look of it, was very heated, and then, with one last exclamation, Captain Morrison jumped to the ground and strode off through the crowd. Miss Haversham had leaned over to the other side of the chaise and was trying to call him back again, but he ignored her. Just then the traffic which had held up the landau began to move forward, and a cry from behind made Miss Haversham start. Her hand was on her brow, as if she had heard some terrible piece of news, but now she forced it down upon the reins and, with a snap, drove off. The same moment brought the end of the knot of traffic, and Maggie was prevented, even had she wished to call out again, from doing so by feeling her own chaise move forward.

"Marie," said Maggie slowly, leaning back in her seat, "did you see that little blue landau that was stopped opposite us just now?"

The maid, who had leaned forward with her mistress to try to discover the cause of the delay, nodded.

"Why, was not it the gentleman we met on our way to Essex, miss? The one who was so very kind? I thought it was, miss—a very handsome gentleman, to be sure! But he certainly looked angry just now!"

"He certainly did, Marie," responded Maggie absently. "Very angry indeed." She said nothing for a moment, but after a while remarked, "I suppose you did not recognize the lady he was with?"

Marie's eyes grew round, and she shook her head. "No, miss—ought I to have done?"

"It was Miss Haversham, Marie—the same Miss Haversham who was at Ramblay Castle with my cousin's other guests."

"Oh, to be sure, miss! I should have recognized her shoulders. Very handsome shoulders she has got, to be sure—but with the veil and all, miss, I could not tell. How very funny, miss," Marie rattled on, now that her mistress had let her know it was proper to speak, "that they should know each other—and so well, too!"

"Why do you say that, Marie?" inquired Maggie sharply.

"Say what, miss?"

"How funny they should know each other so well," repeated Maggie, impatiently.

"Why, miss—it is funny, ain't it? That one of Lord Ramblay's guests should be acquainted with a gentleman you met by chance on the highway?"

"Yes, yes, Marie—" Maggie smiled at the girl's instinctive discrimination between the "haristocracy" and mere strangers met along the highway—"but why do you say they know each other *so well?*"

The question seemed to strike Marie as a bit dim-witted, for she smiled patiently at her mistress.

"Why, Miss Trevor, it was as plain as day! She looked as if she was going to *strike* him! One ought never to strike mere acquaintances! My belief is that one ought never to strike *anyone,* saving only one's own family, and other hintimates."

Marie leaned back against her cushion with a prim look, and Maggie gazed at her, dumbstruck.

"Why, Marie, you are a very genius!"

The maid smiled at this. She did not know the meaning

of the word "genius," but her mistress's tone was ever so complimentary.

"I try me best, miss."

But Maggie was no longer listening. With a long exhalation, she leaned back, but her lips were pursed, and a frown darkened her hazel eyes until the chaise was well out of the metropolis and headed in a southwesterly direction.

The sight of the Dartmoor posting house might have brought up a flood of memories had Maggie not been preoccupied with other matters. Here was the same general commotion of noise, sights, and smells, the same hurly-burly assortment of travelers, from the cream of England's peerage, stopped in their phaetons and elegant private chaises on their way to Bath and their country seats, together with the humblest men and women, their possessions done up in a knotted shawl or ragged valise held together with rope, all intent on acquiring the best fresh horses or a meal to tide them over. The very same lad leaned against the very same rail, perusing a fly, and his face was smudged exactly as it had been on that other day, when Miss Trevor had stopped on her way to Essex. Only a leaden gray sky, portending the first snow, lent a grimmer cast to the scene, and the observer, who felt that she had aged considerably since that other journey, thought fleetingly how it reflected her present mood.

In truth it was a very different young lady who now stepped down from the chaise and made her way through the crowd into the inn. Marie had been dispatched to discover when the next stage left for Sussex, and Maggie herself, having procured paper and writing implements from the landlord, was directed to a private parlor. Here, with a fire newly kindled in the grate, and a glass of hot cider beside her, she sat down at a table to compose a letter. For a while she sat motionless, her pen poised over the paper, uncertain how to begin. That the letter must be written, she was positive, but how much she ought—or even could—say, she was unsure. One or two beginnings were cast into the hearth with an impatient sound before, with a determined look, she began to fill a fresh page. Once begun, her ideas fairly composed themselves. In half an hour she had filled three pages and a half. The

letter was now re-read, and finding only that she wished
to add a final note, Maggie signed her own name and
sealed it up. It was now directed to Miss Blanche Haversham in Grove Street, and laid aside to be posted by a
servant.

Having finished her letter, Maggie took a chair near
the grate and sat for some time staring into the fire. Marie
had come in while she was still writing, to say that there
would not be a stage coach going in the direction of
Sussex until seven in the evening. It was now four o'clock,
and Maggie had instructed the maid to inquire whether
there was a room to be had for the night. She did not
much like the idea of staying overnight in a public inn
without any male servant or companion, but it was pref-
erable to jogging over potholes with a dozen other souls
until the small hours of the morning. In any case, there
was no point in arriving at Sussex in the middle of the
night, for her father did not expect this early return and
it was probable they would only be forced to put up at
an inn there until word could be got to the Admiral that
his daughter was in the district.

Marie came in a moment later to say the landlord had
arranged for a suite of rooms to be got ready, and while
they waited for the place to be dusted, the sheets changed,
and the fire made up, suggested they take some refreshment here. Marie was on the point of running off again
to oversee the business of serving her mistress's dinner,
when Maggie stopped her.

"No, no, Marie—I had rather go downstairs myself and
dine in the public room as we did before. Only go ahead
and put our order in, and I shall be down presently." The
maid curtsied, and did as she was told. In a few minutes,
Maggie followed her.

She had not achieved the bottom of the stairs when she
heard her name mentioned. Glancing up, she saw that the
landlord was speaking to a gentleman in a brown riding
cape, whose face was hidden from her by a top hat pulled
well down at the side.

"Aye, my lord," said the innkeeper, "there is a Miss
Trevor putting up here for the night. I have just come
from her rooms now. Shall I send word you wish to see
her?"

"No, my good man, I shall find her myself, if you will only direct me to her parlor."

For an instant, Maggie's heart stopped. The voice, the stance, the riding cape were now unmistakable. Glancing at the gentleman in alarm, she had only just turned about to rush up the stairs again when Lord Ramblay called her name.

Twenty-one

"MISS TREVOR! I do hope you are not going to rush off again," said Lord Ramblay. His tone was exasperated, but there was a trace of amusement in it.

Flushing, Maggie turned back in confusion.

"My lord?"

"I have had the devil of a time today, Cousin, chasing you about the countryside, and I do hope that now I have finally found you, you are not going to run away." Lord Ramblay regarded her with an ironic smile.

"How—how did you know I was here?" she stammered in response, still with one foot upon the higher step and undecided whether she wished really to look into those eyes, for they seemed to have lost none of their power to discommode her.

"I shall be glad to tell you about it, if you will invite me to dine with you. What with riding to London and then riding halfway back again, I am devilish hungry, I confess."

Maggie looked at him warily.

"You are free to do exactly as you please, your lordship. Only I had better tell you that not six hours ago I insulted your mother."

"Ah, well!" Lord Ramblay did not seem much disturbed by this news. "As I imagine she gave you ample cause, I shall not hold it much against you. I ought not to say so, I suppose, but it has been the great ambition of my life to find a woman who was not frightened of my mother. Nearly everyone is, you know. But enough. If you will consent to coming down these last four steps, I will give you my arm into the supper room."

Maggie was not much inclined to obey him, but seeing there was no alternative, she begrudgingly consented to do as she was told. In short order the cousins were established at the best table in the dining saloon. Maggie noted how quietly her relative had procured it, and how readily his instructions were obeyed, though, from hearing no one use his title, she imagined he had chosen to be anonymous. With some surprise she noticed that there was no servant to attend him, and remarking upon the fact, heard him reply. "It is quite true, Miss Trevor—I am sadly unattended. But I was in the greatest haste, you know, to find you."

"To find me! Why should you be in a hurry to find me? On our last meeting, I supposed you hated me so much that never seeing me again would have been a blessing."

Lord Ramblay smiled delightedly. "And I believe you felt the same."

Maggie admitted she had not been overjoyed by her cousin's treatment of her.

"And it was just on this account that I wished urgently to see you again. In short, I have come to apologize."

"To apologize!"

Lord Ramblay smiled. "For having falsely accused you of hurting my son, when I know now it was not the case."

Maggie stared at him, all amazed.

"He was not hurt, then. Oh! I am so happy! You cannot imagine how worried I have been, how ashamed of myself—indeed, I have been longing to know how he was, only, only——"

The Viscount gave her a deep look, and seemed graver than he had been since first laying eyes upon her. "Only you did not wish to inquire it of *me*—is that not the case?"

Maggie flushed, and looked into her lap. She felt her cousin's intent gaze upon her, and was torn between the uneasiness she always felt when he regarded her, as if he could see clearly through her soul, and the questions which were still in her own mind about him. At last she made herself look up and meet his gaze squarely.

"No," she said simply, with a faint smile, "I did not wish to inquire it of you. But now tell me, he did not suffer from playing with me?"

"Not from playing with you, no—but he did suffer. His nurse left him alone shortly after you saw him, and while she was gone, he must have fallen down from his bed, for she found him sobbing on the floor when she returned. He naturally took fright—for he is not strong, as you must have seen—and, with a chill he had developed already, began to be delirious. The woman was naturally afraid to tell me of her own negligence, and seized upon the first excuse she could think of to explain his tantrum to me. It was only by chance that that very afternoon you had come across them, which, deviating so far from his normal routine, seemed to her a sufficient reason for his illness."

Maggie breathed a little sigh. Through all her other worries in the last days, this one matter had not ceased to torment her, and the guilt and shame she had felt on behalf of the child had not been diminished by a mounting suspicion of the father.

"Oh, I am *very* glad to hear it," she said earnestly. "You cannot imagine how the idea of my causing him any harm has tormented me. Then the woman must have confessed the truth to you at last?"

"Only last evening, when we saw he was completely out of danger. So ashamed was she, that she did not stop at telling me the truth of the matter, but went so far as to add a forceful defense of your opinion of his illness."

"My opinion! Why, what did she say?"

Now Lord Ramblay looked really grave. "Aside from praising your treatment of James, she informed me that the two of you were agreed upon the subject of his surgeons. I suppose she assumed I was about to send her packing in any case, and in the heat of the moment joined her own feelings to yours. She said you were of the opinion that the attention of so many surgeons was worsening his condition, rather than the contrary. She made a most eloquent speech upon the subject, saying that a normal childhood would be the best cure for his ailment and using as an example how much improved he had seemed after only half an hour with you."

"Well, I hope you did not send her packing after expressing so sensible a view," said Maggie, half mockingly.

Lord Ramblay smiled, but there was more in his look than even the gratitude of a father.

"Quite the contrary. I implored her to stay in my service, for the good of my child, as well as my own. There was one condition to her agreeing, however—do not you wish to know what it was?"

Maggie nodded.

"It was that the two of you together should be allowed to essay your own theory of medicine upon him for a little. As I meant in any case to ask your forgiveness for my hideous accusations that night, I promised that I should enjoin you to it."

Lord Ramblay gazed at her attentively, waiting for a reply. But Maggie, feeling a sudden and unaccountable disappointment, did not answer at once. She had not known what she had expected, but it was not this. Now she said, in a firm voice, and looking him square in the eye,

"I really do not think I ought to return to Ramblay Castle, Lord Ramblay, despite my affection for your son and my very real wish to do him any good within my power. Your mother has already ample cause to hate me, and it would be adding insult to injury if I now accepted any further hospitality from you."

"Allow me, if you will, Cousin, to determine that for myself. As for my mother, you need not worry—she and I have disagreed upon many subjects in the past. What becomes of my son, however, and what takes place within the walls of my own home, is for me to decide."

It required some little persuasion to erase all of Maggie's doubts upon this head, but at last, having heard Lord Ramblay as good as beseech her to comply, she agreed to go back to Ramblay Castle and attend the child. But she would not stay above a fortnight, upon this point she stood firm. A fortnight would be sufficient time to see if James responded at all to her own theory of healing. If, afterward, she thought he showed no signs of improvement, she would concede to her cousin and all the surgeons once more. Otherwise, any kind and gentle attendant might do as much as she could.

"Oh, I think not," murmured Lord Ramblay with a smile, upon hearing this. "I think not, indeed."

But Maggie, rising from the table, did not hear him. It had been agreed that she should continue to Essex that very night, in the same chaise which had brought her thus far, and which Lord Ramblay had succeeded in detaining in the yard. The Viscount himself would not accompany her—some pressing business in London required his attention for a day or two. He would return to the castle as soon as he could, however, though he said with a smile as he fastened the door of the chaise after Maggie, "I

cannot conceive you will have any need of me, Cousin—
for a woman less dependent upon the help of a gentleman
I have never known."

Maggie replied that this was untrue, for she had always
stood in need of her father.

"Ah!" exclaimed Lord Ramblay, upon hearing this. "I
had almost forgot!" And reaching into the pocket of his
cape, drew forth a letter, which, from seeing one glimpse
of the hand even in the flickering flame of the carriage
lamp, Maggie knew was from Admiral Trevor. "It came in
the post a day or two ago, and I thought you might like
to have it straight away."

The sight of the letter made Maggie remember the one
she still had for Miss Haversham. She had taken it up
when she left the private parlor to go downstairs to the
supper room, with the intention of finding a servant to
post it. When she had seen Lord Ramblay, she had slipped
it into her reticule, and in the interval had forgotten all
about it. Now she drew it forth, saying, "I wonder if you
will deliver this letter to Miss Haversham when you are
in London, Cousin? I know you are great friends, and are
likely to meet her."

Lord Ramblay looked surprised for a moment.

"Ah! She told you that, did she? I had meant to call upon
her tomorrow, as a matter of fact, and should be glad to
take your letter."

"I would be very grateful if you would. It is something
urgent, and I would be glad if she had it as soon as
possible."

Lord Ramblay seemed a little surprised at this, but saying nothing, took the letter from her and thrust it into the
same pocket where Admiral Trevor's had been. Having
given the order to the coachman to take Miss Trevor and
her maid to Ramblay Castle, Lord Ramblay thanked her
and wished her a safe journey. After one last look at her,
in which were mixed so many emotions and uncertainties
that even he could not have said what he felt at that moment, he stood back to let the carriage pass.

Ensconced once more in the luxury of her cousin's chaise,
the extraordinary events of the day began to do their work
upon Maggie. Until that moment, she had been kept going
by false energy. First there had been her elation after the

happy time she had spent riding in the park with Captain Morrison, and then the great rush of mad energy she had felt after her quarrel with Lady Ramblay. The first surges of anger had not died away before the shock of seeing Miss Haversham and the naval officer riding together in the lady's landau had instantly dashed what certainties she had remaining as to the character and conduct of these people. And now Lord Ramblay's unexpected appearance, his apology for their last meeting, and request for her help, had drained Maggie completely. The swaying of the carriage, the dark, the warmth of the moleskin rug over her lap, and extreme fatigue, all at once began to do their work. Shortly after the carriage drove away from Dartmoor, her head dropped back against the cushions, her lids closed over her eyes, and she was fast asleep, with her father's letter still clutched in her hand.

It was not until some hours later, ensconced in her old apartments at Ramblay Castle, that she had the opportunity to open that letter. She took it up the more eagerly for the doubts she presently entertained about every other man she seemed to know. Lord Ramblay was complicated and difficult; his manner toward herself that afternoon had been radically different from his former style, but there was still no making him out, and Maggie felt, because of this, all the more irritation at herself for caring what he thought of her. She had always prided herself upon her knowledge of human nature, and yet here was a man she could not in the least fathom. Of all men on earth, he seemed the most upright, the most sensible of his duty to family and friends, the most incapable, if only out of a love of correctness, of any despicable action. Yet not eight hours before she had been convinced he had—if not actually committed murder, at least tormented his wife into an early grave. Of Captain Morrison, whose appearance and style were the most open and forthright imaginable, she dared not even think. Too many doubts and questions had risen in her mind upon seeing him so intimately conversing with Blanche Haversham. Those doubts and fears, she knew, must be put aside until her letter to that lady had its reply—till then she would not even think of him.

It was with a great relief that she now turned to her father's letter, calling up in her mind as she did so a picture of that stern old face, so fearsome to his sailors when angry, and so dearly loved by everyone who knew him at every other moment. Even his hand—bold, large, and blunt—was a comforting sight. Laying every other thought aside, Maggie sank into an armchair and opened it up. With a fond smile she noted the several closely written pages, and knew, from her own familiarity with the Admiral's usual epistolary brevity, that he must miss her sadly.

The first and the second pages of the letter were full of trivial news about all their friends and acquaintances in Sussex. The Admiral had progressed farther than he had hoped to do in his memoirs of the War, there was a new curate in the village, and the skill of the cook was not much improved since his daughter's departure. He hoped Maggie was benefiting from her relations' company, and enjoined her not to stay away too long. All this was predictable, and, to Maggie's present state of mind, delightful. She read his phrases as if she could hear his voice, and felt instantly comforted. But all at once the style and tone of the letter changed, as if the Admiral, postponing by every means he could think of the disclosure of some awful secret, had at last reached the end of his resources.

"My dear (read the letter), I was sorry to discover, from the tone of your last letter to me, that you seemed still to hold a grudge against your cousin, the Viscount. From what you said, I gathered he had given you no reason to dislike him, and yet you persist in calling him haughty, proud, and arrogant. He has been kind to you, and yet you cannot find it in your heart to feel a genuine affection and respect for him. I am very sorry for this, Maggie, very sorry indeed, for I believe it is all due to me that you feel as you do. Had I told you the whole truth of our correspondence, I believe you should think altogether differently, and blame *me* for what you now suppose is Lord Ramblay's fault. I should have remedied this unfortunate state long ago—indeed, I ought to have told you the whole truth at once, rather than letting you believe what you now do about him. I hope it is not too late for you to change your opinion of Lord Ramblay, for I have every reason to think him a fine, sensible, and generous man, as unlike his father as any son can be.

"When I showed you his letter, my dear, I am afraid I let you think it was his first attempt to correspond with me.

I did so out of shame, and nothing more, for I had behaved very badly in ignoring an earlier letter, written nearly five years since, in which my old enemy's son first expressed his eagerness to breach the gap made by our old feud. *That* letter was as different from the one you saw as day from night. It was three times as long, and positively begged me to forget our old quarrel. Of course it did not really beg, my dear, that is an exaggeration. Yet it went so far toward admitting his father's mistake, and hoping I would put our old quarrel out of my mind, that, had I not been such a stubborn old termagant, I should have answered it at once. That I did not, Maggie, is a fact I shall regret all my life, the more so if it has affected your own relations with him. I could not hope for a more amiable friend than Lord Ramblay, nor a more sincere one. His letter was everything it ought to have been, and for his second communication being cold and reserved, I can only blame myself. Indeed, he had every reason to be cold, after the disdain with which his first overture was received. I shall speak no more upon this subject, but I hope you will forgive me for letting this untruth go so long unconfessed."

The letter did not end here, but Maggie was too amazed to read any further. In disbelief she perused the last paragraph again, and again, until, with an exclamation, she stood up and began pacing up and down the room. Her promenade was punctuated now and then by a little self-inflicted slap upon the brow, which came with every fresh realization of her error.

"Oh, Papa!" she exclaimed out loud, "why indeed did you not tell me sooner? Oh, dear—I ought to have known it was not in your character to make the first attempt at a reconciliation! I ought to have known you would never, never humble yourself to your old enemy's son! Lord, I have been a fool! To think—oh dear, to think what I *almost* was sure of!"

With every moment, Maggie's confidence in her own powers of perception was weakening. She had been so positive from the first of her cousin's character that she had not paused once to wonder if she was not mistaken. No, with the stubbornness of her nature (and, she thought now with a grimace, of her father's) she had stumbled blindly on, blaming everything upon Lord Ramblay, and never questioning if some other person might have been at fault instead. In the matter of the letter, she had never weighed whether or not her own father might have been the instigator of the insult, and not his relative. At the posting house at Dartmoor, on her first sight of the Viscount, she had been quick to blame him for forgetting her, and leaving her without horses for her journey. Even when it was proved that horses had been sent, and a commodious carriage besides, she had supposed he meant to insult her, never once demanding of herself if perhaps his need was not more pressing, and the urgency of fetching the surgeon from London required a swifter team than one only destined for an easy ride over good roads with a vehicle made for easy pulling. Oh, no—in both these matters, it was clear to her, she now began to see, how it had been she herself who was mistaken and not her cousin. There was still the graver matter of her cousin's wife to be considered, however. But had she any knowledge, other than her own inclination to suspect him, and Captain Morrison's hints to go upon in blaming him for anything greater than an unhappy marriage? It was the latter gentleman's tale which had started her off, and now her certainty of even his character was faltering. Her suspicions of the officer, whose word she had been so quick to trust, were founded upon seeing him in that strange conversation with Miss Haversham. Her maid had been right—one did not argue so passionately with mere *friends*! But if they were not friends, what closer relationship joined them? The idea that they were lovers, hiding from the world behind the guise of other friends and admirers, had rushed over her with a sickening force. But in an instant that thought, however awful, had been replaced by an even more terrible idea. Was not it possible—was not it altogether *probable*—that Captain Morrison was that same brother of whom Miss Haversham had spoken?

Every word that lady had said in description of her sibling now came back to Maggie with a ringing, jeering clarity. "You could not understand me, without seeing him—he could charm a stone into speaking." Was not that almost exactly what she herself had thought about the officer? "His charm was so great that the world took it in lieu of more solid qualities." He had been depicted to her as amiable, handsome, and popular in the *ton*; was not that an exact description of Captain Morrison? Miss Haversham had said he was clever, and a naval captain, besides. He was admired in the service, and circulated freely in the *haute* society of London. All these thoughts had come back to Maggie in the first few moments after she had seen her friend and the officer in Berkeley Street, and had inspired her letter to Miss Haversham. Indeed, she *must* be certain of the matter. So cruel a misunderstanding must be cleared up at once, for until she knew, for certain, she could not trust a word of the Captain's.

Indeed, if she could not trust him on any other count, how could she believe his story of Lord Ramblay's marriage? The link had been long in coming to her, for her brain had been too much muddled by events to allow her to think clearly. But now, standing stock-still in the middle of her bedroom, it dawned over her: Had not Captain Morrison been the only person who had said anything against the Viscount? Had not he, when she had related to him her morbid suspicions, been quick to take them up and to encourage them? All this was plain, and it broke over Maggie with the sudden force of a thunderclap. And yet, try as she might to make some sense of it, she could not comprehend what advantage it would be to the officer to have her think ill of her own cousin! To be sure, it was a most extraordinary, and most perplexing case.

Having turned the matter over in her mind until she was incapable of thinking any more, and so exhausted that she thought she would weep, she sank down into her armchair again with the thought, "I cannot consider this any more, until I have some proof of my suspicions. Indeed, my suspicions have already been the cause of too much trouble. Until I have a reply to my letter to Blanche Haversham, I shall not think about it, but make better use of my time. There is little Jamey to nurse, and a deal of other better occupations for my mind than senseless wondering."

And with this very sensible intention (more sensible, in truth, than most of Maggie's ideas of late), she took up the remainder of her father's letter to read.

There was little left of it, only a paragraph. But this one paragraph, though brief, and written as if an afterthought to the principle subject of the document, was almost more interesting than Admiral Trevor's admission of his mistake.

"My dearest child, I had almost forgot. You made some mention of having met a Captain Morrison. The name struck me as familiar, and by chance I remembered some business that was connected with it. I have since looked further into the matter, and having heard from my old friend Corning, in Portsmouth, hope that indeed you have not befriended a Captain Charles Morrison, if such is the fellow's name. That gentleman, though well thought of in the service for his ability as a commander, has yet a most unsavory reputation among his fellow officers. It seems he is an incurable gambler, and is always in debt. Several duels have been fought over his refusal to pay, and one or two other matters, involving the wives of his comrades, which I shall not go into. There was a business some years ago which seems to have been hushed up, by whom I cannot say—but that it was very serious, and very detrimental to the Navy as a whole, I have reason to believe. I cannot comprehend why he retained his commission afterward, but suppose some very elevated personages must have interferred on his behalf. However the case, I hope you shall have a care in your dealings with him, and avoid him as much as possible. *I* have never met him, or if I have, have no recollection of the fact— you may tell him so if you see him again."

Such was the end to this astounding letter, already overloaded with interesting information, and it was some time before Maggie could contrive to put it down. Suffice it to say, in respect to her thoughts upon the subject, that it was a most mortified young lady who that night lay down upon her bed.

Twenty-two

WHATEVER WAS TROUBLING Maggie in those next two days
—and we may assume that her thoughts were not entirely
comforting ones—she gave no sign of it to anyone else.
All the vast resources of her energy, intelligence, and cheerfulness were directed at the business of curing little James
Ramblay. That child so delightfully, and so instantly, had
taken hold of her heart that no other distraction could
have sufficed as well. Indeed, she was rewarded the first
moment she walked into his nursery by seeing the lad,
wrapped up in his covers and lying full length upon his
bed, greet her with a happy smile. His nurse was no less
welcoming, and before an hour had passed the three were
well attached in friendship and good humor.

Little James was not yet strong enough, after his illness,
to get out of bed. But together Maggie and his nurse contrived to invent such amusements for him as could be
practiced upon his back, without disarranging his coverlets, and these he readily undertook. So willing was he to
be taught, and so sweet in the performance of his various
feats, that Maggie could barely resist hugging him every
few seconds. She attempted to curb her demonstrations of
affection, however, upon remembering how a little son of
one of her friends disliked being toyed over like a girl.
Little James seemed to feel no such injury to his dignity,
however—he was equally warm in his embraces of her as
she was of him.

It was apparent at once to both the child's nurses that
this new form of treatment was having an immediate effect.
His color was already much improved by the end of the
first day, and on the afternoon of the second, he actually
made a sound that was very like a laugh upon seeing one
of his toy soldiers knock another down!

Maggie stared at the nurse, who stared back in amaze-

ment, and together they tried the trick again. This brought
up a similar sound, though a little louder, and on peering
into his face, they saw his eyes twinkling in amusement.
A third essay brought forth an absolute chortle, upon hearing which, the two ladies seized each other's hands and
began dancing about the room, clapping and laughing. This
spectacle was infinitely funnier than anything tin soldiers
could do—and very soon the three were all bent double
with laughing, and tears were streaming out of Maggie's
eyes from an equal combination of happiness and gratitude.
It was as they were clapping each other on the back and
commencing a new jig that a grave voice sounded at the
door.

"I hope I may interrupt this scene," came the unmistakable tones of Lord Ramblay.

Instantly abashed, the ladies straightened up and stared
in mortification at the nobleman. Even little James seemed
to feel the change in the air, and the smile froze upon
his face at the sight of his father.

"Oh dear!" murmured Maggie. "We did not expect you
back so soon!"

"I seem to have interrupted you a second time, Cousin,"
said he, advancing into the room. "I hope it is not quite
so inconvenient as it was *then.*"

Maggie flushed.

"I—I hope you do not mind!" was all she could mumble.
"We were just laughing at the tin soldiers!"

"At the tin soldiers? Dear me—*I* do not think they are
very amusing. Their faces are very dour, and their arms
stick down on either side in a most unnatural fashion."

Lord Ramblay gazed gravely at his son. "Do you think
them funny, James?"

James, not knowing what was required of him, only
stared back. Neither lady, standing awkwardly beside his
bed, knew what to say.

"He did a moment ago, Lord Ramblay," said Maggie,
suddenly overcome with anger at this father who could
so swiftly dampen their victory—had not he seen his son
laugh, had not he seen how changed he was?

But Lord Ramblay, still with the same grave expression,
gazed back and forth between his son and Maggie with a
reproachful look.

"How dare you," he breathed, "how dare you find anything so funny when I am not here to laugh as well?"

And now a huge smile came over his face, and tears sprang into his eyes. A nervous titter issued from the child's lips, which was instantly changed into an outright cry of joy when Lord Ramblay, with a suddenness that surprised everyone, fell down upon the little bed and seized the child in his arms. There followed such a tangle of limbs, such an intensity of happiness and pride on every side, that no words are capable of describing them. Let us simply say that Maggie, having once recovered from her shock, could only stand back and laugh, and smile, and nod her head, with the tears pouring down her cheeks, and her heart so full that she thought it would break.

After a little while, when the Viscount's first explosion of emotion was spent and he had sat up and pushed his tangled hair out of his eyes, and covered up his child carefully, he turned to Maggie, and in a voice made hoarse with feeling, said: "I have you to thank for this, Cousin. No other woman is capable of such a miracle."

On hearing her demur, he only continued, "No—no, I shall not hear you contradict me. It is perfectly true—you have brought joy into the house again!"

A short time after the enactment of this little scene, two figures could be seen walking down one of the garden paths that led into the deer park. Well wrapped up against the inclemencies of the weather—for it was now the first day of December, and a few flakes of snow were falling from the sky in token of the approaching season—Maggie was oblivious to the chill. Her mittens and her cape, however, were not half so responsible for this apparent indifference as the words of her companion. She listened with every nerve in her body, but at last, when Lord Ramblay stopped speaking, she replied,

"I cannot—indeed—I shall not attempt to conceal the very great honor you do me, Lord Ramblay. To hear these words spoken by you, of all men, is certainly astonishing, and more gratifying than I can say. And yet I cannot accept you—no, please hear me out. I am sensible of your feelings, and as that is true, I cannot allow you to go on. In short—I cannot be your wife."

Lord Ramblay regarded his cousin for a long moment.

"How—that is, if you do not object, would you be so kind as to tell me why not?"

Maggie nodded, but walked on a little further in silence, endeavoring to collect her thoughts before she spoke.

"Indeed, you have every right to know the reasons I cannot accept, and there are several. The first—and by far the most important, from my own view—is that I believe you are not asking me to be *your wife,* but rather the mother of your child. I am sure that I have not the eloquence required to convey to you my feelings about your son—he is everything dear to me: precious and dear. I would do a great deal for him, but even for *him,* I cannot consent to be the wife of a man who does not love me."

Lord Ramblay had listened to this speech very attentively, but, on hearing this last phrase, he looked relieved, and smiled broadly.

"Oh! Is that all!"

"Is that *all,* did you say?!"

"Yes," nodded the Viscount, kicking a little pebble beneath his feet in a victorious gesture. "It is all, and I am exceeding happy to hear so, for I must tell you that I loved you from the first moment I saw you, and my feelings have done nothing but deepen since. From that first glimpse I had of you standing at the bottom of the stairs, with your defiant—and oh, so irritating—attitude, my heart was lost. If there had been any doubt about it, it was laid to rest when I saw you fail to tremble on seeing my mother. And since that time, through all the reasons I have had to resent you bitterly, I have only grown more attached to your impudent, maddening ways. Even when I discovered that you had been gadding about with Captain Morrison——"

Maggie, whose heart had skipped a beat on hearing the first part of this and then begun to do a little outraged dance, now absolutely froze.

"Captain Morrison! You know about Captain Morrison!" she gasped.

But Lord Ramblay was gazing at her with a droll expression on his face.

"My dear Maggie—I shall call you Maggie now, if you don't object—I certainly know a great deal more than you would like me to. I know about your foolish infatuation with the man—I shall call it foolish, because I have some previous knowledge of the man's character. And yet I cannot really condemn it altogether, for Morrison has always had an immense power over the weaker sex, especially when they were in ignorance of his true nature. In point of fact, it was only when I discovered that you knew him that I began to understand your bizarre conduct toward *me*—since you came to the castle, I have not had two minutes' rest, endeavoring to make out the reason for your dislike of me. It would have been the cause of some uneasiness in any case, for I did really wish to make up for our family's quarrel—but in view of my own feelings toward you, it was *most* inconvenient that you should hate me."

Maggie gaped back at his ironic smile.

"How—how did you find out?"

Lord Ramblay felt in the pocket of his cape, and drew forth a thick letter.

"It was largely on account of you, my dear girl," he smiled. "I went to London chiefly for the purpose of conferring with my mother upon the subject we were just discussing. I had hoped to persuade her that you were not just such a little frazzle-brain as you appeared to be, and that your father had had some justification for not replying to my first overture, some five years ago—a thing which she has yet to forgive him for."

Hear Maggie was forced to interrupt, in order to explain the misapprehension she had been under as to the cause of Lord Ramblay's later coolness, upon hearing which, the Viscount's face lit up in comprehension, and a laugh escaped him.

"What!" cried he. "You never knew about the first letter? By God! I thought surely *you* had been the force behind its being ignored! Well, well—I can begin to understand a little *now* why you were so quick to think ill of me! In truth, that was my greatest predicament, for I could not understand how a slimy eel like Morrison could have got his first opportunity to persuade you!"

Maggie still had no absolute proof that Captain Morrison was a slimy eel, however, and she begged for a further elaboration. Lord Ramblay was all eagerness to give it to her—and, handing the letter over, which was discovered to be from Miss Haversham, declared that "all the intricacies of the matter were in that." *He* would just give her a briefer narrative, and one less encumbered by female subtleties.

"In short, I went yesterday to visit Blanche Haversham, with your letter in my hand. I was not in the best spirits, for my mother could not be persuaded to think well of you, or to approve our marriage. Naturally, this did not in the least change my *own* mind, but it is always pleasant to have the blessing of one's parent in such a kind of case. Your friend Miss Haversham offered me very little comfort, for she was immensely distracted with some other matter, and kept pacing up and down the drawing room as if she was caged, barely attending to anything I said. She seemed of two minds about telling me what was upsetting her so, for she kept beginning to speak and then stopping herself. At length I rose to go, having unburdened my overflowing heart to the unfeeling girl, and gave her your letter, mentioning that you had called it 'urgent.'

"At once her manner changed. She gave the letter one glance, and commanded me sharply to stay in my chair till she had looked it over. Obedient to the end, I sat patiently, while her mouth worked in shock, amazement and, at last, in anger. She gave a cry and demanded to know whether I was aware you had become on intimate terms with Morrison?

"I must tell you that upon hearing this, I was absolutely dumbfounded. Even before I saw all the ramifications of the thing, I was horror-struck. In order for you to understand why, I shall interrupt myself to tell you the history of my acquaintance with the Captain."

Now Lord Ramblay, who had hitherto spoken with a lightness almost approaching amusement, and whose eyes had been sparkling with delight at amazing his cousin so, grew suddenly grave. They had by this time walked into a little bowery corner of the park, which in the spring must have been lovely with light and shadow and greenery but now was barren and brown, the branches of the willows shuddering in a chilly breeze. Inquiring if his companion was cold, he invited her to sit down upon a stone bench, protected by a hedge from the wind. They were soon arranged together on the seat, and having pulled the hood of her cloak a little closer about Maggie's face, Lord Ramblay recommenced:

"It is not a tale I delight in the telling of," he began, with a very solemn look, "and yet I cannot leave you in ignorance of it any longer. It is one of those matters which, having once gone by, ought by right to be buried as deep as possible out of sight and mind. Only in such a case as we have now before us is there merit in dragging it up again—for the tragedy of others has no benefit at all, if it cannot help to prevent the same kind of unhappiness occurring again.

"As you know, I was lately married. You may have thought it odd that no more mention is made of it by myself or my family, and that we behave as much as possible as though the marriage had not taken place, more so than is thought usual, even where the wife has died an early and an unhappy death. Indeed, my wife's death was more tragic even than an early demise usually is—for she was as innocent as a child, and as sweet. She deserved only the best and gentlest kind of life, and yet fortune must have frowned more cruelly upon her than it is accustomed to doing, for Anna was carried off not only sick in body, but unhappy in her mind. That such was the case, shall be forever a subject of torment for me. I do not believe I could have eased her spirit any more than I did, but I cannot believe there was not something more I could have done to have prevented her unhappiness before it came about.

"Anna was the daughter of a rich West Indian merchant, whose lands make up nearly a third of all the property in the islands. She came to London upon her seventeenth birthday to be presented to Society. It was in that, her first, and eminently triumphant season, that I met her. I was instantly in love with her. Had I been older, I might have had some other considerations besides her beauty, her sweetness, her gentleness—I might have looked for the kind of mind and heart that should have been a just companion for my own, not only in youth, but in middle, and in old age. I might have seen at once that we two had nothing in common—neither tastes nor temperament—and that our ideas of life were perfectly opposed. Be that as it may, I loved her. I was twenty-five, and heady with life. I thought nothing of the future, but supposed our courtship, with its secret meetings and whispered confidences, would last forever. Against the advice of my family and friends, I married her, and despite the knowledge I quickly gained of her, I should have been her faithful and loving husband forever, had not fortune intervened.

"Shortly after the wedding day, we set up in a house in London belonging to my father. There Anna was used to receiving her friends. She had them in large quantity, and they were all devoted to her. But they were not the sort of people I should have liked her to know. Women of much older years and greater experience, officers and court dandies, streamed in and out of her private apartments all day and half the night. When I suggested that so much society was distasteful to me—for I would never have intimated that her friends were not of the proper kind—she laughed and teased me, saying I was as dull as all her friends would have her believe. I tried in every way I could to impress upon her the importance of her station as my wife. That she should live a restrained and a decorous kind of life, at least in the public eye, was every wise desirable. She scoffed at the idea that she should hide her real tastes from the world—within six months she had become as worldly as her friends, as capable of cynicism, and completely unlike the girl I had fallen in love with. Still, I was determined to defend her against the world, and, if need be, against the criticism of my own family. And then at last the solution seemed to present itself—Anna was with child. She could not go out into society any more, and her condition confined her as much as possible to home.

"I thought it was the luckiest stroke in the world, for it provided me a valid excuse to require her at home, and I hoped the birth of a child would tame her spirits a little. But Anna was exceeding vexed. She did not wish a child yet, she said—and refused, until the very last moment, to modify her life in any way. When she grew too large to be seen in public, she came willingly to the country, for she could not bear the idea of being glimpsed as she was, and called it 'a great hole in her life.' She lived out the last months of her confinement with hardly any interest in anything. She never spoke of the forthcoming child, never hoped for anything save to be back in town with her acquaintances. She avoided me as much as possible for having put her in such an unhappy state, and began to loathe everything about myself or my family. All she ever talked of was going back to London, all she ever wondered was what balls were being given, and what fashions worn in the *ton*. Naturally I hoped all this would change the moment she saw her child—I have heard it is often the case with women. But, as the day grew closer, she was more and more in dread of it, and bemoaned the day she had ever been married.

"James was born at last—and with what joy I beheld him, I cannot tell you! Here was a new reason for my existence, a new hope for my old age; whatever had been lost of hope in the married state, was five-fold made up for by one glance at his face. Anna felt no such ecstatic trembling. She accepted the child, but only as her fate, as her personal albatross. She was not a bad mother—her natural instincts were too well placed. And yet she took no delight in dandling him upon her knee, none of that happiness in seeing his first smile, his first gesture, that mothers generally have. And as soon as he was capable of being left alone for an hour, she was impatient to be back in London.

"I do not mean to paint for you the picture of a hardened woman, a cruel or a heartless one. Anna was still the loveliest lady in England. Her sweetness, her gaiety had not left her—her manner was as artless as a young girl's. But it was just this quality that made her selfish—I cannot call it less. She was used all her life to getting her own way. No toy was ever denied her as a child, nor any amusement when she grew older. She expected just this same kind of laxity in later life. Any little hardship or difficulty would make her weep with unhappiness and incomprehension. She really did not believe the world had the right to deny her anything. I canot tell you how often that look of wide-eyed incredulity won me over! *I* had not the heart to make her miserable, and so, like her father, I gave in to her every whim. Would *now* that I had not!

"Anna returned to London, with the child. We set up once more in our town house, and once more the stream of visitors commenced. I had by now given up the idea of making her understand any other way of life. I was only grateful when she vouchsafed the child and me an hour together of her company. For the rest, I made it my business to see James well cared for, and absented myself as much as possible from the house. It was during this time that an officer by the name of Morrison began to be a more and more frequent visitor. I did not notice at first— there were so many faces, so many uniforms, and I had given up trying to recognize them all. In truth, it was not until too late that I saw anything improper in this growing alliance."

Lord Ramblay was silent for a moment, staring at the ground. Incapable of making him continue this painful history, Maggie touched his shoulder with her gloved hand.

"Oh dear!" she breathed, "poor man! And so they planned to go away together?"

"No impropriety was ever committed," he said sharply, glancing up. "I found them before they reached Gretna Green. From there they had determined to go to the Continent, under false names, and live forever upon Anna's legacy. I am convinced the whole plot was worked out by Morrison, and only conceded to by Anna out of weakness. She had no more notion of evil than a child has—but neither had she any notion of strength. She was instantly penitent, and begged to be forgiven. She wept like a baby, and claimed that she could never have left me and our child. However, all my old faith was gone. I could never again look at her with complete trust.

"My father, alas, had learned of the scheme, and of its outcome. He was outraged. Where I had been too weak to deter Anna from anything, he was not. He ordered her to the country, closed up our house in London, and commanded her to live as quietly as a nun. Anna took her punishment with surprising docility. It was as if she had accepted the end of her life. From that day forward, she was a different woman—more compliant, and absolutely inscrutable. She did everything she was meant to do, but all the joy had gone out of her. She took to working needle-point, and finished a whole tapestry before her death. I am convinced her body was commanded by her mind to die, for she had not interest left in anything."

Lord Ramblay's last words hung in the air between them for a moment, with only the sound of the wind and the distant tinkle of a cow bell to disturb the absolute silence. Maggie spoke at last, as gently as she could.

"And what of Captain Morrison? I suppose he is Blanche Haversham's brother?"

The Viscount nodded.

"For her sake, as much as for my wife's, the matter was kept quiet. Morrison was bought back into the service—for he had deserted his command to elope with my wife—and no hint was ever made of the subject again. I wish now

I had had more courage to defy him openly, despite the cost in dignity, for it might have prevented a second attempt to use the innocence of others to his own profit."

Now Maggie looked really frightened. Her lips began to form a question, which her cousin, seeing, instantly understood.

"Have no fear. Your letter was just in time to prevent that second attempt. When Miss Haversham read it, she saw at once the link between Morrison and the Italian count my sister had fallen in love with. To be frank, she had already some suspicion that her brother was devising another scheme for his advantage, for when she told him she intended marrying young Montcrieff and that their mutual secret was soon to be dashed, he was not so angry as she had expected. He hinted, in fact, that he was soon to be out of England and that his fortunes would no longer depend upon *her* whims and fancies. She saw him by accident talking to the Italian, whom she already had some aquaintance with, and heard my sister had been seen riding with him in the park a few days before. As soon as we guessed their plan, we drove over to Grosvenor Square in time to prevent the elopement—for in fact it was already planned, and Fanny was so besotted with that foreign snake that she was perfectly willing to do anything he asked."

"Oh Lord!" cried Maggie, in real anguish, "and to think *I* was the cause of it!"

Lord Ramblay looked at her and smiled, saying gently, "No, that is not true; you were only the victim of a cunning mind, and not nearly so clever as you thought you were."

"For *that* I shall be truly sorry all my days."

"No, no—you may be sorry now, if you like, but only enough to understand the lesson you have had, and to realize that the world is neither so complicated, nor so simple, as you think. If you learn this one lesson well, you will be the best woman upon earth—for there is not another lady in England with your strength, your courage, or your honesty. After all, had not you the courage to admit your mistake? That is a kind of heroism seldom seen among either males or females, and do not think *I* hold it light!"

Maggie had been staring very hard at the ground, condemning herself in no uncertain terms for the stupidity, the foolishness, and very nearly, the cruelty, she had been

capable of, in thinking one man evil, and the other fault-
less, when in truth they were almost exactly the opposite.
She raised her eyes now in a humble and beseeching look
to her cousin's steady gaze.

"I wonder you have the heart to forgive me so easily,"
she murmured.

"Oh! I have the heart for much more than that!" responded the Viscount. "And now, if you will let me prove
it to you, I should like to kiss that impudent mouth of
yours, which in truth has been tormenting my sleep these
past three weeks."

There was very little resistance offered to this idea, and
it was not for some moments that Maggie's lips, impudent
or otherwise, were freed for any other occupation. At
length, however, having grown almost immune to the racing of her heart and the burning of her cheeks, she was
able to get a little of that old irritating light back into her
eyes, and to say, with something of her old mockery,

"If I am to be a different kind of woman altogether—
that is, more sensible and clear-thinking, less given to
impudence and nonsense—do you think I may require one
change from your lordship?"

Lord Ramblay looked at his cousin in some confusion.
"Why, what is that?"

"Nothing more than an occasional attack of mirth at
yourself, my lord," she murmured, with a lowering of her
eyes.

Lord Ramblay seemed a little taken aback by this, but
in a moment he grinned.

"Done, your ladyship. I shall agree to a regular attack
of laughing at *my* stupidity, if you shall agree to——"

"To what?"

But Lord Ramblay had no need to elaborate any further.
His eyes spoke eloquently to that question, answered as
silently as it was asked, with a long, a deep, and a heartfelt
look.

It was not for some time that those two figures, which
had shortly before walked away from the castle, returned
and, stopping behind a hedgerow for a last stolen kiss,
slipped quietly into the mansion.

Twenty-three

"BY JOVE!" GROWLED Admiral Trevor, staring down into the hedgerows from his position at the library window. "By Jove! Has not the fellow any idea of when to have done?"

"I beg your pardon?" stammered Lord Ramblay.

The Viscount had been pacing back and forth before his desk while he made his speech. He had felt some nervousness, it is true, upon requesting the Admiral's permission to marry his daughter. Some hesitancy he had expected, though the older man had *seemed* complacent enough upon emerging from his conference with his daughter earlier that day. But so emphatic a denouncement of his plea, he had not forseen. Now, seeing the fierce look in the Admiral's eyes, he moved closer the window himself, and peered downward.

"Have you ever seen such a knave in all your life?" demanded Admiral Trevor, without glancing up.

"Oh!" Lord Ramblay looked relieved. "I take it you are speaking of Mr. Wayland, sir."

"None other, my dear fellow—look at the idiot now, waving his arms about for all the world as though he would like to be a windmill! And look at that pompous face! Have you seen anything to top it?"

Lord Ramblay grinned. "Seldom, in fact. I wonder what he is saying to her?"

Even Mr. Wayland might have astounded his audience, had they known that he was once again in the midst of proposing to Miss Trevor. The idea had been eating away at him ever since that pleasurable walk they had had together in the park on the first day of his arrival at Ramblay. He had hemmed and hawed for some little while, uncertain if he really wished to encumber himself with as troublesome a wife as the Admiral's daughter would no doubt make. But at last vanity and ambition had won out

over good sense, and he had managed to secure a moment
alone with her. This was no mean feat, to be sure: Miss
Trevor was much in demand by her cousins of late, and
there had been a great to-do in the castle, what with visitors
coming and going and the arrival of the Admiral himself.
But at last he had seized his chance, upon glimpsing the
young lady walking alone in the hedgerows with a most
docile and dreamy expression upon her face. This expression had persuaded him that her thoughts were not far
removed from his own, and when she started a little upon
hearing his voice, and then smiled up at him very sweetly,
he was convinced of the fact.

"My dear Miss Trevor," he had commenced, falling into
step beside her, "I hope I am not disturbing some very
deep reflection of your own." This was accompanied by a
significant look. "Love is a wonderful thing, is it not?"

"A most wonderful thing," agreed Maggie softly, but
a little astonished to find how clearly Mr. Wayland had
read her mind.

"Surely the closest thing to Heaven we are granted here
upon earth," continued the Vicar, with a comprehending
look.

Maggie made no reply, for none seemed needed. She
saw that the clergyman was about to embark on one of
his rhapsodic speeches, which in truth required no encouragement from any outside source. She continued to
walk along, gazing before her with a starry-eyed look,
which Mr. Wayland promptly interpreted as a maidenly
attention to his words.

"It is the manna of our existence, the very honey of
our lives. Without love, what are we but savages, uncivil-
ized and sordid creatures, incapable of any fine feeling?
Love, indeed, strikes me as the very oil of life. When our
hearts are lifted up by such a kind of sentiment, our minds
are clearer, our thoughts purer, we are driven to do good,
as surely as the murderer is driven to do evil. All foulness
and baseness is vanished from us, we are purged and
cleansed, as white as lilies of the field, as clean as snow."

Here Mr. Wayland, who had been inspired by seeing
some white particles beginning to descend from Heaven,
attempted to seize one in his fingers with the idea of laying
it in Maggie's hair. His attempt was futile, but he persisted

in catching at snowflakes for a while, waxing eloquent as he did so.

He was amazed, after a little, to see that Miss Trevor had not made a sound. She still gazed straight before her with that same starry-eyed expression, which was beginning to strike the clergyman as unnatural and making him wonder if she were not ill. To be sure it was unlike her not to make even *one* impudent retort! Peering at her, he broke off his soliloquy to murmur, "Are you absolutely well, Miss Trevor? You look a little ill, I think."

But he was quickly assured that she had never been better, and with such a delightful radiant smile, that it seemed to him this was all the encouragement he could ever wish for. Plunging in, therefore, he commenced to steer his own speech in the direction of matrimony, as the highest expression of that love he had already lauded to the Heavens. He was in the midst of this lecture, which in truth had some very pretty metaphors in it, though not of his own invention, when he was startled by a gurgle from behind him.

The sound may not have been a gurgle—it might have been a growl, or even a gargle, but nonetheless, it made the curate jump up in the air and spin about, thinking they must have crossed the path of some wild beast.

But the figure which now emerged from the clump of trees just behind Mr. Wayland bore more resemblance to a thunder cloud than an animal. Admiral Trevor, his cheeks puffed up with indignation, his great hammy fist lambasting the very air, came lumbering out from his hiding place with such a roar that Mr. Wayland almost fell down in terror.

"Here, here, you young pup!" roared he now, advancing upon the pair with his jowls wagging, "what d'you think you're doing?"

"What—what?" cried Mr. Wayland, positively shaking in his boots.

Admiral Trevor did not deign to repeat himself. He stood his ground, as if he were holding off a fleet of brigadoons, with his fist still raised in the air. He seemed to be on the point of shouting something else, when a mild voice from behind him said:

"Why, Admiral—do not you see? Wayland here is just rehearsing what he is going to say at the pulpit, on the day your daughter and I are made man and wife!"

Lord Ramblay took a step or two forward and secured the hand of his betrothed, who was smiling up at him in delight.

"Just so, Papa," she said with a twinkle. "Mr. Wayland has very kindly offered to do our honors at the wedding ceremony. He is just deciding what he ought to say on the points of love and marriage for our edification."

Mr. Wayland blinked back and forth between them. "At your wedding?" he stammered.

"Right-o, Mr. Wayland. Only do try to keep it short and crisp, if you will," Lord Ramblay suggested mildly, "for we shall be in something of a rush to suit our actions to your words."

Admiral Trevor nodded gravely at this, regarding the bewildered curate with a keen look. "Excellent advice, my dear fellow, excellent advice—I pray you will take it to heart, Wayland."

ABOUT THE AUTHOR

JUDITH HARKNESS was born in San Jose, Costa Rica, the daughter of parents in the diplomatic service. After a childhood spent in eight countries in Europe and South America, she attended Brown University in Providence, Rhode Island, where she studied literature and theater. Six years as a starving actress and a successful fashion model led unexpectedly to a free-lance career in journalism. She currently lives in Providence, where she divides her time between writing fiction and magazine profiles of artistic personalities. THE MONTAGUE SCANDAL, her first Regency romance, is also available in a Signet edition.

SIGNET Books by Clare Darcy

Recommended Reading from Signet